Praise for Ma

"Abundant details turn this A_____
thriller...into a work of art."
    —*Publishers Wee___*
                (starred review)

"Crisp writing and distinctive characters make up Perry's latest novel. *Where Secrets Sleep* is a truly entertaining read."
          —*RT Book Reviews*

"*Leah's Choice* is a story of grace and servitude as well as a story of difficult choices and heartbreaking realities. It touched my heart. I think the world of Amish fiction has found a new champion."
  —Lenora Worth, *New York Times* bestselling author
                of *Code of Honor*

"Perry's story hooks you immediately. Her uncanny ability to seamlessly blend the mystery element with contemporary themes makes this one intriguing read."
       —*RT Book Reviews* on *Home by Dark*

"Perry skillfully continues her chilling, deceptively charming romantic suspense series with a dark, puzzling mystery that features a sweet romance and a nice sprinkling of Amish culture."
      —*Library Journal* on *Vanish in Plain Sight*

"*Leah's Choice*...is a knowing and careful look into Amish culture and faith. A truly enjoyable reading experience."
   —Angela Hunt, *New York Times* bestselling author
               of *Let Darkness Come*

**Also available from Marta Perry
and HQN**

For additional books by Marta Perry,
visit her website, www.martaperry.com.

AMISH SECRETS

MARTA PERRY

HQN

HQN

ISBN-13: 978-1-335-41854-8

Recycling programs
for this product may
not exist in your area.

Amish Secrets

This edition published by arrangement with Harlequin Books S.A.

For questions and comments about the quality of this book,
please contact us at CustomerService@Harlequin.com.

HQN
22 Adelaide St. West, 40th Floor
Toronto, Ontario M5H 4E3, Canada
www.Harlequin.com

Printed in Spain

This book is dedicated to my dear husband, Brian.

AMISH SECRETS

CHAPTER ONE

RACHEL HURST PAUSED outside the back door of the huge Victorian house, uncertainty slithering down her back like an icicle. Did she really have courage enough to do this?

She glanced back at her younger brother, waiting for her in the buggy, his straw hat shielding his face. She caught a glimpse of bright blue eyes and an encouraging nod. Sammy believed in her, and it wouldn't set a good example for him if she backed out now.

Besides, what was there to fear? Geraldine Withers needed a housekeeper, and Rachel needed a job. She'd be taking on the same position her own mother had held, years ago. If Mammi could do it, surely she could.

And what other choice did she have? Move in with one of her brothers' families and be the spinster aunt? Neither Joshua nor Sammy deserved to have his big sister planted on him when they were both newly married. This was the only way forward that she could see.

Stop dithering. She could almost hear her mother's brisk voice in her mind. *Just do it.* Mammi had always gone straight at whatever was next to do. She would want her only daughter to do the same.

Rachel raised her hand and knocked. The door opened before she could take a breath, and Ms. Geraldine Withers stood confronting her.

Ms. Withers made an intimidating figure—straight as

the trunk of a pine tree despite her seventy-some years. Rachel didn't know whether she needed the cane in her hand, but the woman certain sure wasn't leaning on it. Steely blue eyes gave Rachel an assessing look. Then something that might have been a smile softened her stern mouth.

"Well, come in. What are we standing here for?" The voice was an echo from the past. Sometimes she'd come with Mammi to work when she was a small girl, and she'd found the voice frightening.

Mammi's response had always been a smile and a quiet, "Ach, her bark is worse than her bite." At the age she'd been when she first started coming with her mother, she hadn't found that reassuring.

Ms. Withers turned and stalked down the hallway, the cane clicking on the wide, polished floorboards. Rachel had to scurry to keep up, giving her no time for second thoughts.

They passed a huge kitchen and several other rooms before emerging into the front of the house. Archways on either side led to a dining room on the left and what she remembered Mammi calling the parlor on the right. She had a flash of memory—herself a small, shy child, standing awestruck at the sight of the immense portrait over the mantel of a man who frowned disapprovingly at the room and anyone in it. He had bushy white eyebrows and an equally bushy white moustache. The image had appeared in more than one childish nightmare.

The elderly woman seated herself in a high-backed armchair and turned to Rachel. Her frown was only slightly less intimidating than that of the man over the mantel.

"You were looking at the portrait." She gestured with the cane. "My father, Davis Withers." Her voice was surprisingly deep for a woman, and it struck another echo in Rachel's mind that she didn't bother trying to track down.

"Yah, I remembered it. From when I was here with my mother a long time ago, I mean."

The elderly face softened. "Lydia was a special person. You have a look of your mother about you."

"Denke." Rachel's voice wavered. Even after ten years, the mention of her mother could do that to her.

"Yes, well, the question is whether you'll suit me as well as she did." Ms. Withers seemed to be sizing Rachel up. "Lydia never argued. I can't stand people who argue with me."

Since she thought it highly unlikely she'd want to argue with this woman or anyone else, Rachel just nodded. Seizing the opportunity, she assessed her prospective employer in turn.

Gray hair swept back from Ms. Withers's thin face to hug her head, making her face appear even thinner. Her blue eyes weren't quite as forbidding as those in the portrait, but her thin lips formed a straight line that suggested firmness, maybe even stubbornness.

"You'll have a bedroom and bath to yourself along with your salary," the woman went on, "and I don't expect you to act as a nurse. I don't like people fussing over me." She paused as if for emphasis, but she was speaking like everything had been settled. "And no heavy cleaning. There's a service…"

She stopped at the sound of the front door opening and the click of heels on the hall floor. A second later a woman appeared in the archway, already talking. "I've brought those papers, Aunt Geraldine." She gave Rachel a quick, questioning glance before putting a glossy folder on the lamp table next to Ms. Withers. "I'm sure you'll be impressed by all this new housing complex has to offer."

Rachel knew the woman by sight, as she knew most people in River Haven. Lorna Withers's husband was Richard Withers, and his father had been Ms. Withers's younger brother. Everybody knew about the Withers family. They'd been the founders of River Haven, and its most important residents for a long time.

Richard ran the largest real estate agency in River Haven, probably in the whole county, and his wife had her finger in every civic event in the area. Amish women didn't pay much attention to women's fashions, but Rachel knew expensive clothing when she saw it.

Ignoring Rachel as if she were a piece of furniture, Lorna plunged ahead. Not sure whether she should stay or go, Rachel took a step back. Trying not to listen, she gazed out the large front window. The house was on a rise overlooking the whole town. It seemed almost isolated from the town, with only two other houses along the street and the ground rising behind them to the woods and the ridge.

She moved restlessly from one foot to the other. Lorna had picked up the folder and was now urging her aunt by marriage to look at it. Rachel could see Ms. Withers's face setting into rigid lines… The more Lorna insisted, the deeper the stubbornness grew.

Well, Rachel could handle stubbornness, that was certain sure. After ten years of managing her daad and brothers, there was nothing Ms. Withers could teach her about being stubborn. Daad had been compared to a mule more than once by her irreverent younger brothers. But not in his hearing, of course.

"You can see what lovely facilities they're building over at Green Lawns. It would be perfect for you." Lorna thrust what seemed to be a colorful brochure into Ms. Withers's hands. The woman responded by letting the brochure slip through her fingers to the floor. Rachel's lips twitched.

"Green Lawns, indeed." Ms. Withers snorted. "Sounds like a cemetery to me."

Now she had to hide a smile at the woman's tactics, so Rachel bent to pick up the brochure. A quick glance told her it advertised the new retirement community being built over near Fisherdale. She held it out to Ms. Withers, who waved it away. Lorna snatched it from her hand and put it down on the table carefully.

"Now, Aunt, you know Richard talked to you about this, and you agreed you'd consider it." Lorna sounded like her patience were wearing thin. If they were going to quarrel, Rachel thought maybe she should excuse herself.

She gestured toward the door. "If you'd like me to come another day…" she began, but Ms. Withers struck the floor sharply with her cane, ensuring silence. She drew herself up, her eyes flashing.

"Lorna, you can tell my nephew that I've already solved the problem of living alone. Rachel Hurst is coming as a live-in housekeeper, and she'll take care of everything. So you can stop trying to put me in a home."

"It's not a home—"

Ms. Withers ignored her to address Rachel. "You go have a look around the place. Come back in about half an hour."

It appeared she was hired. A little stunned at the turn of events, Rachel nodded. She decided not to risk saying anything to either of them and slipped out. The voices, momentarily silenced, started up again as soon as Rachel was in the hall.

Rachel escaped into the kitchen. Now, this was more familiar territory. Much of her day was normally spent in a kitchen, after all. This one had old-fashioned glass-paned cabinets combined with what looked like brand-new appliances. She blinked at the number of knobs and buttons on the electric range, but if it cooked food, she'd manage it. They didn't use electric at home, except for the generator that powered the milking equipment, but using it here would be part of her job.

Among many other things, she hadn't yet learned what meals she'd be expected to prepare. Still, whatever her tasks, it would certainly not be more than she'd been doing for the past ten years, taking care of Daad and the boys.

She glanced back as the sound of a raised voice penetrated the parlor door. It was obvious what had been going on between Ms. Withers and her kin. They were concerned about her living alone in this big house, and Rachel could hardly blame them. But Ms. Withers was just as clearly used to managing her own affairs, and the effort to push her into something had backfired.

Would they give up at this point? Or would the nephew be back with a more convincing argument? If so, her job here might be fairly short-lived. She suspected Ms. Withers had announced Rachel's employment only to silence her niece. Still, it was a place to start, and she couldn't let herself be discouraged.

The click of heels again announced Lorna Withers was leaving. The footsteps headed toward the front door, stopped, hesitated briefly, and came back toward the kitchen. When she appeared in the doorway, Rachel closed the cabinet door she'd opened and managed to smile.

"May I help you with anything?"

She got a frown in return. "You probably don't know that my aunt has been having problems living alone. She wouldn't tell you she's had several falls, and I hardly imagine having you in the house is going to prevent that. You may want to think twice about this position. If you like, I'm sure I could find something else for you."

Rachel discovered in herself a dislike for having other people tell her what to do. "I already have a job, thank you."

Lorna's face stiffened, showing her age despite the careful makeup. "Very well," she snapped. "Just realize that if anything happens to Ms. Withers, the responsibility is on you."

She spun and stalked back to the front door, closing it firmly behind her. A moment later Rachel heard a car pulling out.

Rachel stood where she was, surprised by her own reaction to the woman. But was she right? If Ms. Withers needed more care than she could provide, she might have made the wrong decision in coming here.

Still, she didn't regret it—at least, not yet.

Standing there brooding wasn't going to help any. A glance at the clock showed her that she had a good forty minutes before she would talk to her new employer again. She couldn't very well keep Sammy waiting that long, so she headed out back.

Sammy was leaning against the buggy, staring up at the house's fanciful curlicues and turrets. He jerked his head at them, grinning a little.

"Pretty fancy, ain't so? Well, what's the verdict? Did you get the job?"

"I did." She couldn't help returning his grin.

"Good going!" Sammy wrapped his arm around her in a hug. "I knew you could do it. Wait until everybody hears."

By everybody, she supposed he meant Daad, who was off on a wedding trip with his new bride. She'd agreed she'd be moved out by the time they came back, and so she would.

Dad's marriage had shocked everyone, but her most of all. She had resigned herself to staying at home and taking care of him, and to discover all at once that she wasn't needed had shocked her—shocked her so much that she hadn't been able to think straight. Only one thing had been clear to her, and that was to move out as fast as possible.

"I'll have to go back to the house to pick up my things, but Ms. Withers seems to want me around this afternoon. Are you okay if I call the phone shanty later and let you know when to get me?"

"For sure." He gave her a questioning look. "Are you okay about all this?"

"I'm fine," she assured him, hoping she meant it. "It's natural that Evelyn will want her new home to herself. And it's much better for me to be independent."

A shadow crossed his face, making her think he had been as shocked as she had when Daad had announced out of the blue that he was marrying again after ten years of being a widower.

"If it doesn't work out, just remember you'll always have a home with Sarah and me." He would always be the little brother she'd helped raise, but he seemed solemn and grown up all of a sudden.

"Denke, Sammy." It was her turn to hug him, and her throat was tight. "I'd best get busy. I'll call later and leave a message." She turned away quickly, not wanting him to see her face while she blinked back tears.

Sammy climbed up to the buggy seat, picked up the lines and then glanced at her again. "Rachel, I'm not so sure about this. Did you know—"

"Go on, now. Go. I'll see you later. It will be fine." Her confident smile wouldn't last much longer, so she waved and hurried to the door. She wouldn't look back to see him drive away. Much better to do as Ms. Withers said and get familiar with her new home. And keep her mind off the past.

An hour later Rachel had seen much of the house and had a chat with her new employer. The tour had left her wondering how many people had once lived in such a huge place. Amish had big families, but they did it without a house the size of this one.

It must have been built in part to show the community that Davis Withers had been a man of wealth and importance, at least in the town's eyes, she supposed. He and his wife had had four children—one boy and three girls—information she obtained from the extensive framed family tree in the upstairs hall. Ms. Geraldine was the oldest of the girls. They'd certainly had enough bedrooms for a couple more.

Some of the rooms were closed up, and her talk with Ms. Withers had assured her that she wouldn't be expected to keep them clean. A cleaning service would take care of that. Rachel's job—cooking, laundry and light cleaning— was far less than she'd been doing at home.

She mentally added another job as she walked out onto the back porch. According to Lorna Withers, she was responsible for keeping Ms. Withers from falling, and that might be the most challenging job of all. Somehow she couldn't see herself telling the woman what not to do.

She'd called and left a message for Sammy, but it would take a little time before he received her message and drove over. Rachel decided she'd take a look around the grounds. She'd have no responsibilities there, but she could still enjoy them.

The plantings that made the Withers place the star of the annual garden tour were filled with an array of spring flowers. The early bulbs were past, but a variety of tulips stood proudly along the porch, including a rich lavender hue she'd never seen before. She walked slowly along the back of the house. A small kitchen garden drew her eyes, already green with early lettuce and the spears of spring onions. She'd have to ask if she could pick what she needed for meals, wondering whether the gardener might disapprove.

The sound of hammering drew her on around the building, past a thick row of lilacs in full bloom, ranging from deepest purple to pure white. As she rounded the corner of the house, a grape arbor came into view. She stopped, entranced by the memories that seized her.

Her mother had sometimes sent her outside with instructions to play quietly until she'd finished her work. If Ms. Withers's nieces and nephews had been there, quiet play had been questionable, but she'd found a haven in the grape arbor. She'd never seen one quite like it, extending for what she now saw was a good twelve feet in length and wide enough to have benches down either side. She'd loved to hide there in the cool shade, making up stories with the tiny dolls she'd created from hollyhock blossoms.

It was too early for hollyhocks now. Smiling, Rachel shook her head and recalled herself to the present. According to her mother, she'd always been a dreamy child, happy to entertain herself with her imagination, although the advent of two younger brothers had sometimes made that impossible.

The grape arbor had been her place, and the pounding was coming from inside it. The gardener, maybe? She certainly hoped it wasn't being torn down.

Walking on, she reached a point at which she could see the inside. She came to a dead stop. Someone was working on the arbor, someone who stopped and stared at her as if he didn't believe what he was seeing.

Fair enough, because she didn't want to believe what she was seeing either. Jacob Beiler, the one person in the Amish community that she didn't want to meet here or anywhere else. Jacob Beiler, the man she'd jilted nearly ten years ago. And he was staring at her with a look cold enough to freeze her on the spot.

IT TOOK JACOB just a second to recover from the unexpected sight and project the attitude he had maintained toward Rachel for years—the attitude that had gone a long way toward getting him through glimpses of her at worship or at community events.

Calm, polite acceptance of another member of the Leit— that was all she was to him. At least, that was what he told himself, suppressing the sense of resentment that came without warning.

"Rachel. I didn't expect to see you here." If he had, he'd have been better prepared.

At least he could take pride in the fact that she looked even more affected than he thought he had. He'd have to count that as a point in the odd game of not caring they'd been playing for years.

Rachel straightened, seeming to force a smile. "I didn't either. Expect to see you, I mean." She nodded toward his toolbox. "You're doing some work here, ain't so?"

She had to know he specialized in the restoration of old houses, a popular trend among the Englisch. She was probably thinking that mending a simple grape arbor was a comedown for him.

Shrugging, he gestured at the arbor. "This is just a little extra job for Ms. Withers. Anyone could fix this. I've been restoring and refinishing the woodwork in the house."

"In the house." She repeated the words as if needing to be sure of them. "I…I didn't know."

Did that mean she wouldn't have been here if she'd known he was? Well, she couldn't be more eager to avoid him than he was to avoid her. The bitterness he'd been trying to conquer for years welled up as fresh as if it had been yesterday. It looked like he had some more work to do on the whole forgive-and-forget idea.

"Your turn," he said. "What are you doing here? A little far from home, aren't you?"

Her rounded chin came up, reminding him of the way she'd looked at him long ago. She hadn't changed much, not externally, anyway. She still looked like the sixteen-year-old she'd been, with the warm, peachy glow to her smooth cheeks and the gentle smile.

"Ms. Withers just hired me to be her housekeeper." She said it as if expecting an argument, or at least surprise. Or maybe she was the one who was surprised at where she'd ended up.

His bitterness surged again. "I did hear that your daad remarried. I guess that threw you out of a job, ain't so?"

That hurt her—he could see her wince. He told himself he didn't care. She was the one who'd thrown all their happiness away for what she called her duty. And where were they now? Both unmarried, both without the family they could have had.

Rachel had regained her control. She wouldn't want him to see that he'd gotten through to her, and he had a moment's regret. What good was it, going over and over the past? He'd be better off pretending he didn't mind the fact that her new job would force them into seeing each other every day.

He searched for something reasonably polite to say. "Do you think you're going to like it?"

"I...I suppose so." She seemed troubled, and the old longing to take her burdens on himself surged and had to be forced down again.

"You don't sound convinced."

She shook her head slightly. "I don't know. Her niece—Lorna, I mean—came in while I was there. She didn't like the idea."

"I'm certain sure she didn't." He smiled in admiration of Geraldine's spunk. "Geraldine out-maneuvered them and their ideas that she should move out and let them do what they wanted with her house. She hired you so they couldn't complain she was alone. Good for her."

"I'm sure they didn't mean it that way." Predictably, Rachel defended them, just as she'd always defended her father's selfishness. "I'm sure they're just worried about her living alone at her age."

"You always expect the best of people, don't you?" He looked at her with honest curiosity.

"Why not?" Her eyes, looking more green than blue with the green dress she wore, opened wide. "Don't you?"

"No," he said bluntly. "And you won't, either, once you've been out in the world a bit." He gave a short laugh. "And once you've seen a little more of Ms. Withers's family. As far as I can tell, they all just come here to see what they can get from her."

Distress darkened her eyes. "Ach, Jacob, you shouldn't talk that way about people you don't know."

"I might not know them, but I've seen and heard them around her. That's enough to tell me what to think. There's a sister who spends all her time whining because their father left Geraldine in control of the family money. And the sister's precious son, Gerald, who must be forty if he's a day and hasn't done a lick of work in his life."

Something in Rachel seemed to respond to that. "I think I remember Gerald. He was around a lot when I used to come with Mammi to work." She paused.

"Looking for something nice to say about him?" he asked, sarcasm underlying the words. "You can't, can you?"

She flared up at that. "I was only five or six…hardly at an age to give an opinion about what he's like as a grown man." She hesitated. "Is that all of them? I've forgotten most of what I knew, and I guess I should know what to expect. Or who, if I have to deal with them."

Maybe Rachel wasn't quite as naive as he'd thought. There was some wry humor in her words.

"There's a niece, Julianne, daughter of Geraldine's other sister. She didn't stay in the area. Geraldine mentions her now and then—mostly to say she's moved to another city or found another husband. I think she has a daughter."

Rachel gave him a questioning glance. "How is it you know so much about them? I wouldn't think—" She stopped, as if not sure she wanted to complete that sentence.

"You wouldn't think she'd confide in me." He had no trouble finishing it for her. "I wouldn't think it either." He shrugged. "Sometimes she watches me work and talks. More like talking to herself, most of the time."

"It sounds as if she's lonely," Rachel said with that quick sympathy of hers.

"I'd guess that's where you come in, Rachel. Not just to cook and clean, but to keep her company." Rachel would probably be good at that, he'd think, after dealing with that cross-grained father of hers all these years.

"She liked having my mother around, I know. I used to hear them talking sometimes." She seemed to shake off the past. "Is that all of the family?"

"I think so. Lorna and Richard you know of already, yah? And they have a teenage boy"

"Lorna was just here." She said the words as though they left a sour taste in her mouth, and she met Jacob's eyes, her face troubled. "She was trying to talk her aunt into going to that new retirement place they're building. I don't think she liked the fact that Ms. Withers had hired me."

Something in him responded to the feeling beneath the words. All of a sudden it was as if they were talking the way they used to, when they'd hardly needed words to communicate with each other.

"If she doesn't, it's not your fault. She wouldn't be happy with anyone who might get in their way."

"You shouldn't talk that way about them. They're probably just worried about her being all alone in this big house."

"That's not what Ms. Withers thinks." He'd heard enough to know that.

"Maybe so, but…did you know she'd been falling?"

That startled him. "No. She never has when I've been around. She didn't say that, did she?" It would be very unlike the woman to admit to any weakness on her part.

"No, but Lorna did. She said that was why they wanted her to move. To be somewhere safe." She sucked in a breath, her distress deepening. "She said having me in the house wouldn't keep her from falling. And that if she were hurt, the blame would be on me."

"That's ferhoodled," he snapped. "Even if she did fall, it wouldn't be your fault. You can't keep the woman from doing what she wants, and neither can Richard and Lorna. Have you asked Ms. Withers about it?"

"No. Do you think I should?"

"I think you might get your nose snipped off." He grinned, hoping to lighten the mood. Rachel was starting to make him worry right along with her. "But if you're going to worry about her, maybe you should ask her. Just see what her opinion is."

"I suppose." She didn't sound convinced.

"Anyway, even if she did, you're there to get help if she needs it. And if she's having trouble getting around, there are plenty of solutions short of moving out. She could have safety bars put in the bathroom, for instance. I could do that easily. And you might check for any tripping hazards. Better to try that than to push her into a place where she doesn't want to live."

Some of the worry left her face. "Would you do that, Jacob? That's an idea. I'll try to find a moment to bring it up. I'd feel better if I knew we'd done what we could."

We. Did Rachel even realize she'd coupled their names together the way she used to? He didn't think so, but she was looking at him as though he'd helped. He'd like to think it was a good sign that they were able to talk easily again.

"It's no trouble to set up safety bars and things like that. See what you can do with her and let me know."

"Denke, Jacob." She reached out toward him as if she'd touch him, but then quickly pulled her hand back, flushing a little. "I…I should go. Sammy's picking me up to go home and move my things over. He might be here by now."

She turned, taking a step and abruptly freezing. A cry came from the house—sharp and piercing. For an instant he was frozen, too. And then they were both racing toward the door, hearts pounding.

CHAPTER TWO

RACHEL RAN INTO the house, hearing the thud of Jacob's footsteps right behind her. Her heart hammered in anticipation of what she might find.

Silence dropped around them, and for a split second she almost thought she'd imagined that cry. But they couldn't both have imagined it.

"Ms. Withers? Where are you?"

"Here." The voice came from the stairs, sounding faint. But at least she could respond.

Rachel lunged for the stairs, jostling with Jacob as they flew up them. The wide staircase took a turn halfway up, and Ms. Withers was just around the bend, out of sight from the bottom. Jacob moved instinctively to lift her.

"No, stop." Rachel grabbed his arm before he could complete the act. She knelt next to her employer. Ms. Withers seemed composed, but her face was white as paper and her hand was clenched around the spindle, the blue veins standing out and the bones visible under the skin.

"Where does it hurt? Don't try to move, just tell us." She touched the rigid hand, and the woman switched her grip to Rachel's warm one. Rachel saw her make an enormous effort to control herself.

"I'm sure I'm all right. Give me a minute." She glared at Jacob as if he'd been rushing her, but his stoic expression didn't change.

"As much time as you need," Rachel soothed, realizing her employer needed to feel in control. "We'll help however you tell us. Should I call a doctor?"

"No." The answer was sharp, and some of the color came back into Ms. Withers's face. "I can just hear that nephew of mine if he heard I'd had a fall. He'd be trying to cart me off to a nursing home the next minute."

"Never mind about Richard," Jacob said, and Rachel wondered if he knew that dislike sounded in his voice. "If you're hurt, you need a doctor."

"I'm not." There was more sureness in her voice, and her expression challenged them to argue. "Just maybe a few bruises, that's all."

Rachel exchanged glances with Jacob before turning back to her employer. "What about resting on your bed for a little?" Was that where Ms. Withers had been? Maybe she'd gone up while Rachel was outside. She felt irrationally guilty.

"Nonsense. I'll go down to the parlor and be comfortable in my usual chair. If you want to fuss, you can just give me your arm to hold."

"For sure." She stood, but as she moved into position, her right foot slid a few inches despite the rubber-soled shoes she wore. She regained her balance in an instant, but the misstep started an unpleasant train of thought. She glanced at Jacob, but he didn't seem to have noticed.

Clearly the first thing to do was to see the woman settled and comfortable. She held out her arm, remembering how her grossmammi had hated it if anyone grabbed her arm to help her. No matter how old, a person wanted to feel in control of her own body.

Jacob, watching her, copied her movements. With one on either side, they moved slowly down the steps. To Rachel's relief, by the time they reached the hall, Ms. Withers seemed to be regaining her strength. Still moving slowly, they proceeded into the parlor and settled her in the chair that was apparently her favorite. Rachel found an extra pillow while Jacob slid the footstool into place.

"All right?" she said, as Ms. Withers leaned back in obvious relief.

"Better. You can make me a cup of tea."

"Of course." Rachel wanted to caution her not to move until she returned but feared having her head bitten off. "I'll be back in a moment."

"Fine." She closed her eyes. "You can go back to work, Jacob."

Apparently that was his dismissal. Jacob followed Rachel out, pulling one of the double doors to, and then paused in the hall. "A thank-you would be too much to expect," he muttered.

"Denke, Jacob," she said softly, smiling at his exasperated expression. "That would be admitting she'd needed you." With a quick shake of her head, she turned toward the kitchen. "I'd best get that tea started."

"I'm going up to check on the stairs. Yah, I saw your foot slip. I want to see why. Distract her if she asks what I'm doing."

Before she could ask him anything, Jacob was gone, moving silently up the stairs. Now she understood why he'd pulled one of the doors partially closed. At this angle, Ms. Withers wouldn't be able to see him.

But how she was supposed to distract the woman, she couldn't imagine, so she fled to the kitchen.

When she came back through the hall with the tea tray a few minutes later, Jacob was just coming down the stairs.

She looked at him with raised eyebrows. "What do you think?"

He was frowning, his eyes intent. "Some sort of slick polish on several of the steps. Not just something spilled. It's been smoothed out. It's hard to imagine how it got there."

"No one would use that type of polish on steps." She thought of the way her foot had slipped. "It could have been a mistake, I suppose…"

"Come in here, both of you." Ms. Withers's voice was abrupt. And loud.

Exchanging glances with Jacob, Rachel led the way into the parlor, then set up the tea on a side table that seemed intended for it. The table was equipped with a couple of shelves, one of which held books and the other a workbag of some sort—embroidery, she thought, noticing the glint of a steel hoop.

Ms. Withers let her finish before speaking. "Now, then." She surveyed them. "What's going on? What's wrong with the steps?"

Rachel decided Jacob should field that one, and she looked at him. The strong planes of his face tightened as he seemed to consider what to say.

After a moment, he spoke. "Like I was telling Rachel, it looks like there's some kind of slick polish on a couple of the steps. Right where you fell."

"Nonsense. No one with any sense would do that."

He shrugged, looking annoyed that she doubted him. "It's there."

"Someone might have dropped it, I guess," Rachel said quickly, before he could say anything. "You told me it was smoothed out, but someone might have tried to clean it up, not realizing it was still slippery. It's certain sure my foot slid on it when I tried to help you up."

"Some safety treads on those steps—" Jacob began, but Ms. Withers cut him off.

"Never. I won't have that beautiful wood ruined. And that's final."

"I can scrub the polish off without harming the wood." Rachel began to think her main job was going to be mediating between Ms. Withers and other people.

"That's not your job," Ms. Withers began, but this time it was Rachel's turn to cut her off.

"It makes no matter," she said calmly. If she let herself be intimidated by her new employer's growling, she may as well quit now. "Ach, that must be my brother coming for me. Excuse me."

She hurried toward the back door, not waiting for an argument. She couldn't leave when Ms. Withers was in such a state. She'd have to get her things later.

"Hold on." Jacob got to her before she reached the door, catching her arm. "Ms. Withers says you're to go. You were going to cancel, weren't you?"

"I was. I still am. I can't leave her alone right now." She pulled her arm free of his warm clasp.

"She won't like it," he warned. He seemed to struggle with himself before he spoke. "Look, I can stay in the house until you get back. I won't let her do anything. Just go." His face relaxed in what was almost a smile. "I have sisters, remember? I can't stand to listen to women arguing."

Rachel hesitated. She'd already found, in her brief employment, that Ms. Withers didn't want to be thwarted. "All right," she said reluctantly. "I'll hurry. It won't take me long."

"Not a problem," he said easily. "No point in upsetting her any further."

"I guess not." She hated the thought of leaving, but Jacob

was right. She moved toward the door, more reluctant than she would have expected. What was she worried about? Jacob was perfectly capable.

But the feeling persisted. She forced herself to hurry out to the waiting buggy. It might not make any sense, but she didn't think Ms. Withers should be alone. Not at all.

THE HOUSE SEEMED very quiet with Rachel gone. Jacob paused, wondering if he should look in on Ms. Withers again, knowing she wouldn't like it. Probably best to keep busy within earshot of the parlor. The door was partially open, so he'd hear her if anything happened.

After getting a pail out, he filled it with soapy water, hoping he wasn't going to get in trouble with Rachel for going ahead with what she'd planned to do. Well, whether she liked it or not, he intended to have those steps clean before he did anything else. And he'd check the rest of the way up to be sure there hadn't been any more accidents.

He tried not to speculate on how this had happened, but he couldn't stop himself. Strange as it seemed, he'd gotten fond of the crotchety old woman in the four or five weeks he'd been working here. He liked her spirit, and he didn't want anything to happen to her.

It took some time, but when he came back down, Jacob was satisfied that the staircase was as safe as it could be. He figured Ms. Withers could easily afford one of those chairlifts. That would be a lot safer for someone her age, but he sure didn't want to be the one to suggest it, given the way she'd reacted to his suggestion of stair treads.

"Jacob!"

He hadn't made it past the door without being heard. Setting the pail down carefully, he headed into the parlor. "Anything you need, Ms. Withers?"

"I need to know what you found on my staircase." She tapped the shining mahogany cane on the floor. "Come over here where I can see you."

Suppressing a smile, he went. Spirited, like he'd told himself.

"I found pretty much what I said before. It looked like someone had slopped wax or polish on a couple of steps. I checked every one, and it was just that one place." A place where she might have had a good long fall if she hadn't caught herself, he added silently.

"That dratted cleaning crew." The tip of her cane hit the floor again. "How they have the nerve to call themselves that, I don't know. There's not one of them knows a thing about keeping a house clean. I have to keep after them all the time."

"In that case you wouldn't think they'd even try to shine the stairs," he commented. He'd seen the crew on their twice-weekly visits and hadn't been impressed. "More likely to sweep the dust under the carpets than to try polishing anything."

She snorted. "Probably because I told them what I thought of their excuse for cleaning the last time. I can't stand people who don't even try to do what they're being paid for."

He had to agree with her. If you took a job on, you did your best. "Why did you hire them anyway?"

"Lorna set it up. I had Lois Potter for years, but she wanted to quit, for some reason."

Probably because Lois Potter was eighty if she was a day. He suppressed a smile. "Why don't you fire them and get somebody else?"

"Lorna kept after me, saying with antique furniture and expensive silver around, I should have a company that was bonded, so I'd be covered if anything was missing or broken." Her fingers tightened on the head of her cane. "Truth is, I didn't want the hassle of looking for someone."

"That's easy enough," he said, suppressing any comment on Lorna's interference. "Ask Rachel. She probably has a cousin or a friend who'd like a job. And she'd make sure they did it, too."

"Humph. Guess that's a thought. Rachel should be a big help—I can see that already. Just like her mother was." She seemed to gaze into the past for a moment and then she zeroed in on his face. "Didn't I hear the two of you were sweethearts once?"

It wasn't easy to resist that penetrating look, but he managed, shrugging it off. "That was boy-and-girl stuff. A long time ago."

"Neither of you is old enough to make it a long time," she said. "I wouldn't know, but they say people often come back to their first love. Isn't that right?"

She was trying to get a rise out of him, and he wasn't going to let her. She could go try this technique on Rachel.

An instant later he was sorry for the thought. For all he knew, Rachel might be sensitive on that subject, and Ms. Withers wasn't exactly tactful.

"I wouldn't know either. Anyway, like I said, I'm sure Rachel can find someone. It's a rare Amish woman who doesn't know how to keep a house clean."

She nodded, seeming thoughtful, so apparently he'd diverted her thoughts.

The tea tray Rachel had brought earlier still sat on the side table. "Do you want me to take that to the kitchen? Or get you a refill?"

"That's my bone china. You might be a good carpenter, but I'd rather trust Rachel with it."

"Good thinking." He smiled, then turned his head at a sound. "There's a buggy coming. Rachel must be back already. I'll see if she needs any help."

Just as well that Rachel had turned up to give him a reason to head for the kitchen. He always felt as if he should go back out and wash his hands again when he went in the parlor. And maybe clean his shoes on the mat, too.

To Jacob's surprise, he found that instead of Rachel's brother bringing her back, she was alone in a single-seat buggy. "What happened to your brother?" he asked, lifting a black suitcase from behind the seat.

"We decided I should take the old courting buggy for my own use." She sounded a little doubtful, as if wondering whether she'd done right.

"Sounds like a gut idea. You'll need something to get around in. You could walk downtown, but you wouldn't want to be carrying stuff up the hill." He put the bag on the porch. "You can keep the mare in the small barn where I stable mine when I'm here working. Komm. I'll show you."

He didn't make a move to get in with her, but just led the way past the garage to the outbuildings that were still standing from the time when Withers property extended across the whole hill. They were in good shape, too. Ms. Withers wasn't one to let her property go.

When he shoved back the door, Blackie, the rawboned gelding he drove, looked up and whickered. "No, it's not time to go home." He patted the horse and pushed his head out of the way to open the adjoining stall door. "We're bringing you some company."

"Denke, Jacob." Rachel slid down from the seat. "I'll have Bessie set up in no time." She started to unbuckle the harness.

"Here, I'll take care of that." He grasped the mare's head-stall. "You go see about Ms. Withers."

"Is she all right?" Rachel's face clouded. "I knew I shouldn't leave her."

"Forget it. She's fine, just her usual cranky self. She wouldn't let me touch her precious china."

Rachel's lips twitched at his reference to the china. "I'm not surprised. I expected a lecture the first time I touched the set." She rubbed the mare's muzzle, and Jacob noticed that the brown was touched with gray, a sure sign of age.

"I hope I did right to bring Bessie over here. Daad might not like it, but Sammy said—"

"Whatever Sammy said, I agree with him. The least your Daad owes you is an old horse and buggy, kicking you out of your own home after all those years of work."

He was surprised at his own vehemence. What did he care whether her father was fair to his daughter or not? But he found he did.

He expected her to jump to her father's defense, but she took off in another direction. "Don't you call Bessie old. Don't listen to him, sweetheart." She crooned in the mare's ear as she stroked the muzzle. "You're the best little buggy horse anyone could hope to find." She gave a disdainful look at Blackie, and Jacob couldn't help grinning.

"You're thinking I'm a good one to talk. Blackie's not much of a looker, I grant you." He lifted Bessie's harness away and hung it next to his own. "One of my brother Matt's finds. He never could judge horseflesh. But Blackie's as strong as an ox, so we get along okay."

"Bessie forgives you, then." The twinkle in her eyes reminded him of the schoolgirl she'd been. "We won't insult each other's taste in horses, yah?"

"Yah." For a moment they stood there, smiling at each other across the mare's head.

Then Rachel seemed to shake herself and spun toward the door. "Denke, Jacob. I'll see you later, ain't so?"

He nodded, trying to remind himself that it didn't matter to him if Rachel had a twinkle in her greenish blue eyes or a smile that a person just had to return. Not one bit.

RACHEL WOKE WITH the sun the next morning, glad that the room assigned to her faced east. Ordinarily she woke to the sounds of Daad heading out to the barn before daylight, but quiet gripped the Withers house. Hurrying through getting dressed and ready for the day, she went quietly down the stairs to the kitchen.

She'd had a restless night, but a mug of strong coffee would soon get her moving. And the aroma of coffee perking should take away the sense of desertion in the functional kitchen.

Once the coffee was on and the sunlight streaming through the kitchen window, the room did seem a bit more welcoming. In any Amish house, the kitchen was very much the heart of the home. Constantly busy, often filled to bursting with talk and laughter. Obviously the same was not true here.

Maybe that was why she'd had such a restless night—the quiet, and also the fact that she'd been trying to settle in a bed that, however comfortable, wasn't the one she'd slept in since she'd been big enough to sleep in a regular bed.

The previous evening, she had finally been able to settle the extent of her responsibilities. Ms. Withers wanted her to prepare the meals, clean up and do whatever daily cleaning needed attention. A laundry service, a lawn service and the weekly cleaning service supposedly took care of everything else. The grocery store in town would deliver anything she ordered.

It seemed simple enough and was certainly far less than her usual workday in her father's house. In fact, she'd begun to wonder how she'd fill the hours in the day. She had to smile at the idea of not having enough to do. That was a problem she'd never even considered.

At that moment she heard the sound of footsteps on the stairs and swung into action. A three-minute egg couldn't be made ahead of time, but she figured by the time Ms. Withers was settled, she'd have breakfast ready to set in front of her.

Her employer must not be a morning person. She didn't say a word, eating in silence at the oval table in the dining room while Rachel, also in silence, finished her meal in the kitchen. This was going to take some getting used to, she decided. Nothing more different than her usual breakfast could be imagined.

"I don't suppose you usually have breakfast all alone." Ms. Withers's sudden entrance startled Rachel, and she leaped to her feet.

"May I get you something else?" She moved in front of her dishes. Nothing looked worse than an eggy plate, after all.

"I'd like some more coffee, but I'll have it here with you, if you don't mind."

Rachel whisked her dishes into the sink and brought the coffeepot. "I surely don't." She waited until the elderly woman had taken a seat before pouring the coffee and sitting down across the table. She hadn't expected this. Did Ms. Withers want to tell her she'd done something wrong?

"It wasn't always this quiet." Ms. Withers sipped her coffee and then added a little more sugar. "Those summers when my nieces and nephews came to stay… I couldn't have done without your mother."

The momentary tension slipped away. Was it possible that Ms. Withers just wanted to reminisce? She'd seemed so cool and self-contained that Rachel hadn't expected it. Still, it was nice to have someone remembering her mamm that way.

"Yah, I remember. She brought me sometimes, but there was one summer when Mammi brought me with her most days. I remember it best." She smiled, her thoughts drifting back. "She said it was so I could help her, but I think mostly she wanted to get me away from my little bruders for a while."

"I'd guess my nephews could be just as annoying to you as your brothers were. Especially Gerald." Her face tightened a little when she mentioned him.

Rachel certain sure didn't want to add fuel to the fire. "Ach, he just liked to play tricks." Especially on someone smaller and weaker than he was, but she could hardly say that.

"Sometimes I wonder if he'll ever grow up." Her voice was tart. "He should have a decent job and a family by now."

Rachel did some mental arithmetic. Gerald would be younger than Richard, but not by all that much, so he must be in his thirties, at least. Richard was enough older and kinder that he'd sometimes stopped Gerald from teasing her.

"Nothing to say to that?" Ms. Withers gave what might have been a slight smile. "Never mind."

"I…I guess I remember Julianne and her bruder a little better. William, that was his name, wasn't it?" They'd all been in their teens while she'd been just old enough to be a nuisance, she supposed.

She could remember being fascinated by how pretty Julianne had been. And how much time she'd spent on her looks. That young Rachel had never seen makeup before, and Julianne had let her watch her fix her hair and her face sometimes.

"Yes, William." Ms. Withers's face had softened in a way Rachel had never seen. "He was the best of the bunch."

"He was good-looking, I remember." She had a mental image of a tall, tanned boy with sun-bleached hair and an engaging grin. He'd clearly captured his aunt's heart, judging by her expression.

"He had it all." Ms. Withers seemed to have forgotten her as she looked into the past. "Handsome, intelligent, talented…" She paused, her face drawing tight against the bones. "And then he threw it all away, and his family with it."

She rose, steadied herself against the table for a moment, then walked away without another word.

Baffled, Rachel looked blankly at the swinging door. What had happened? Obviously something very drastic. Rachel hadn't seen him since that summer, but there was no reason why she should have. Both he and his sister had, she supposed, gone on to live their lives elsewhere. If there had been some scandal, she'd never heard about it.

Reminding herself that it wasn't any of her business, she washed the breakfast dishes, ignoring the dishwasher under the counter. She might have to use it sometime, but she could do these faster by hand. And maybe cleaner, as well.

After she'd made beds and tidied the bedrooms, Rachel explored the second floor a bit more. There were four bedrooms on this floor—Ms. Withers's large suite across the front of the house, three others toward the back, along with what seemed to be a large sewing room.

She eyed the electric sewing machine doubtfully, but she could figure it out if necessary. Her good friend Joanna had an electric machine in her quilt shop for the use of the Englisch customers who came for quilting lessons.

At the thought of Joanna, Rachel found herself longing to have a good long talk with someone she understood. Someone who understood her. Well, she could always drop in on Joanna when she went to town to do any extra shopping. Ms. Withers wouldn't mind, surely.

Beyond the sewing room were two other rooms at the back of the house with closed doors. A quick look told her they'd once been bedrooms, but the beds were stripped and the rugs rolled up. The room was clean, but obviously not in use.

She returned to the part of the house in use. She'd walked past the third bedroom this morning, having seen it yesterday, but now she was drawn by a noise. The floor creaked… as if at a step. But old houses always creaked, didn't they?

Did she have time… A gentle thud came from inside the room. Her nerves jumped. Quickly, before she could talk herself out of it, she threw the door open.

And then laughed at herself when Jacob, kneeling by the baseboard, looked up at her, startled.

"I didn't realize you were working up here. I thought you were still outside." Rachel realized she was flushing. She wouldn't want him to think it mattered to her where he was.

He didn't seem to notice. "I finished the arbor yesterday, so it's on to the next thing. Much of this woodwork is due to be refinished and repaired." He paused. "How's Ms. Withers? Any problems after her fall?"

"Not that she's willing to admit, anyway." She walked to the window that looked out over the driveway and the field beyond. "She started talking to me about the past— remembering the summers her nieces and nephews used to spend here."

Jacob eyed her in a questioning way. "She's probably going to chat with you a lot because of your mother."

She wasn't sure she liked the idea that she was accepted for that reason, but she knew better than to respond. "She thinks I remember about them because my mother brought me with her in the summer. I hope I don't disappoint her. I was quite young the first time she brought me, but each summer I came more often. Still, it's been a long time to remember."

"More likely she just wanted to talk about them herself." He shrugged, turning back to the woodwork. "Older people like to talk about the way things used to be."

"And she doesn't seem to have much family to talk to." She thought again what an isolated life the elderly woman led. Although Geraldine Withers probably wasn't the type for a lot of chitchat, young or old.

"Maybe you ought to work on remembering more, then." He didn't look at her this time, maybe losing interest in the subject.

"There's a car pulling in the drive." She was galvanized into action. "I'd best get the door."

Rachel hurried out, not looking back at him.

When she was halfway down the stairs, she saw that Ms. Withers had taken care of that herself, opening the door to a woman and a young girl. Rachel had time for a good look at the visitors while greetings were being exchanged.

She'd have to amend her opinion about Ms. Withers not getting much attention from her family. The woman had changed a great deal from the teenager she remembered, but she knew her. It was Julianne, sister of the boy Ms. Withers had referred to in such bitter terms.

CHAPTER THREE

FOR A MOMENT they all stood there, saying nothing. Then Rachel reached out for their bags. Julianne surrendered her suitcase readily, giving Rachel the warm smile she remembered. The young girl pulled her overstuffed backpack away as if Rachel might run off with it.

The silence ended in a babble of talk as Julianne rushed at her aunt with hugs and overflowing affection. Ms. Withers offered her cheek for a kiss and then drew back warily.

"Well, it's just delightful to see you, Aunt Geraldine." Julianne released her. "I'm so sorry I didn't let you know when we were arriving. After all, no one likes to have unexpected company. But once we were on our way, I was so eager to be here again that I drove straight through. You remember my daughter, Holly, don't you?" She pulled the sulky-looking preteen forward.

Ms. Withers surveyed the child. "I wouldn't have known her. She was only about four or five when I saw her last."

Her tone was dry. Clearly, for all her professed affection, Julianne hadn't been staying in touch with her aunt. The girl was looking around the hallway as if she'd never seen it before and didn't think much of it now.

Rachel stayed where she was, not sure what to do. Julianne was just what she'd have imagined she'd grow up to be—beautiful and well-dressed, with a big-city flair that Richard's wife would probably find distasteful. Her heart-shaped face was still young-looking, but as a ray of sunlight from the window touched it, the fine lines in Julianne's face reminded Rachel that she was no longer a teenager.

As for her daughter, Rachel couldn't decide. Was that sulky look always there, or had she been brought to visit her elderly relative against her will? It was certain sure she wasn't making much effort to be pleasant, but with her mother's golden hair and bright green eyes, she had the promise of beauty once she was a few years older.

Julianne was still babbling away, telling her aunt about every stage of her trip from Atlanta. There seemed little point in standing here holding a suitcase. As Julianne paused for breath, Rachel cleared her throat.

"Would you like me to take the bags upstairs, Ms. Withers?"

Her employer replied with a slight shake of her head. "Just leave them in the hall for now. You might see what we have that you can fix for lunch." She turned to her niece. "You will stay for lunch, won't you?"

Rachel wondered about that while Julianne accepted the invitation very prettily, with apologies again for not notifying her aunt. It struck Rachel that Julianne wouldn't have brought her suitcase inside unless she'd planned to stay overnight, at least, but if the lunch invitation disconcerted her, she didn't let it show.

But none of that was her business. She stowed the case against the wall so that no one could trip on it, and then she hurried off to the kitchen, her thoughts busy with what she could produce for a company meal on such short order.

At least there was plenty of chicken left from last night's supper. Engrossed in finding the ingredients for chicken salad, she turned from the refrigerator and nearly dropped an armload of produce on the floor. Jacob had appeared behind her.

"Where did you come from?" She put everything on a nearby counter. "I didn't see you come down the stairs."

He lifted an eyebrow at her surprise, a talent she'd envied as a girl. "You don't know about the back stairs?"

"There's another flight of steps to the second floor?" She'd have been glad to know that before carrying things up and down that polished, elegant stairwell.

Jacob's face actually cracked in a smile. "You probably thought it was a closet. It comes down into the pantry. See?"

She followed him through the large pantry to an unobtrusive door past a row of shelves. He opened it, revealing a narrow set of steps going up, lit faintly by a small window at the top.

Jacob gestured. "They figured this was good enough for the servants, I'd guess. If you're going up and down, be careful. They're narrower than they look."

She gazed up for another moment, shaking her head. "I'd never have guessed it was there." She headed back into the kitchen, her mind on lunch.

"Oh, that's not the only surprise in this rambling old place. You wouldn't believe some of the nooks and crannies I've found looking around. If you want me to show you…"

"I have lunch to fix," she said firmly, not giving in to the temptation to grab a little more time with him. "This is no time for a tour."

Rachel expected him to take the hint and disappear, but he leaned against the counter, watching as she chopped celery and onion.

Apparently tiring of the repetitive movements, he shifted his weight and looked toward the swinging door. "Wonder what brought Julianne here. She's not exactly a regular visitor."

"Do you know her?" She couldn't help but ask.

He shrugged. "Only from her photograph in the upstairs hall. Do you?"

"Not exactly, but I remember her from the last summer I came with my mother. She was a pretty teenager then, and she's even prettier now."

"Our grossmammis would say, 'Pretty is as pretty does.' She hasn't visited here in years from what Ms. Withers told me."

"I don't think we should…"

The swinging door opened hard enough to hit against the wall if not for the doorstop. Julianne's daughter walked in, looking from one to the other of them, her expression not giving anything away.

Rachel turned to her, wiping her hands on a tea towel. "Can I do something for you? I'm Rachel, by the way."

Holly was too busy staring at Jacob to answer. "Who's he?" she demanded, not bothering to sound polite.

It was probably best to ignore the rudeness. "This is Jacob. He's doing some carpentry for your great-aunt."

Holly surveyed him carefully. "Is he your boyfriend?" she asked.

Jacob's eyebrows lifted so high they almost disappeared under his hair.

"Just a friend," she said firmly, while Jacob muttered something and strode out the back door. "Did you come into the kitchen for something?"

Holly shrugged. "My mother said to come out here and get something to drink. You got any soda?"

"Sorry. How about milk?" She reached for the refrigerator handle, but Holly made a face. "Lemonade?" Holly hesitated and then nodded.

Thankful that she'd thought to make a pitcher of it this morning, Rachel poured a glass and set it on the table. Holly sat down, stared at it for a moment and then took a gulp.

Deciding she'd done all she could, Rachel turned back to the chicken salad. What a challenging child Holly was. Thank goodness she didn't have to deal with her.

Rudeness set her teeth on edge. Those years between childhood and adolescence could be difficult for a girl, but even so…

"I guess you know what my mother wants."

Rachel blinked and glanced at her. Holly was staring into the glass as if something were written in her lemonade.

"I'm sorry?"

"I said, you know what my mother wants." Holly's eyes narrowed so much that Rachel could hardly see the green.

"I have no idea," she said.

Holly was silent, and Rachel was glad. If the child was in the midst of a quarrel with her mother, it wasn't Rachel's concern, and she'd rather not know.

Another moment passed, and then Holly shoved back her chair and shot to her feet. "She wants to leave me here, that's what!" she announced. "That's what she does. Takes me to visit one of her friends and talks them into having me. She doesn't want me around when school's out."

Startled, Rachel could only stammer, "I'm sure it's not—"

"You don't know. I tell you she wants to dump me here, in the middle of nowhere. Well, I'm not staying. I don't care what she wants, she's not going to dump me out here in some hick town nobody ever heard of. And you can tell her I said so!"

She stormed out the back door, letting the screen door slam, leaving Rachel staring. It took her a moment to regain her senses, and then she hurried to the door. She wasn't responsible for what the girl did, but she'd best make sure she wasn't running off toward the woods. Or the highway.

But Holly was apparently content with kicking gravel from the driveway into the grass. Shrugging, Rachel went back to her salad. She'd thought Holly wasn't her concern. She'd thought she wouldn't have to deal with her.

Maybe she was wrong on all counts.

JACOB, FEELING HE'D just as soon be alone as be questioned by a sassy child, took himself to the temporary workshop he'd set up in the old stable. Once, there'd been a fancy carriage here, he supposed, kept shining and ready to be pulled on the road by a team of prime horses.

Now the dark sedan that Ms. Withers used sat in its own garage, polished and gleaming. He'd seen Ms. Withers drive off in it, sitting as erect and cautious behind the wheel as her ancestors would have in the carriage.

He glanced into the two stalls they were using. He'd turned both horses out into the adjoining field, intending to come back and be sure the stall for Rachel's mare was all right.

The wide planks of the floor were fine. They'd be sound against almost anything. He double-checked the latch on the stall, knowing an elderly mare would be familiar with every trick of getting out of enclosures. It wiggled slightly when he touched it, so he went over to the workbench to fetch a screwdriver.

A movement on the other side of the car caught his attention, startling him. Gerald Withers slid out and walked around the car to join him at the workbench. Jacob watched, his face impassive but his mind moving quickly behind the facade.

It was nothing new to find Gerald, Geraldine's nephew and namesake, on the property. Not visiting his aunt, necessarily, just there. He didn't seem to have anything better to do, like work, for instance.

"Want something, Gerald?"

Jacob took his time about picking up the tool he needed, watching the man. Gerald had the Withers features, but they seemed a little blurred in comparison to the portrait of his grandfather. He'd begun to put on weight around the middle.

Gerald didn't meet his eyes. "No. Just…no."

Taking the screwdriver and a couple of extra screws, Jacob turned away.

"Wait." Gerald came a step closer. "I was coming to see my aunt, but looks like she has company."

"Yah?"

"Well, who is it? Somebody on business? Her lawyer?" His voice sharpened.

If it had been, Jacob wouldn't have spoken, but since it was a relative…

"It's your cousin. Julianne," he added.

"Julianne?" He sounded disbelieving. "What's she doing here?" He muttered something to himself.

"I don't know." And it was none of his business. Tiring of the subject, Jacob returned to the stall. As he did, he saw Gerald slip out of the garage.

He'd probably add himself to the family party, Jacob assumed. But instead, Gerald sauntered over to the hedge, moved behind it and disappeared.

Strange. Almost as if he didn't want his aunt to see him. Still, it wasn't any of his business.

Jacob turned back to the stall door only to be interrupted again. This time it was the kid.

"Who was that?" she demanded, leaning on the workbench.

Taking his time, Jacob glanced at her. "That was Gerald. Your cousin, isn't he?"

"He is?" Holly looked blank. "I didn't think I had any cousins."

"Well, your mother's cousin, I guess. Your second cousin, maybe." He wasn't sure, not used to troubling with such distinctions. When you were related to half the community, it didn't matter much the exact degree, he figured.

"Oh."

She was silent for about a minute and a half before asking the next question. "Why isn't he coming in? Did you tell him to go away?"

"Why would I do that?" His patience was wearing thin. Maybe Rachel had time to answer endless questions, but he had work to do.

She stared moodily at the latch he was fitting on the stall door. Then he felt her gaze switch to his face. It was like having a fly buzzing around his head when he was working.

"What?" he demanded.

"Are you Rachel's boyfriend?"

He was so surprised he almost blurted out the truth— that he had been, once. He caught hold of himself. "None of your business. Why don't you go find something to do?"

"I don't want to."

He tried ignoring her.

"I asked Rachel that, too."

"What did she say?" he asked involuntarily.

"None of your business," she said, grinning. It was the first smile he'd seen from her, and it disappeared fast.

"Look, I'm busy," he growled. "Why don't you…"

"Holly! Holly!" A woman came past the edge of the wide door into the stable. Holly's mother, obviously.

"Lunch," she sang out, and then her eyes focused on him. "Well, hello. I didn't know anyone was here." She approached, her gaze sweeping over him. "I'm Ms. Withers's niece. Who are you?"

It didn't sound quite as rude coming from her as from her daughter, but she was looking at him the way a kid would look at an ice cream cone.

Before he could answer, Holly burst out, "He's the carpenter, Mom. And besides, he's Rachel's boyfriend, so you don't need to flirt with him."

Julianne's laughing gaze invited him to share her amusement. "The things kids say, honestly."

He remained expressionless. She didn't act like his image of a mother, he decided. Pretty, yes, but…

Holly grabbed her mother's arm. "Come on, Mom. You don't want to annoy Aunt Geraldine by being late for lunch, do you?" She tugged her away, acting as if she were the mother.

Jacob wiped his forehead on his sleeve when they'd disappeared from view. Given the relatives Ms. Withers had, maybe it was just as well that they didn't come around very much. He realized he was wondering what Rachel would have to say about them.

Shaking his head, he began tightening the latch, pushing them out of his mind. Including Rachel.

WHEN SHE'D FINALLY finished clearing up from lunch amid a number of interruptions, Rachel stepped out onto the back porch, sucking in a breath of air. It was a lovely spring day, with the fields growing greener almost while she looked at them. On the ridge, a faint green haze gave notice that the trees would be in full leaf soon. That ought to refresh her, but it wasn't working. The thing Julianne had said clung to her thoughts like a burr on her skirt.

Julianne had come to the kitchen ostensibly to thank her for the delicious lunch. It soon became evident that something else had been on her mind. She'd been talking to Jacob. About her. Her cheeks burned at the memory. Embarrassing enough that they'd been talking about her, but if Jacob thought he could get away with such a thing—

She took another deep breath. She couldn't let it upset her. What happened between her and Jacob was in the past, gone and forgotten. At least it should be.

Attempting to reassure herself, she decided she must have misunderstood Julianne's comment. Or maybe it was someone's idea of a joke. Either way, it was best forgotten.

Rachel turned at the sound of Ms. Withers calling her name and hurried back inside.

"I'm right here. Do you need something?"

"Not exactly. I have something to tell you." The woman's face was tight, her skin stretching against the fine cheekbones. Rachel wasn't sure whether that was annoyance in her eyes or something stronger.

"I've just been talking with my niece. She's asked me to have Holly here for the summer while she goes out to California."

"I see." It seemed clear to Rachel that Ms. Withers wasn't happy with the suggestion, and who could blame her? At her age, the idea of assuming sole responsibility for a young girl, even for a few months, couldn't be easy. "Is there no one else who could have her?"

Ms. Withers's thin lips twisted. "It seems my niece has

run out of people who are willing to take care of her child while she goes off looking for yet another husband."

Rachel's breath caught at the tart words with the ring of truth behind them. Before she could speak, Ms. Withers made a gesture of silencing her. Or maybe herself.

"I should not have said that. Please forget it. In any event, I have agreed. I realize this will make your work more challenging, so if you want to reconsider my offer, I'll understand."

Rachel was shaking her head already. Where else would she go? She had to be established before her father returned with his bride.

"It's fine. I'll do my best." Well, maybe not fine, but she'd manage.

"That's all either of us can do, I suppose. Julianne plans to leave in the morning, and she'll tell Holly." Her lips thinned even more. "We'll have to comfort the child."

Ms. Withers said it as if it were an unfamiliar concept to her. Then she turned and went back through the swinging door.

Rachel suspected if comforting were needed, it would have to come from her. After raising her younger brothers, she felt capable of doing so, but given what Holly had said earlier in the kitchen, she was afraid they'd have an open revolt on their hands.

Now she had two things to disturb her precarious balance. The situation with Holly, and the foolish and hurtful thing Jacob had apparently said to Julianne.

It was no good. There was no way of ignoring it. She couldn't do anything about poor Holly, but she certain sure could tell Jacob just what she thought of him. Driven by an unaccustomed anger, Rachel headed back to the stable, where Jacob had set up his work area.

The anger kept her going across the backyard. But as

soon as she saw him, Rachel found her anger ebbing. No matter how much she might think it justified, she just couldn't flare up at him.

Or at anyone. It wasn't part of her personality. Her outspoken friend Joanna was constantly trying to get her to stand up for herself, but even she didn't understand.

Jacob glanced up, looking surprised to see her. "Was ist letz? What's wrong?"

"I... What makes you think something's wrong?" She took a few steps toward him and stopped.

A smile tugged at Jacob's firm lips. "I've known you most of your life. I know when something's wrong. What is it? That pesky kid again?"

"No." She hesitated. "Well, maybe." She sucked in a breath. "Did you tell Julianne that you were my come calling friend?"

Come calling. It had been a long time since anyone had come calling for her in the way those words meant. The Englisch teenagers said *going steady*, she'd heard.

He looked at her steadily for a moment, his gaze intent. "Is that what she said? No. Why would I? Your friend Holly was the one who said it."

"I should have known." She felt foolish. "She'd asked me that, and I told her no. So why would she say that to her mother?"

Jacob leaned back against the workbench, frowning in thought. "I don't know. I couldn't figure out what was happening between them." He hesitated. "It was odd."

Quite suddenly, watching him, Rachel knew why. He was embarrassed. He'd been right about one thing. They did know each other too well to hide.

"What did she do to upset you?" Surely he wouldn't be

embarrassed because of what Holly had said. Then she understood.

"Was Julianne flirting with you?"

She had to hide a laugh at his expression.

"I guess that's what you'd call it. Probably wanting admiration. I should think that's important to her. And stop laughing. It's not that funny."

Rachel managed to wipe away her smile. "I'd like to have seen it." She sobered. "But Holly…well, they're not like any mother and daughter I've ever known."

He shrugged. "I've heard Ms. Geraldine talk about her niece. Seems like Julianne always has a new boyfriend."

"That would be hard on Holly." She tried to imagine the effect on a girl Holly's age, balancing awkwardly between child and woman.

"Yah." He didn't sound very sympathetic.

"It is," she insisted. "She's at a difficult age, and who does she have to show her what kind of person she ought to be growing into?"

He studied her face for a moment, and she wondered what he was thinking. Then he spoke. "At least it's not your concern. Or mine. They'll be leaving soon, I'd guess. Especially if Julianne got what she came for."

That startled her. "What do you mean?"

"Money, don't you think? That's what Ms. Withers's relatives usually want when they come to see her. And I could hear them arguing in the parlor when I was working on the second floor."

"I guess," she said slowly. Ms. Withers hadn't mentioned that, but most likely she wouldn't. "But if so, that wasn't all Julianne wanted."

"No? Well, it's no business of mine. Or yours, ain't so?"

She shook her head slowly. "I'm afraid it is. Mine, at

least, and maybe yours, too." She'd got his attention now. "Ms. Withers told me that Julianne wants to leave Holly here for the summer."

"Leaving a woman Ms. Withers's age responsible for a young girl?" His reaction was the same as hers had been. "Surely Ms. Withers didn't say yes."

Rachel shrugged. "She said she felt she had to. There was nowhere else for Holly to go."

"Great." Jacob pushed away from the workbench, looking as if he needed to vent his feelings on something. "It's not enough to have Richard and his wife pestering her to move, and Gerald sneaking around the place—"

"Gerald? You mean he's in town?" They'd been talking about him, but she'd assumed he'd grown up and gone about his life somewhere else.

"He's around, all right. He was here earlier, curious about Ms. Withers's visitors."

"Why didn't he come in? I'd think he'd want to see his cousin."

"Who knows? Anyway, it's annoying to look up and find him watching you. And now we'll have that kid wandering around, poking her nose into everything."

That irked her. "You don't know any more about her than I do, and that's not much. She thought that her mother intended to leave her here, and she wasn't happy about it. I should think we ought to feel sorry for her instead of being annoyed."

"Fine." His tone was short, and he turned back to the workbench. "You feel sorry for her, then. But keep her from bothering me."

"Fine," she snapped in return. "If that's how you feel." She couldn't remember when she'd been so out of sorts with Jacob.

CHAPTER FOUR

IT SEEMED TO RACHEL, serving breakfast the next morning, that the room was fraught with tension. Clearly Holly had already been told that her mother was leaving her here. She sat sullenly, not looking at anyone, paying no heed to the plate of scrambled eggs and fried scrapple Rachel set in front of her.

Julianne was the exact opposite. She sparkled and chattered, using wide gestures as she interspersed comments about the travels she had planned with accounts of how much fun Holly would have this summer. Although how Holly was going to have fun staying with an elderly aunt and her housekeeper, Rachel couldn't imagine.

After each unresponsive frown from Holly, Julianne talked even more vivaciously. Maybe she thought she could infect Holly with her own excitement.

Ms. Withers indicated her cup, and Rachel refilled it with coffee. They exchanged glances, and Rachel wondered if Ms. Withers found Julianne's performance as disturbing as she did.

Escaping to the kitchen, she took a long gulp from the mug of tea she'd left on the counter before filling a basket with the sweet rolls she'd been warming in the oven. If they got through breakfast without a major explosion from Holly, she was going to be surprised.

When she returned, Julianne had switched to memories of her own summer visits to the Withers house.

"...so many things we found to do. Hunting for wild strawberries along the edge of the pasture, hiking in the woods, taking a picnic basket up to the cliff above the quarry..."

"I seem to remember telling you children not to go playing around up there." Ms. Withers put down the butter knife and frowned at her niece.

"You told us not to swim there, Aunt Geraldine. You didn't say anything about having a picnic."

"Well, I should have," Ms. Withers said tartly. "I suppose you went in swimming, too."

Julianne shook her head. "Not I. I can't speak for the boys. You remember those picnics, don't you, Rachel?"

Suddenly having Julianne address her like an old friend startled her. Rachel managed to smile, nodding. Julianne gave her the impression that she was putting on some sort of performance, one designed to convince Holly to let her leave without a ruckus. She didn't really want to participate, so she slipped away as quickly as possible, busying herself with a sink full of dirty utensils.

Somewhat to her surprise, the predicted explosion didn't come. Rachel heard the sound of goodbyes from the hallway, promises from Julianne to call frequently, and then the door closed and the house grew so silent she could imagine that everyone had left.

She was just putting away the last dish when the back door opened. Jacob came in with a toolbox in his hand.

"I see Julianne's car is gone," he said, opening the door to the back stairs but making no attempt to go up.

"Yah, she left after breakfast." She cast a glance toward the ceiling. "It's awfully quiet."

"The calm before the storm?" Jacob suggested.

"I hope not. If Holly is upset…"

Ms. Withers pushed open the swinging door and came through. "Good, you're both here. I'd like a word."

Her face was tired already, Rachel decided, and the day had hardly begun. She reflected again that it was asking a great deal to expect someone Ms. Withers's age to entertain a young girl for the summer. But no one had asked for her opinion, that was certain sure.

"Of course."

Rachel glanced at Jacob. He still stood at the foot of the back stairs, one hand on the door, the other holding his toolbox. He looked like a man eager to be elsewhere.

Ms. Withers clasped her hands together. "Julianne seems to think that her daughter will be fine after a day or two. I must say, I hope she's right. In any event, I'd like to ask you to be particularly patient with Holly for these first few days. Staying here will be a difficult adjustment for the child."

"I'm sure." Rachel's voice warmed when she thought about being left with someone who was a virtual stranger, especially at Holly's age.

Jacob's expression didn't change. "As long as she doesn't tamper with my tools, we'll get along fine."

Rachel shot him an annoyed look. He might have sounded a little more welcoming than that.

"It will be lonely for her," Rachel said quickly. "Especially with nothing to do. Perhaps she'd like to learn how to bake. I'd be happy to teach her."

Ms. Withers nodded. "That would be kind of you, Rachel. All we can do is our best, I suppose." She sighed. "I never did understand girls that age. Boys are different."

"They are, that's certain sure." Rachel smiled, thinking of some of her brothers' misadventures. "At least I don't suppose she'll go off risking her life climbing the highest tree or trying to balance on the ridgepole of the barn."

That brought a smile to Ms. Withers's face. "I hope not. Thank you."

No sooner had she vanished into the other part of the house than Rachel turned on Jacob. "Jacob Beiler! That was not very helpful. Couldn't you have found anything else to say?"

"I'll leave that up to you." His face tightened. "You're the one who's so good at sympathizing with anybody and everybody."

"You—" Before she could find the words, he interrupted.

"My job is carpentry, and that's what I do. I didn't sign on to be a babysitter. Julianne should take care of her own kid, not expect other people to do it."

"Maybe that's so, but she isn't. That poor child… Can't you see how hard this is for her?"

Rachel watched as the annoyance drained from his face. "I suppose you're right," he grumbled. "I'll try, but I've got a job to do. You go ahead and teach her to bake. Just don't expect me to teach her how to wield a hammer. She'd probably brain someone with it."

Yanking the door open, he stamped on up the stairs, leaving Rachel smiling to herself. For a moment there, she'd thought that Jacob had changed entirely from the kind, helpful boy she'd known. Maybe a person just had to dig a little bit to find him now.

Not that she was interested, she added quickly.

The rest of the morning passed peacefully enough. She could hear the occasional noise from the room where Jacob was working, but otherwise, all was quiet. After an hour of no sound from the bedroom where Holly had taken refuge,

Rachel began to be concerned. She found Ms. Withers at the desk in the corner of the parlor, apparently paying bills.

She glanced up at the sound of Rachel's footsteps. "I thought perhaps you were Holly."

Rachel shook her head. "I haven't heard a thing from her. I can see that she might want to be alone if she's upset, but do you think someone should check on her?"

After a moment's consideration, Ms. Withers nodded. "Perhaps you should go up and let her know what time lunch will be served. That way, it won't look as if we're checking on her."

She realized that was uncertainty she saw in her employer's face. Ms. Withers seemed so sure and confident about everything, but clearly not about handling an eleven-year-old girl.

"Yah, that would be gut."

Leaving the parlor, she started to go up the front stairs, but then reconsidered and went through the kitchen. Holly hadn't eaten much breakfast. Maybe a snack would be welcome. Fetching a glass of orange juice and a couple of oatmeal cookies, she went up the back stairs.

Jacob glanced at her as she passed the room where he was working. "I don't suppose those are for me?" he asked, seeming to have overcome his earlier irritation.

"I'm certain sure you can fetch your own cookies," she said, smiling. "Have you heard Holly go out of her room?"

He shook his head. "She was on her cell phone the last I saw her."

Relieved, Rachel went on to the bedroom next to hers. At least that sounded fairly normal. From what she'd heard, Englisch kids all had phones and were on them constantly, texting each other even when they were together.

The bedroom door stood ajar. She tapped on it and went in. "Holly? I brought you a snack…"

But the room was empty. Funny. She hadn't heard the child come downstairs. Where was she?

JACOB HADN'T HAD time to finish removing a section of baseboard before Rachel was back, still holding the juice and cookies. She stood in the doorway for a moment, looking as if she feared having her nose snipped off for disturbing him again.

Feeling a little ashamed, he put down his tools and stood. "No takers for the cookies?"

"It's not that. Holly isn't there, and I didn't hear her come downstairs." She looked as if she expected him to have some answers.

"If you were in the kitchen, you might not hear her come down the front steps." The reassuring words didn't seem to have the desired effect, and Jacob had to tamp down irritation. "What are you worried about? She's not a little kid. And anyway, she's not your job."

An answering annoyance showed in the way her eyes narrowed. He could hardly miss it. After all, he'd once known every single sign of emotion in her expressive face.

"My job is whatever Ms. Geraldine says it is. She asked us to help with Holly. I remember that, even if you don't."

Obviously there was no use arguing with Rachel—not when she thought something was her duty, anyway. "Okay, okay. I'm sure she'll turn up, but if she doesn't, I'll help you look for her. She probably won't appreciate it, not at her age."

Rachel's quick smile chased her concern away. "You've got that right. I do remember being eleven, I guess." She put the tray with cookies and juice on the table. "Here you are. I'll just have a casual look around downstairs."

Shrugging, he decided he might as well take a break. Munching an oatmeal cookie, he wandered toward the top of the front stairs. If she found the kid, he'd be able to hear, and then he could forget about it.

From above, he could look down the stairwell to the hall below. Rachel passed through the hall and from here he could see only the smooth, silky hair swept back behind her ears and the top of her white kapp. She went into the parlor, and he could hear a murmur of voices. Rachel must be passing on her concerns to Ms. Geraldine. She was the proper person to worry about the kid, ain't so? Like he'd said, it wasn't his job.

And if it turned out to be Rachel's, she might very well end up regretting that she'd taken it on. If she quit, he'd be relieved of seeing her every day. Funny, it didn't sound as good as he'd have thought it would.

Firmly dismissing the whole thing from his mind, he returned to the bedroom to finish removing the length of baseboard. It was a job to get it off, but in a way, that was a tribute to the craftsman who'd put it there a century or more ago. In a modern house, it would have come off with a single pull, and probably broken to pieces in the process.

Gathering what he needed, he headed out to his makeshift workshop, where he'd be able to repair and refinish without annoying everybody in the house with the sound and the smell.

As always, once he was engrossed in the work, he didn't even notice time passing. It was always that way, and he could only be thankful he'd found the job that made work a pleasure.

The clanging of the bell on the back porch sounded over

an hour later. Frowning, he put down the fine sandpaper he'd been using and went out. He hadn't heard the bell rung since he'd been working here. Was something wrong?

Rachel was still wielding the bell rope when he reached the porch. Grimacing, he gestured to her to stop.

"Was ist letz? Is something wrong?"

Rachel frowned, her gaze moving around the back premises. "Ms. Geraldine says she told Holly that I'd ring the bell for meals. Jacob, we still don't know where Holly is, and I don't see her anywhere. Have you?"

He shook his head. "What does Ms. Geraldine say?"

"That it's normal for kids to run loose when they're out here in the country." She looked a little shamefaced. "But I can't help being worried."

"Why?" He stepped up onto the porch next to her.

She looked at him blankly, as if expecting him to understand.

"What worries you so much about it?" He asked carefully, "If you were at home and one of your little bruders didn't come when you rang the lunch bell, you wouldn't be worried, would you?"

"If one of my brothers didn't come when the lunch bell rang, I'd know he was sick," she said, a spark of amusement in her eyes. Then, just as quickly, she sobered. "I know what you mean, though. I…I can't explain it myself. I think it's this place." She glanced around, and she actually shivered a little.

He frowned at her. "I don't get it. You're familiar enough with the house and grounds, ain't so? You spent time here with your mother often enough. Why is it bothering you?"

"I don't know." Impatience edged her voice. "If I did, I could explain it. But I just keep feeling there's something wrong." She shook her head, seeming exasperated with herself, but he could see she was troubled.

"Look, I'm sure the kid is okay. She's probably enjoying making everybody worry about her. But I'll help you look. You take the downstairs and the cellar, and I'll do the upstairs and the attic. Whoever finds her gets an extra cookie, okay?"

"Find her and I'll give you a whole batch," she muttered. "All right. Denke."

As he headed up the steps to work his way methodically through the upstairs, he could hear her murmuring something soothing to Ms. Geraldine. His jaw tightened. He'd have a few words for Miss Holly if he found her.

Nothing in the upstairs. He hadn't thought there would be—that was too obvious. The attic was more likely.

He went up the steps two at a time. It was hotter than he expected up there, and the term *attic* wasn't really right. It wasn't one big room. The attic was composed of a number of small rooms, most of them crowded with furniture, boxes and trunks of all description. It looked as if everything anyone didn't want from the whole mansion had been shoved up to the attic and forgotten.

It would take an army to search the whole place thoroughly, he realized, but he looked into or around everything capable of hiding a skinny eleven-year-old without success. By the time he started back down, he was beginning to share Rachel's concern, not that he intended to tell her so.

Rachel met him at the bottom of the steps, followed a moment later by Ms. Geraldine. "Anything?"

He brushed off a length of cobweb from his sleeve, shaking his head. "She's not up there, I'm certain sure."

"I should have listened to you." Ms. Geraldine's face had tightened. "I should have known nothing could be that simple, not where my niece is concerned. Where could the child be? Do you think she really meant what she told you, Rachel? Would she really run away?"

"Let's not move too fast," Jacob interrupted before Rachel could answer. "We're going to look foolish if she's just somewhere reading or exploring and we're overreacting."

Rachel's eyes flashed at him. "We have to do something."

"Right." He controlled his impatience. "We'll go through the outbuildings first. Then, if she's not there, we'll think of something else."

She wasn't, and by then Ms. Geraldine had regained her usual air of control. "I don't want to call the police unless I have to," she announced. "If she is trying to run away, she's likely set off for town, where she might get a bus or pick up a ride. Or she could have headed up the trail through the woods, thinking that would lead to town."

Jacob nodded his agreement. "I'll take the buggy and drive toward town. If she's there, I'll spot her." He turned to Rachel. "You—"

"I'll go up the trail to the woods." She rubbed her arms with her hands as if she was cold despite the warmth of the spring day. "Ms. Geraldine, your lunch—"

"Never mind my lunch," she snapped. "Just go find that child."

RACHEL STARTED UP the trail through the woods, watching for any sign that Holly might have gone that way. It might have seemed logical to the child, knowing that town was on the other side of the ridge, that it would be a shortcut. It wasn't—unless you were a crow.

How strange it was that her feelings about this place hadn't surfaced in her mind until she'd said what she had to Jacob. Somehow the words had come out without her thinking it through, but once said, she knew they were true.

But why? She'd been focused on the thoughts and memories of coming with Mammi…of helping her, talking to her without Daad and the boys around, of having that special time alone with her. All that was true, so why, underneath, did she have this apprehension?

The feeling had probably been there all the time, hidden under other memories. Holly's presence seemed to have stirred them up, and she couldn't imagine why. Why Holly, and why the uneasiness?

Her feet had been following the trail while she thought, but when she stumbled over an encroaching tree root, she came out of her absorption. She'd best focus on what she was doing. Searching for the basis of her feelings might be important, but not while she was trying to find a lost child.

The path grew steeper as it wound up toward the ridge, and the thick undergrowth petered out. The dense growth of pine and hemlock trees made such a heavy canopy that very little grew on the forest floor but moss. She vaguely remembered collecting various kinds of moss to make a terrarium in a gallon jar—a project inspired by her schoolteacher.

The terrarium hadn't survived the trip out of the woods. The boys—William and Gerald—had come racing each other down the path and the jar ended up smashed on the ground. It had been Gerald, she thought, who knocked it free, but it had been William who'd knelt to help her pick up all the pieces of glass so no one would get cut.

The memory came so clearly at this moment. The tall, gangling teenager, his hair glinting gold when a stray beam of sunshine hit it, had been the kindest of the bunch to her young eyes. Small wonder that he seemed to have been Ms. Geraldine's favorite, at least until he'd started to rebel.

Teenagers did that, she knew. Even Amish teenagers. Still, Holly wasn't a teenager yet, and she didn't really have enough knowledge or sense, surely, to get far. How on earth did she think she was going to find her mother, or even get out of town? She might have money, but would the bus driver allow her on without an adult's say-so?

Rachel stopped for a moment to catch her breath, and she shivered again. It was cool under the pines, she told herself. That was all. Probably Holly was fine. She'd seen no sign of her so far. Maybe by this time Jacob had already picked her up on the road to town.

She pictured that, smiling a little as she wondered what he would say to her. Or, more importantly, what Holly would say to him. What could he do if she refused to get into the wagon? She could easily imagine his baffled frustration at that.

Maybe she should go back. Rachel hesitated, longing to head back down the trail into the sunlight and to find Holly perfectly safe. She glanced up the trail, feeling reluctance growing as she drew nearer to the quarry. Holly wouldn't have gone this far, would she?

But she couldn't take the chance. She'd have to continue on, at least to the top of the ridge. If she hadn't found a sign of the girl by then, it would make sense to go back. Ms. Geraldine might have to call the police and get a search party started, and in that case, the sooner the better.

Realizing she hadn't been calling out for the girl, she chided herself. If Holly had strayed off the path, she might well be hoping for someone to find her. She'd allowed the darkness and silence under the pines to intimidate her into matching silence, as if any noise she made would bring out something to fear. Silly.

Shouting Holly's name, she listened. Nothing but a faint echo disturbed the stillness, so she climbed steadily on. She must be fairly close to the top now. It had been a long time, but she knew she was nearing the quarry.

Her breath came a little faster. The quarry had been a scary sight the first time she'd seen it, and she wouldn't have ventured any closer if someone—Julianne, she thought— hadn't taken her hand and held it while she peered over the edge. It was a deep gash in the hill, the sides of gully jagged where at one time they'd quarried stone for building. Even when she was a child, those days were long past and the quarry abandoned.

Impelled partly by her own fear of the quarry's depths, she hurried on, calling Holly's name. No Trespassing signs still dotted some of the trees, prominent among them a large Danger—Quarry sign that she couldn't help but see.

Rachel sucked in a breath and called again, sure she'd hear nothing in return but the echo of her own voice. She heard that, all right, but she also heard another voice.

"Help! Help me!"

Rachel ran toward the sound, her heart thudding and fear clutching at her. Stumbling through brambles that caught at her clothes, she burst into the sunlight at the clearing along the quarry.

"Holly! Where are you?"

"Here." Holly's voice, choking on a sob, was nearby.

Rachel moved forward cautiously, a vivid memory of the sharp drop-off filling her mind, past a bush whose branches had been shoved back. Suddenly there was nothing in front of her but air.

Sucking in a breath, she took a firm hold of the bush

and leaned forward, looking down. Down a long way to where water gleamed at the bottom. Thank the gut Lord Holly hadn't fallen straight down. She was standing on a ledge no more than ten feet below the top.

Rachel's breath came out in a whoosh of relief. "Holly! Are you all right?"

The child's face was tearstained, but she nodded. "I can't get up. I was calling and calling, and nobody came."

"It's okay. I'm here now." The first thing to do was to calm her down. "I'll get you out. But are you hurt?"

Holly shook her head, seeming to lose some of her fear now that Rachel was there. "I'm okay." Talking steadied her, Rachel realized. "I didn't know the edge was there, but I slid down."

Studying the predicament, Rachel realized that the drop-off wasn't as sheer as she'd feared. It was on the opposite side that there was a sheer drop to the bottom. Here the cliff went down at more of a slant, though still too steep to climb easily.

She could see the dislodged small stones that must have slid under the child. Fortunately, the ledge was wide enough to stand comfortably, and she wasn't in any immediate danger that Rachel could see. But how to get her up?

"I think I'd better go for help..." she began, only to be answered by a cry.

"Don't go! Don't leave me! Can't you call somebody?"

She repressed a smile. "Amish people don't usually carry cell phones."

"That's dumb." Holly dismissed Amish customs.

"Where is your cell phone?" That was more to the point. She'd thought it was firmly attached to the child's hand.

"I didn't bring it. I didn't want anybody tracking me by my cell phone."

Rachel hadn't known that was possible, but she stowed the information away. "Listen, Holly, I think it's best if I go for help."

Her small face crumpled. "Don't." The word broke on a sob, and Rachel knew she didn't have the heart to go, even to get help.

"Okay, it's all right." She paused, thinking. Holly wasn't really that far down, and the slope wasn't too sheer. "If I lie down on the ground and grab your hand, do you think you can scramble back up?"

"I don't know."

Rachel heard the edge of fear in her voice and reconsidered, looking around for a better spot. A few feet farther along the ledge, two small shrubs had found root in the steep ground above Holly's head.

"Holly, if you can move along the ledge to where those bushes are, it should be easier to get up." She sought for something else that would reassure the child and then untied her apron. Making her way through the brambles to what she thought was the right spot, she dropped to her hands and knees and crept forward. When she looked down, Holly was right below her.

"Looks better, doesn't it?" Not waiting for an answer, she lowered one end of the apron down to Holly. "I'm tying the other end to a good strong sapling." She was doing it as she spoke, trying to sound sure of herself. "It'll give you something else to hang on to. Okay?"

She crawled forward as she spoke. A glance down assured her that she could have scrambled up easily with the available handholds. But could Holly, scared as she was?

"What do you think?" she asked, studying the girl's face. With the apron grasped in one hand, Holly's expression firmed. "I can do it. Easy," she added with a flash of bravado.

"I know you can." Rachel reached down with one hand, murmuring a silent plea for help. If this didn't work, she'd have to climb down herself and boost her up.

But Holly, encouraged, grasped Rachel's hand tightly, the apron with the other, took a deep breath and scrambled upward.

"That's it. Put your foot against that bush. It'll hold all right." She hoped she sounded calmer than she felt.

Holly hesitated, then moved her foot upward to the shrub. With a shove, she was up to the point where Rachel could grasp her shoulders and heave her over the top. They fell back, hanging on to each other.

"It's okay. You're safe." Rachel half-expected a sassy retort now that the child was safe.

Instead, Holly burst into tears.

CHAPTER FIVE

RACHEL SAT ON the ground, holding Holly in her arms, and felt the sobs that shook her whole body. The tears weren't just for the narrow escape, she knew. The poor child wept for the grief and fear of abandonment. Rachel felt like crying with her, but she wouldn't. She'd just be thankful Holly was safe.

The quarry gaped just beyond them. The gash in the earth had always looked like a giant mouth to her, open to grab anyone who ventured too close.

A memory slid into her mind. She'd followed the Withers children up to the quarry, lingering as far away from the edge as possible. Someone…Gerald, maybe…had pulled her closer, laughing at her fear.

Richard had scooped her up and put her down safely away from the edge before grabbing Gerald and shaking him.

Odd, how clear that image was now when she hadn't consciously remembered it in years and years. If Holly felt as she did about the quarry, small wonder she'd been afraid and desperate.

"It's over now," she murmured as Holly's sobs diminished. "I know it was scary, but you're safe now."

The crying stopped except for a convulsive sob now and then. Holly stirred and seemed to recall who she was leaning on. She pulled back, looking up at Rachel. Then she averted her gaze.

"I'm okay." She sniffed a time or two. "It wasn't a big deal."

Rachel nodded, smoothing the tangled hair back from Holly's smudged face. "You're fine."

"I am," she declared, as if to convince Rachel. Or herself. "I'd have got up by myself in another few minutes."

Rachel suppressed a smile and nodded. Holly's embarrassment was understandable. She wouldn't want to have anyone thinking she wasn't as tough as she claimed.

"I'm sure," Rachel said, her own nerves calming after the fear and panic of the past ten minutes. "Your jeans don't look so good, though."

Holly put her finger through the hole in the knee of her jeans. She shrugged. "It's the style, anyway. No problem." She scrambled to her feet.

Studying the girl as she got up, Rachel decided she couldn't be hurt if she moved so easily. She got up more slowly, telling herself that she wasn't in shape for such a rescue. She dusted the skirt of her dress. It was dirty, of course, after she'd lain on the ground, but otherwise all right.

The apron dangled half over the edge of the quarry. Rachel picked it up, trying not to look down as she did. The apron was fit only for a dust rag now, and it had been a fairly new one. She'd have to find time to do some sewing.

"If you're okay, maybe we should be getting back. Your aunt will be worried."

Holly frowned down at the hole in her jeans, and then the familiar pout formed on her face. "Guess I have to now," she muttered. "But don't think I'm going to stay there, 'cause I'm not."

This last was said defiantly, but she darted an apprehensive look at Rachel when she said it.

She didn't try to argue. "It's not up to me. Where were you headed?" she asked casually, wondering if Holly would answer.

But the girl looked at her in surprise, as if she should know the answer. "To find my mother. She can't just go off and leave me anymore. I'm too old to get parked with anybody she can find."

"Do you know where she is?" She tried to remember what, if anything, Ms. Geraldine had said about it. Something about the West Coast, she thought.

"I know. I texted her." Holly grimaced. "She finally got around to answering me. She said she was in Las Vegas, of all places. That's not where she said she'd be."

Holly sounded resigned to that fact. How often, Rachel wondered, had Julianne actually been where she should have been?

"That's a long way off. I'm afraid you couldn't walk there," she said mildly.

"I'm not that dumb. I'll hitch a ride." She spoke with utter confidence, totally disregarding the danger she might be in. "Truckers go across the country all the time. I can get one to take me along."

When Rachel didn't respond, she scowled. "I will. I told you I'm not going to stay in this boring place the rest of the summer." She glanced back over her shoulder. "I don't think I'll go this way."

"No, I wouldn't." Her mind scrambled for answers. Holly wasn't her responsibility, she reminded herself. Still, she couldn't just do nothing when the child proposed to put herself in danger.

She suspected argument wouldn't do the least bit of

good. Holly seemed to be as well-endowed with stubbornness as her great-aunt. She didn't want to tell tales, but she'd have to let Ms. Geraldine know what the girl planned.

Maybe just changing the subject would be best for now. "I was up here a few times when I was a little girl." She glanced back at the quarry, much as Holly had done. "I never got as close as you did, though. It scared me, even when somebody was with me."

"When you came with your mother, you mean?"

"When I came to the house with my mother," she said. "I don't remember Mammi ever going up to the quarry. That was your mother and her cousins."

"Like Gerald, you mean? He's Mom's cousin. I guess he's Aunt Geraldine's favorite, being named after her and all."

Somehow Rachel doubted it. From what Jacob had said, it sounded as if Gerald was his mother's favorite but not Ms. Geraldine's.

"I remember the boys used to talk about swimming in the quarry, but they never did. It's a long way down, and nobody knows how deep the water is. Your aunt Geraldine said she'd send them straight home if they tried it."

Funny how clear that memory was. She'd been sitting in the kitchen waiting for Mammi to be ready to leave, and the voice from the parlor was loud enough to be heard all over the house. She'd asked Mammi why Ms. Geraldine was so angry, and Mammi said she wasn't angry at all. She was afraid—afraid they'd get hurt doing something so foolish.

That must have been a new concept to her then—the idea that fear might sound like anger. More years of experience had shown her Mammi had been right.

They came to a place where the trail split, with one

branch leading off around the flank of the hill. She grabbed at an excuse to talk about something other than the quarry.

"If you went that way, you'd come to a place where the woods thin out. Wild strawberries grow there…little tiny things, but really sweet. And later on, black raspberries and blackberries."

"Can we go there and pick some now?" For a moment Holly dropped her bored, worldly air and became a kid again.

"Not today. They probably wouldn't be ripe yet. Anyway, we have to go back and let people know you're okay."

Holly didn't argue, but the sullen look descended on her face again. "I can take care of myself. Why can't people understand that?"

She couldn't take care of herself, but at her age, Holly wanted to believe it. If Rachel could just think of something to turn the girl's mind in another direction…

"You know, maybe the problem is that your mother doesn't realize how grown-up you're getting."

"That's for sure." She looked gratified that Rachel understood. "She'll know how old I'm getting when I show up on her doorstep. Mature." She said the word with pride.

Rachel almost shook her head, but she stopped just in time. She wanted to persuade Holly, not antagonize her.

"I don't know. She might just think that was…well, irresponsible. Taking off like that and leaving everybody scared to death that something had happened to you."

Oddly, Holly didn't flare up at that. Maybe that meant that she really was becoming mature. She seemed to think about it.

"What else can I do? She's not here to see, and it's hard to argue by texting."

Rachel saw a chance and grabbed it. "What if you made

a deal with her? Maybe you could say you'd give it a fair try for a period of time, maybe a couple of weeks, and then if you still couldn't handle staying here, she'd agree to have you join her."

Holly considered it, at least, her expression serious. "I don't know. Mom probably wouldn't agree to it. She thinks she's got me off her hands for the summer."

The words sounded bitter, but underneath Rachel could hear pain, and it made her heart clench.

"She might. She probably doesn't want to risk upsetting her aunt." After all, Ms. Geraldine was the wealthy one in the family, and none of her relations seemed to forget it.

"Yeah, well, maybe. I'll think about it."

Rachel took a relieved breath. At least if Julianne agreed, it could give all of them a spell of peace. Maybe something would happen to make Holly more reconciled to being here.

They came out into the open, where the lawn spread out in front of them, and Rachel's momentary relief vanished in an instant. Jacob had evidently just come back from his trip to town. He looked toward them, and he was close enough that Rachel could make out the expression on his face. Jacob was angry.

JACOB STOOD WHERE he was, watching as Rachel and Holly emerged from the woods. They were talking to each other and seemed, if not happy, at least agreeable. Nothing about Holly's expression suggested that Rachel had given her the scolding she deserved.

Not his business, he told himself. But it was, in a way. He'd wasted most of the afternoon in a futile search for that kid. If he'd been the one to find her, she wouldn't be looking so calm.

As they came closer, he noticed they looked the worse

for wear. Rachel seemed to have done something to her apron, since it dangled from her hand. And there was a long, dirty streak down the front of her skirt. So something had happened. It only made him more eager to give the kid a piece of his mind.

On second thought, given that she was his employer's kin, it might be better that it was Rachel who'd found her. Better that he hadn't said a word to the kid. That didn't mean he wouldn't, if she irritated him.

They didn't give him a chance to vent any of his frustration with the girl's behavior though. With a small wave from Rachel, they went straight on into the house. Why that should irk him, he didn't know, but it did. Rachel knew he'd been out looking, too. The least she could do was tell him what had happened.

On second thought, he'd best get back to his own work and forget them. Maybe that would put him in a different frame of mind.

It took him a few minutes to put the buggy back in its place. Then he was back at his workbench, the strip of molding in front of him, trying to forget the annoying interruptions to his work.

He couldn't say it had the calming effect he'd hoped for, though. Ever since Rachel had shown up here, things had been upside down, especially his disposition. And that was just plain ferhoodled.

He'd finally succeeded in losing himself in his work when a shadow crossed the bench and a voice spoke.

"Why do you look as if you're mad at that molding?" Rachel asked, sounding amused.

Since he didn't want to admit his feelings, he didn't try to answer. "I see you brought the runaway back. How far did she get before you caught up with her?" He put the sanding block down to give his full attention to Rachel.

Her face lost its amused expression. "All the way up to the quarry." Her voice seemed to shake on the last word. For a second, he thought…well, he didn't know what he thought.

"At least she didn't get clear to town," he said, annoyed at the whole situation. "Maybe this will convince Julianne that Ms. Geraldine is too old for this nonsense. Her kid could easily have gotten hurt. Or worse."

Rachel reached out to grasp the edge of the workbench, and he realized that her hands were trembling. What on earth? He reached across the bench and touched her arm, feeling the tension in her.

"What is it? What's wrong?" Obviously they'd both come back in one piece, so what was she upset about?

She blew out a breath and made an obvious effort to regain her poise. "That is more real a possibility than you'd think. When I found her…oh, Jacob, she had fallen over the edge of the quarry. For a moment I thought…" She gulped, and he realized that tears weren't too far away.

"Here, take it easy." He led her to a bench near the stalls and sat down beside her. The horses looked over the horizontal stall bars as if vitally interested in what was going on.

He couldn't help clasping her hand in his the way he used to. "Make sense, Rachel. She couldn't have fallen into the quarry or she wouldn't be here now. Come on, pull yourself together."

He spoke sharply on purpose, knowing that would bring her alert and probably mad, as well. He was relieved to see a spark of annoyance in her eyes.

"She didn't fall all the way down," she snapped. "I didn't

say that. She must have stumbled right at the lower edge and the ground gave way under her. She went sliding down where it's not a sheer drop-off. But if she hadn't been caught on a ledge, she'd still have been badly hurt, if not—"

"Well, she wasn't," he pointed out. "I guess that scared her enough to scramble out again."

But Rachel shook her head. She pressed her lips together for a moment. "When I found her, she was stuck. The ledge was too far down for her to get out without help." A shiver went through her, and he seemed to feel it, too. For a moment he couldn't speak, and then anger came to his rescue.

"How… You're not telling me you got her out. Rachel, you should have come for help. You could have ended up at the bottom of that quarry yourself." An image shot into his mind, and his stomach roiled. "Why didn't you come for help?" He felt like yelling at her.

And then tears shimmered in her eyes, and he felt something else entirely. He wanted to protect her, comfort her…

He shook himself. That was no way for him to be feeling about Rachel, of all people. Still, even a friend could be concerned.

"If I'd left her alone—" A shudder went through her again, and this time he put his arm around her, giving her a reassuring squeeze.

"Well, you didn't. And maybe you were right at that." He managed to smile. "Komm. There's no need for crying. You're all right, and that pesky kid is all right, too. And I've wasted a half a day's work, but that's not important, right?" He couldn't help that touch of sarcasm.

A tiny smile lit her face, and her eyes laughed at him. "Go on, now. It wasn't that bad. It's not like you're losing money by taking a trip to town in the middle of the day."

"Maybe so." He couldn't resist smiling back. They were

friends again. "I promise I won't take it out on the wood-work any more, okay?"

"Gut. And don't take it out on Holly either."

"Rachel, that girl needs a good talking-to. And I don't suppose you said a word of scolding."

"No, I didn't. And you wouldn't either, I hope. That child is so unhappy. She needs understanding, not scolding."

He snorted. "If either of us had done something like that, we'd have gotten more than a scolding from our folks."

"Yah, but we did have our folks. Just think about it. She doesn't have anyone she can count on. Julianne just left—"

"Julianne's no better than a kid herself in some ways," he admitted. "Why neither she nor Gerald ever properly grew up is a mystery."

Rachel nodded, and she looked at him the way she used to, back when they were kids. Like he was a big brother who would help her.

"I don't understand it either. But I'm sorry for the child. She doesn't deserve to be dumped on other people. That's how she thinks of it. Dumped."

"Okay, I'm sorry for the child, too. Are you satisfied now?"

"If she'd had a mother like yours or mine, she'd be a dif-ferent person." For an instant a shadow crossed her face at the mention of her mother, but it disappeared just as quickly.

"Yah, all right. I'll stay out of it. It's not my business to scold her or anything else."

"Gut." Rachel smiled at him, her face warming, and he felt himself smile in return. The moment seemed caught in time, and he didn't want to move for fear of breaking it.

But he had to. They couldn't sit here and look at each other. And he certain sure couldn't start thinking about times past and things that had never happened.

He stood up so abruptly that Blackie jerked his head back in alarm. Carefully not looking at Rachel, he took a step away.

"I'll tell you one thing I'd do if I were you." He spoke almost at random, saying the first thing that popped into his head. Anything to break the silence of that moment. "I'd tell Ms. Geraldine that it's either that kid or you."

Rachel flew off the bench so fast he knew it had been the worst thing he could have said, but it was too late now.

"Jacob Beiler! You said you understood. You said you were sorry for her. Don't you have any feelings at all?"

Frustration made his voice sharp. "I guess not. I learned a long time ago that having feelings just leads to being hurt."

Okay, that really was the worst thing he could have said. He was an idiot around Rachel. He always had been. It looked like nothing had changed.

THOROUGHLY ANNOYED, Rachel walked away as fast as possible, trying to focus on anything but Jacob. With the afternoon half-gone, she wasn't sure whether to serve lunch or start supper, but she needed something to keep her busy.

Ms. Geraldine took the decision out of her hands when she reached the kitchen. "Holly went up to shower and change, and you look as if you'll need to do the same." Her gaze rested on the twisted, crumpled apron and the dirt streaking Rachel's dress.

Rachel took a quick swipe at the bodice but just succeeded in making it look worse. "I…" She didn't know what to say, so she changed the subject. "If you'd like me to serve lunch…"

Ms. Geraldine wiped the suggestion away with a sweep of her hand. "No need. We'll just help ourselves to a snack to last us until supper." She hesitated. "Holly told me how you helped her. Thank you, Rachel."

Ms Geraldine shook her head, seeming to turn inward, as if she'd forgotten Rachel was there. "I hope I'm doing the right thing," she muttered, almost to herself.

Rachel wondered which version of Holly's adventure she'd told her aunt—the one where she'd have been fine without any help or the truth. It sounded as if it had been at least partly truthful.

"I'm glad Holly talked to you about it," she said finally.

"As am I." Ms. Geraldine's cool confidence seemed to have been shaken, and she looked almost as if she wanted to ask Rachel's opinion, presumably about the wisdom of having Holly to stay.

But the moment passed. Ms. Geraldine wasn't one to look to others for her opinion. She didn't speak until Rachel had reached the door to the back stairs. "Holly said you thought she should offer her mother a deal."

Rachel winced. "I promise, I didn't put it that way. And it's not my business, I know. I just thought it might make things easier."

Ms. Geraldine's rare smile appeared. "It's all right, Rachel. I realize anything Holly says should be taken with a grain of salt. And given that you apparently ruined your dress rescuing her, I'd say you were involved. Naturally I'll reimburse you for the dress," she added a little stiffly.

"That's not necessary. The dress will be fine once it's washed." She certain sure didn't want Ms. Geraldine trying to pay her for the dress she'd made out of some fabric Mammi had laid by. She grabbed the knob, eager to get out of what was turning into an awkward conversation.

"You may be right about the situation with Holly's mother," Ms. Geraldine added, almost to herself. "I think

I'd best talk to Julianne myself. If the child is going to be unhappy all summer, it won't do. At least, Julianne should give her a voice in the decision."

She gave a quick nod, as if satisfied with her conclusion, and walked out of the kitchen, leaving Rachel free to head upstairs.

Rachel started up the narrow steps, smiling a little as she looked down at her dress. A dress and apron were a small price to pay if it led to a happier resolution for both Ms. Geraldine and Holly. Whether Julianne would see it that way, she didn't know. Still, she probably couldn't afford to antagonize her wealthy aunt, since money seemed to mean so much to this family.

People were certainly showing themselves in a different light today. Holly, Ms. Geraldine and especially Jacob. Her thoughts stuck on that exchange with Jacob, and she frowned.

Jacob had always been headstrong and determined on having things his own way. She knew that better than most, because she'd been closer to him than anyone had outside his family. But she found it hard to reconcile his harsh words with the boy she'd once known. Once loved, if she were to be honest with herself.

He'd sounded so…well, rigid, she guessed. Uneasiness slid along her nerves and tightened her stomach. He'd blamed the fact that they hadn't married for the person he'd become. From his viewpoint, she'd abandoned him to take care of her family. Could she really be responsible for the change in him? It was an awful thought. She tried to push it away, but it wouldn't go.

By evening, Rachel had become convinced that this day had been far longer than usual. Fortunately, both her employer and Holly seemed to feel the same way, so she was able to get to bed early.

When she closed the door behind her, her room felt like a sanctuary, even though Holly was right next door. With an intuition she'd never thought her younger brother possessed, Sammy had dropped off several more things for her, including the quilt for her bed. Made by her grandmother when Rachel had outgrown the crib quilt, it was a Sunshine and Shadows design done in shades of light and dark green that made her think of the fields in July when clouds drifted across the sun, sending shadows on the land.

Rachel slipped into bed, thankful that the evening breeze coming through the window made it cool enough to pull the quilt over her. Maybe with this comfort, she could forget about the close call at the quarry today.

Snuggling the quilt around her, she relaxed. She might almost pretend that Grossmammi or Mammi was there, tucking her in. *Have happy dreams*, Mammi had always said. She'd try.

She was in the woods again, looking for someone. Was it Holly? She wasn't sure. She just knew she had to get to the top of the hill. Had to, even though something waited there that terrified her.

Was she a child, or was it the adult Rachel who struggled up the path, sick with fear?

Footsteps sounded nearby. Someone was following her, someone who seemed to come closer and closer. She hesitated, not knowing which way to go. Were they above her or behind her? Another frightened moment, and then she was rushing down the hill, heart pounding, desperate to get out of the woods. Trees crowded around her. Brambles reached out, snagging her skirt, entangling her legs. She had to get out, had to...

A cry ripped through the air. For an instant she thought her younger self was screaming. And then she came fully awake, clutching her quilt. Her throat was tight, but she hadn't cried out. The scream still sounded—and it came from Holly's room.

Rachel shot out of the bed, fumbling for the bedside lamp and only succeeding in knocking it over. Leaving it, she raced for the door and plunged out into darkness. Where was the night-light she'd put in the hall socket?

But even as she thought it, she'd fumbled along the wall to the door next to hers. After turning the knob, she felt for the wall switch, found it, clicked it and the room flooded with brightness. The light turned it from a nightmare to a pleasant, normal room.

Normal except for Holly, sitting bolt upright in bed, her eyes wide and staring, her mouth still open wide.

For an instant Rachel froze, uncertain. What was happening? Then memory came flooding back. Sammy, at six or seven, screaming in the night. *Night terrors*, Mammi had called them. Mammi had soothed Sammy gently, talking to him. She comforted him until he had finally blinked those staring eyes and waked.

Afterward Mammi had explained that despite the fact that his eyes were open, he was still caught in a nightmare. Just like Holly was now.

Closing the door and hoping the sound hadn't roused Ms. Geraldine, Rachel hurried to the bed. Gently, now, gently. She sat down slowly, easing herself next to the girl.

"Holly, it's all right. It's just a bad dream. You're okay." Still the eyes, wide and dark, stared, but at least the screaming had stopped.

"It's me, Rachel. I heard you calling. You can wake up now. You're safe. I'm here."

With a shuddering gasp, Holly closed her fingers on Rachel's wrist, grasping it so tight it hurt. She blinked, interrupting that dreadful staring just as Sammy had done. Finally Holly's eyes began to focus.

"Rachel," she whispered.

"That's right. I'm here with you. It's okay. It was just a bad dream."

Holly shook her head violently. "No. The footsteps—didn't you hear them? Someone was coming. Someone was after me."

The words jolted through her. It was almost as if the child had shared her dream. But she couldn't have, and there were no footsteps.

There hadn't been, had there? They were just in her dream, and it seemed in Holly's.

"No one is coming after you, I promise. You're right here in your own bed, and no one is in the house but you and me and your great-aunt, ain't so?"

Taking a deep breath, Holly brushed her tumbled hair back from her face and glanced at the long, loose braid Rachel wore at night. "Sorry."

"There's no need to be sorry." Since Holly didn't seem to object to Rachel's arm around her, she ventured to hug the child. "You just had a bad dream—night terrors, my mammi used to call them when my little brother had them."

"He did?" She seemed more interested in Sammy than her mother's words.

"Yah, he did. Made so much noise he'd wake the whole house up, he did. Sometimes we had to take him clear out of his bedroom and walk him around until he woke up. Once Daadi carried him outside in the middle of winter. That woke him up in a hurry."

She was pleased to see that actually got a smile from

Holly. Then the child was silent, looking down at their clasped hands. "Your mom didn't go away, I guess."

Rachel knew she couldn't make anything up that would reassure Holly her mother's behavior was normal. It wasn't.

"No, she didn't. Not until she died when I was just seventeen. That was hard." She hesitated, wondering how far she could go. "I guess we all have some hard things to deal with. I know it's not easy to have your mother so far away."

Holly's face twisted as if she tried to hold back tears. "It's not the going away so much. It's—" Her fingers dug into Rachel's hand. "Rachel…" She hesitated, as if she didn't want to say anything more. Then the words burst out of her. "Rachel, what if she doesn't come back?"

CHAPTER SIX

ONCE SHE'D SERVED breakfast the next morning, Rachel felt like putting her head down on the kitchen table for a nap. She hadn't had such a restless night since—well, she didn't know when. She'd spent a good half hour trying to reassure Holly, talking and soothing and listening. Eventually Holly had settled back on her pillows, and Rachel had tucked the quilt around her, whispering softly as the child finally drifted off to sleep.

Holly didn't seem any worse for wear this morning, and Ms. Geraldine apparently hadn't heard a thing. Scraping eggy plates, Rachel considered that. She didn't see how anyone could sleep through those piercing shrieks. They'd been terrifying, but maybe that was partly because she'd had a bad dream of her own.

But she didn't see how Ms. Geraldine could have missed it. She wondered, not for the first time, whether Ms. Geraldine was a bit hard of hearing. Given her age, it seemed possible. If asked, she would probably deny it.

Still, it was just as well in this case. If Ms. Geraldine had been roused, Rachel would have had both of them to deal with. It had been difficult enough as it was. If it hadn't been for her own experience with Sammy, she'd never have known what to do.

Terror certainly described the state Holly had been in last night. She'd never known what imaginary monsters her little brother had conjured up, but it was only too clear what terrified Holly. How could any child cope with the fear that her mother…the one person she should be able to count on…might desert her?

She didn't know the answer to that question, but she did know one thing for certain. No matter what anyone thought, she couldn't walk away from people who needed her. The anyone, in this case, was obviously Jacob, she thought wryly. They seemed destined to repeat that same pattern over again.

The swinging door swished, and Ms. Geraldine appeared in the doorway carrying her coffee cup, which she put on the counter. She glanced around the kitchen.

"Is Jacob not here yet?"

"I think I heard his buggy earlier, but he hasn't come in this way." She plunged the cup into hot, soapy water and stood on tiptoe to peer out the window toward the barn. "Yah, he's there. Must be he's busy at his workbench on that molding he was refinishing."

"Fine, fine." She sounded distracted. "I have some phone calls to make, and I don't want to be disturbed."

Still clearly thinking of something else, Ms. Geraldine marched off toward the parlor, leaving Rachel speculating as to what calls were so important. Something about Holly, most likely. Ms. Geraldine hadn't asked for her opinion, so she'd keep it to herself, but she did hope poor Holly wasn't in for another upheaval in her young life.

Rachel glanced out at the barn again, just as happy that Jacob hadn't appeared in the kitchen this morning. After the way she'd lost her temper with him yesterday…well, she was mortified every time she thought about it. No matter what the provocation, she should not lose her temper. She didn't, not with anyone else. So why with Jacob?

She didn't know the answer to that one, but she'd best figure out how to apologize before she saw him again.

From the window over the sink, she had a view of the rose bushes just coming into bloom. Actually there was one, a climbing rose, that had already burst into clusters of small pink blossoms. She should cut a stem or two and bring them in to perfume the kitchen. After she finished the dishes, she'd do that.

A movement on the back porch just caught the corner of her eye, and she stepped back for a better view. Maybe Jacob…but no, it was an Englischer, and probably not yet out of his teens. He must have started inside, because she saw the doorknob turn, but then he apparently spotted her and changed the gesture to a knock.

Drying her hands on the tea towel, she hurried to grasp the knob. It turned easily in her hand, and she opened the door with a smile. "Were you wanting someone?"

"I'm Ricky." He stepped inside, his face crinkling in a smile that made his hazel eyes dance.

"Ricky?" Apparently she should know him, but she didn't.

His grin widened. "Sorry. I'm Richard Withers. Junior, that is. Ricky. Aunt Geraldine—I mean, Ms. Withers—is my great-aunt."

"Ach, I'm sorry." She felt herself blush, but how would she have known? He wasn't much like his father at that age, and he had a laughing, carefree expression that she didn't recall ever seeing on Richard Senior's face. "I didn't realize. Richard. It's a pleasure to meet you."

"Ricky," he corrected. "My dad is Richard. And you must be Rachel. I heard about you from my mother."

She had a moment of wondering what Lorna had said

about her. Probably nothing favorable, given how annoyed she'd been at Ms. Geraldine's having hired her.

She dismissed the thought in an instant. "You'll want to see your great-aunt." She hesitated, remembering that Ms. Geraldine didn't want to be disturbed.

Holly came in from the hall before she could think of an answer.

"Holly, is your great-aunt still on the phone, do you know?"

She nodded, eyes intent as she studied Ricky. "Yeah, I could hear her when I passed the door." She didn't take her eyes off him. "Who're you?"

"Ricky, your cousin." He looked pleased at her obvious admiration. "And you're Holly. I heard you were here. How do you like it?"

She shrugged. "Okay, I guess. Not much to do here. Sort of boring."

"Why don't you two sit down and have some shoofly pie," she interrupted before Holly could launch into a litany of all the things that bored her. "When Ms. Geraldine is off the phone, I'll tell her you're here."

"What, no whoopie pies?" Ricky grabbed the pie plate she'd reached for and switched it to the table. "That's my favorite."

"Next time," she said, laughing a little. "You must have a sweet tooth."

"Yep. All of them."

Holly seemed to find that hilarious. Apparently she didn't have to worry about Holly being rude to her new-found cousin. Maybe Ricky's charm would distract her from the idea of running away.

"What's a whoopie pie?" she asked, but she was asking Ricky, not Rachel.

Good, she thought. At least Holly wouldn't think this was boring.

Rachel busied herself at the sink, listening with half an ear to the conversation going on behind her. It was easy to see that Holly was flattered by the attention of the older boy. Apparently Ricky attended a nearby boys' school and was soon to graduate, so of course Holly would be gratified by the attention he was paying her.

Rachel slid a glance toward him. Funny how much he reminded her of Julianne's brother, William, at that age— much the same open face and easy charm. She'd have expected Richard's son to be more like him, but family likenesses were tricky things.

Take her own family, for instance. Grossmammi always claimed that Rachel was the image of a great-aunt who'd died long before Rachel was born. With no photographs, it was impossible to tell. She'd had to rely on memory.

At the sound of the parlor door opening, Ricky jumped to his feet, seeming to forget whatever he'd been talking about. "Aunt Geraldine must be off the phone. I'll let her know I'm here."

He'd dashed out before Rachel could consider whether she should have checked with Ms. Geraldine or not. Well, he was a family member, and she could hardly keep him out, could she?

As she turned, she caught a glimpse of Holly's face. Holly sat with her mouth half-open, caught in the middle of what she'd been saying when Ricky had suddenly vanished. She looked tactfully away. Not very kind of Ricky, she decided. He might as well have announced outright that he wasn't interested in what Holly had to say.

"Would you like some juice with that shoofly pie? Or cider?" She kept her gaze averted from Holly.

"Um, yeah, cider, I guess."

By the time Rachel had put the glass in front of her, Holly had pulled herself together, careful not to show it if she felt hurt. But the way she glanced at the door to the hall told her exactly what Holly was feeling. She'd tumbled headlong into a crush on her handsome older cousin.

Poor thing. Rachel couldn't mistake that look. Stuck in strange surroundings, Holly was ready to idolize anyone who paid attention to her, and Ricky had stepped right into that spot. Rachel's fingers tightened on the dish towel. He'd just better be nice to her, or Rachel would have something to say about it.

Unfortunately, when Ricky returned, it seemed his talk with his great-aunt hadn't been satisfactory. Two red spots burned in his cheeks, and his quick movements expressed barely concealed annoyance.

When he looked as if he'd charge right out without a word, Rachel intervened. "Have a nice talk with your great-aunt?"

"Nice?" He growled the word, then seemed to pull himself together, the flush fading from his face. "Not when she's in one of her moods. I—" He clamped his mouth shut.

"When you're her age, folks will put up with your moods, too," she said lightly. "Will you have something else to eat?"

"No. But thanks." He glanced from her to Holly. "Gotta run. Listen, Holly, I'm sorry I have to go. I'll come back another day and show you some good places to find wild berries. Okay?"

The sullen look vanished as if it had never been, but Holly managed to appear casual as she answered. "Yeah, sure. If you want to."

"It's a date, then." Lifting his hand in a wave, he flashed a smile and reached for the doorknob.

Rachel beat him to it, opening the door for him. But as she closed it again, she knew what it was that seemed odd to her when he first came in. She had locked the door last thing before they all went to bed, and she hadn't unlocked it yet this morning. No one else had been in the kitchen. So why was the door unlocked when Ricky tried it?

JACOB STOOD BACK and looked at the length of molding he'd been working on. That old oak molding had come up a treat now that the paint was gone. The grain shone where he'd been polishing it. Ms. Geraldine would be pleased, he knew. She'd hated the painted woodwork in that room, insisting it be returned to its original look. Funny how fads changed. Somebody must have thought the paint was a great idea.

One of the horses whickered, as if agreeing with his thoughts. He stretched and turned to look at them. He'd best put them out in the paddock before he went back into the house.

"All right, all right, take your time." He unlatched one stall and then the other, grasping the halters. "About time you were out, yah? And about time I went back to the work upstairs, too."

Bessie came out mincing, her feet stepping daintily, while his Blackie clomped along on the plank floor. Jacob knew perfectly well why he hadn't started inside first this morning.

"I was uncomfortable seeing Rachel, that's what," he informed Bessie, and she nodded her head in response to his voice, as if she agreed.

He may as well be honest with himself. He'd been out of line yesterday—way out of line. Rachel had been annoyed enough over his lack of sympathy for young Holly, and then he'd compounded it by trying to tell Rachel what to do. She'd never have taken that from him even when they were first tumbling into love.

Leading the horses, he headed out. He'd have to apologize, and—

He came to an abrupt halt as he and the animals nearly walked right into Rachel, who was coming in.

"Sorry," he exclaimed. "I didn't mean…"

"It's all right. The horses have more sense than to step on my toes." She moved back, letting them come out. "I wanted to tell you something."

"Let me be first," he said, thinking he'd never get the words out if he didn't do it now. "I'm—"

"—sorry," she said, and they spoke nearly in unison. Rachel's lips twitched in amusement. "We both have the same idea, ain't so?"

His tension relaxed in an instant as he realized Rachel wasn't angry. He nodded toward the paddock gate. "Let me get the horses off my hands, so we can talk."

She fell into step with him and seized Blackie's halter. "There's not a lot to say. I lost my temper, and I'm sorry."

"No need. I deserved it. Some days I don't have the sense I was born with. I should never have tried to tell you what to do. You must know more about girls than I do. I certain sure never understand my sisters. So if you say that kid needs help, not scolding, I trust your judgment. All right?"

"Good enough." She pulled the gate open and stood back, watching, while he shooed the two horses into the field. "We'll leave it at that."

She sounded ready to walk away, and he tried to think of something that would keep her there a little longer. Not that he was trying to start again with her, but he'd like to hold on to their friendship.

"I see you had a visit from Ricky, ain't so?" He'd noticed Rachel letting Richard's son in earlier. With school out, they'd probably be seeing more of him.

"He came to see his great-aunt. Did you realize that he hadn't even met Holly before? They're not a very close family, ain't so?" Her face grew pensive as she seemed to survey her own array of cousins and second cousins, most likely a couple hundred of them.

"Guess not. At least they all turn up to see Ms. Geraldine from time to time." He'd learned that since he'd been working here. "When they want something."

Rachel's eyes flashed, making him wonder why other people seemed to think her a quiet little mouse. "That's not a nice thing to say about them."

"Isn't it true?" he countered. "Just in the last few days you've had Lorna wanting to move Ms. Geraldine out of her house, and Julianne wanting her to take care of Holly. So what did Ricky want?"

"I don't know. But whatever it was, he didn't look as if he got it," she admitted, appearing thoughtful. "He did seem like he wasn't satisfied with the result of his conversation with her."

"Probably wanted money," he said. He lifted his hands as if to defend himself. "And I'm not making it up, so don't get mad at me. Ms. Geraldine complained about Ricky's expensive habits before this. Not really complaining to me, I guess, but just talking."

"I suppose it costs more to be a teenager now than when she was a girl. Or when we were that age for that matter."

"We didn't go to an expensive school," he retorted. "And

if we wanted something, we earned the money for it. That's a gut lesson for a kid to learn."

"Yah, I guess so." She twinkled suddenly. "I'd guess Ricky can talk people into things pretty easily. He certain sure had Holly eating out of his hand. But not Ms. Geraldine, I think."

"That doesn't surprise me." He'd seen Ricky turn on the charm before. "Not my business what Ms. Geraldine's family does, I guess. But I've gotten to admire that stubborn old woman—she's determined to hang on to her independence as long as she can. I like to see that. Reminds me of my daad's mother. She'd never let anyone else do what she could do herself."

"I know, remember? That's why I'm here. To make sure Ms. Geraldine is all right."

He'd been leaning on the gate, absently watching the horses while they talked, but now he turned toward her, alerted by something in her voice.

"What is it?" His thoughts flew back to Ms. Geraldine's fall. "There's been no more wax on the stairs, has there?"

Rachel looked about ready to speak, but she pressed her lips together. "It's nothing."

"If it's nothing, you wouldn't look like that." He knew her too well to be fooled. "Come on, tell me."

She shook her head. "Nothing. At least…well, it's odd, that's all. I don't know what to make of it."

Without thinking, he clasped her hand—to encourage her, he told himself. "If you share it, maybe I'll have some ideas."

Rachel tilted her head, her eyes troubled. "Don't laugh," she said. "But sometime in the night I had a bad dream. I'm too old to be frightened by a nightmare," she added hastily. "But this was so clear. I could hear footsteps coming after me." She put up her free hand and brushed it across her forehead, as if wiping away the remnants of the dream. "Anyway, just then Holly cried out in her sleep. It waked me, and I rushed into her room."

She seemed to run out of steam. He suppressed his urge to scoff at her being scared by a dream. "Was she all right?"

Rachel attempted a smile. "You'll think we're both ferhoodled. But she was obviously having a frightening dream—night terrors, my Mammi always called them. And she kept saying someone was after her. That she could hear the footsteps."

He saw where this was going. "So you think maybe the two of you did hear footsteps in the house, right? But it could be anything. Old houses make a lot of noises, and—"

Yanking her hand away, Rachel glared at him. "Do you think I don't know that? Just be quiet and listen to the rest of the story."

"Yah, teacher," he said, as if he were back in school again. He didn't dare smile.

Rachel gave him a skeptical look. "I didn't think any more of it, and Holly was fine this morning. Like she'd forgotten all about her nightmares. But after breakfast, when Ricky came to the back door…well, he turned the knob and it was unlocked. Nobody had been near that door since last night. So how did it get unlocked?"

He'd have to watch what he said. Rachel was certain sure upset. He risked taking her hand again. "Are you sure the door was locked last night? Maybe in all the fuss over Holly's escape from the quarry, you missed it."

"I'm sure." Her voice was firm. "Locking up the house is one of my jobs, and I'm very careful. I go around the whole downstairs when the others head upstairs, and I check every door. I have to check, because there are so many ways to get into the place. It was locked. I know it was."

She was so certain that he couldn't doubt her. Rachel was conscientious, and if she said a thing, he could be sure she'd done it. Still...

"What about this morning? Isn't it possible you unlocked it yourself without thinking when you first came in the kitchen?"

"I don't think so." He'd obviously planted a doubt. "I went straight to the counter to start the coffee, and then I heard Ms. Geraldine's door and I hurried with her egg. I just don't remember going anywhere near the door."

"But it could have happened. Lots of times we do things automatically and then don't think of them."

"I suppose." She crinkled her nose. "It's all your fault, you know. With your talk about how all her family wants something from Ms. Geraldine."

In an instant he was transported back to the past—standing next to Rachel and seeing that lively, laughing look that was just for him. His hand tightened over hers, and he felt the return pressure of her fingers.

"Rachel?" Holly called from the back porch and waved. "My aunt wants you."

"I'll be right there." Rachel took her hand from his quickly. "Forget it. I'm being silly."

"Imagining things, maybe," he said lightly, trying to find his balance after that challenging moment. He might be the one imagining things. "It could be an issue with the latch, though. I'll check all the locks today, all right?"

She smiled, and he thought there was a little extra warmth in that smile. "Denke, Jacob. I'd appreciate it."

Rachel hurried off, and he stood looking after her. What was happening here?

Rachel had not been able to banish all thoughts of Jacob from her mind the rest of that afternoon. Strange, because she'd spent the last years doing exactly that. It had been the only way she could get through that bad time. First she'd lost her mother, and then, when she'd needed him the most, she'd lost Jacob. He wouldn't see it that way, that was certain sure. He'd say that she refused him.

She bent to dust the lower legs of the dining room table, noting that whatever else the cleaning service had done, they hadn't managed to touch anything below the surfaces. She could imagine what her aunt Anna would say about their cleaning—Aunt Anna was noted for having her house so spotless when they hosted church that lunch could be served on the floor. Not that every Amish household wasn't a hive of cleaning the days before hosting worship.

Ms. Geraldine paused in the hallway and then came in, heading toward the huge mahogany china cabinet that took up half the outside wall. She bent to look in the lower cabinet, then reached for something that slipped out of her hands with a thud.

"Let me get that for you." Rachel was there in an instant, seizing the heavy, leather-bound album that sat on top of a stack of similar ones. "Just this one?"

"Yes, that's fine." Ms. Geraldine's face softened as she touched the cover. "I thought I would show Holly some of the family pictures. She ought to know her own heritage, and it seems Julianne hasn't told her anything." Her voice grew dry on the last words.

Privately Rachel thought that wasn't surprising. Julianne was too busy with the present, probably, to think about the past. She guessed there were a lot of people like that.

She hefted the heavy album. "Shall I put it somewhere for you?"

"I can manage it. I'm not helpless yet." She took the album from Rachel's hands, reminding her of what Jacob had said about his grandmother. "Holly tells me Ricky visited with you in the kitchen before I saw him."

Rachel had to adjust her thoughts to the change of subject. "Yah, he did. We knew you were on the telephone, and I didn't want him to disturb you until you had finished."

"Yes, that was the right thing to do. Not that all my calling did that much good, but I wanted to finish. It doesn't hurt Ricky to learn to wait for things."

Rachel didn't respond to that jab at Ricky. "Holly seemed happy to get to know her new cousin, ain't so?"

Ms. Geraldine sniffed. "Ricky charmed her. I suppose he charmed you, too."

Ricky must have upset her in some way to bring on this response. Rachel decided it was best to remain neutral. "He has very good manners, ain't so?"

"That's what Lorna considers important, that's why. She's always concerned with what's on the surface, not underneath."

She couldn't argue with that, since it was the impression Lorna had left on her, as well. She'd heard people say that Lorna wanted to be on the board for all the local charities but wasn't there when there was work to be done.

"You think that it's none of my business who Richard married, don't you?" She swept on. "Maybe it's not, but I have to be concerned about family."

Rachel nodded. "I can understand feeling that way." The conversation was making her uncomfortable, but she didn't have any choice but to listen.

"As for Ricky, she's thoroughly spoiled him. Richard has, too. I suppose because he's their only child. As a result, that boy has no more sense of responsibility than a mouse." She emphasized the words by slapping her hand on the album. "Well, he doesn't need to think I'm going to follow suit and spoil him, because I'm not."

Not sure what to say, Rachel kept quiet, but that didn't satisfy her irritated employer. "Aren't you going to ask me what he wanted?"

Clearly what she wanted was someone to vent her annoyance to.

"What did he want?" Rachel asked obligingly.

"Money, of course. That's all any of them ever want. I suppose an Amish boy that age would work for what he wanted, not expect someone to give it to him."

It looked as if part of Rachel's job was to be a buffer between Ms. Geraldine and her family. "Different families expect different things, I guess. Did Ricky say what it was about?"

"Just hinted around. I'd rather people come right out with it." This time it was Ms. Geraldine's cane that hit the floor in emphasis, but Rachel thought she was winding down. She might be ready to hear a conciliatory word.

"I suppose Ricky is graduating from school this year, isn't he?" She'd heard him say that to Holly. "Maybe he was hinting that cash would be a good gift for a graduate. Especially if he's going away to school." Hinting about presents was surely normal, wasn't it?

"I guess that could be what was in his mind," she said grudgingly. "Actually, I was thinking of giving him my father's watch for a gift. After all, he's the only boy of that generation. I suppose I could include some cash, too. And I'd better warn him not to sell the watch."

"I'm sure he wouldn't do such a thing." Thank the gut Lord Ms. Geraldine was calming down. The whole house seemed affected by her mood.

"Humph. Well, you might as well get the watch out for me while we're thinking about it. After you carry this album into the parlor for me." She unloaded it back into Rachel's arms, seeming to forget her earlier insistence on doing it herself.

"Where is the watch you want me to find?" She hoped she wasn't going to have to search the whole house. That could take days.

Her employer didn't answer until she was settled in her chair with the album on the table next to her. "Well, now, let me think. I believe the last time I saw it, it was with some other family trinkets in a box my mother used for her second-best jewelry. Now, where did I put it?"

Rachel did her best to look patient, thinking that wherever Holly had disappeared to, she was wise.

"Of course," Ms. Geraldine exclaimed, so loudly Rachel jumped. "It's in the trunk that belonged to my father. In the attic."

Rachel's brief foray into the attic on her rounds of the house didn't encourage her to be optimistic about finding it. That attic had been jammed with furniture and boxes, as she remembered.

Ms. Geraldine actually chuckled at her expression. "It's not so bad as that. When you go up the steps, turn to the right. The trunk is in front of the big dresser with the triple mirror. You can't miss it. The jewelry box is right in the top. Just bring the whole box down."

"Shall I go now, before I fix your afternoon tea?" She glanced at the small gold clock inside a glass dome that sat on the mantel. Ms. Geraldine liked a cup of tea around three o'clock, and it wasn't quite that yet.

"Yes, yes, never mind about the tea. I want to see that watch."

Nodding, Rachel hurried out, wondering how Ms. Geraldine would react if she mentioned that she sounded just like Holly, wanting everything right now.

The second floor was very quiet. Holly, she knew, was out in the grape arbor with her phone. Sometimes she thought the thing was permanently attached to her hand… at least, Rachel didn't seem to think she could get along without it. ↑Holly

Jacob had been inside working earlier, but she didn't hear anything now, so he might have gone back out to the workshop. She opened the door to the attic, thankful that it had a staircase instead of a ladder, as some old houses did. The wooden steps were narrow, but there was enough light filtering down from above that she'd have no trouble seeing.

She started up, one hand on the railing, only to find that it shook under her grasp. She didn't need to hold on, but she certain sure hoped Ms. Geraldine wouldn't venture up here.

As she reached the top step, she felt it wobble under her foot. She'd best mention this—Jacob would probably be happy to fix it and the railing, as well. They were both dangerous.

The sound of a car pulling up in the driveway reached her through the window that looked out the front of the house, and she hesitated. Someone coming? If so, she should probably go down and get the door.

The car doors slammed, and voices floated in the window—Lorna's high-pitched voice countered by a bass rumble that might be her husband. They must have turned toward the house, because Lorna's next words were perfectly audible to her.

"You can judge the girl for yourself and see if she's fit for the job. I really don't think so."

Rachel realized that her stomach was clenching. Lorna

seemed to have that effect on her, and she didn't have any doubt who Lorna had meant. She'd have to get down there, like it or not. Finding the watch would have to wait. Ms. Geraldine would be distracted by her company, anyway.

A few quick steps took her back to the stairs. Hurrying now, she started down. The step—she'd forgotten—wobbled under her. It tilted, and she flung out her arms for balance. She reached, grabbing for anything to hold on to, but it was no good.

In a moment she had pitched forward and hit the steps, her arms flying out. She was falling. She should have been more careful… Her head struck something hard, and her thoughts whirled into blackness.

CHAPTER SEVEN

As THE SPINNING in her head slowed, Rachel realized where she was—sprawled on the attic stairs, head at the bottom and her legs on the steps. No wonder she was dizzy. How did she get upside down?

She moved slightly, feeling the rough wood under her, and memory surged back, bringing with it the sensation of the stair tilting under her foot. Then her head cleared a bit more, and she focused on the faces surrounding her. How did they know…

Someone bent over her—Richard, that was who it was. And Jacob, holding her head in his strong hands. Other faces—goodness, had she brought the whole house running?

"Sorry," she murmured, struggling to sit up. Hands restrained her.

"Hold still, Rachel." Jacob supported her, not letting her move.

"That's right." Richard patted her hand. "Stop and tell us where you're hurt before you try to move."

"These dratted steps. I'd forgotten the railing is loose. I never should have asked her to fetch that box." Even seen upside down, Ms. Geraldine looked pale, and she leaned on her cane heavily.

Rachel shook her head and winced. Better not to shake

her head. "It was my fault. I was hurrying, and I knew the step…"

"Never mind the step," Richard said. "We should get you to a doctor. Maybe paramedics—"

"Ach, no! Just let me sit up. I don't need paramedics."

"She's not the best judge of that." Lorna stood a step behind Ms. Geraldine. "She'll have to be checked out, for everyone's sake."

Richard frowned at his wife. "We need to listen to what Rachel says. Let's help her sit up."

Jacob nodded, and together they assisted her to sit upright on the bottom step. With Richard and Jacob helping, she felt safe, and after one more spin of her surroundings, her vision settled. Aware of the men's arms around her, Rachel felt herself flushing.

"Better?" Ms. Geraldine bent over her, frowning.

Rachel's embarrassment grew. She felt certain that her mammi had never done anything to upset the whole household. Would Ms. Geraldine think she was more trouble than she was worth?

"I'm fine. Just let me sit for a few minutes, and I'll be ready to go back to work."

"I'm sure my aunt can get along without you for the rest of the day." Richard patted her shoulder, smiling.

"Richard, don't be silly." Obviously Lorna was as tart with her husband as she was with other people. "Aunt Geraldine has to have someone to take care of her, and I insist that Rachel be checked out by a doctor at once. You don't want to be in a situation where something comes up later."

Her words might have expressed concern for Rachel, but it didn't sound that way to her.

"Why? Do you think she's going to sue me? Don't be

ridiculous." Ms. Geraldine could be just as sharp-tongued as Lorna when she wanted.

"That's right," Richard added.

Lorna sent Rachel a look of active dislike, but she didn't argue the point. "You and Holly had better come to us for dinner today, then," she said.

"I'm sure I can fix supper…" Rachel began, but she didn't have a chance to finish before Ms. Geraldine vetoed her.

"Now, don't you be foolish. I'm perfectly capable of heating something up for myself and Holly. If nothing else, we'll order a pizza. Holly would like that. I wouldn't mind myself," she added, leaving everyone looking at her in surprise.

Rachel tried to dismiss the image of Ms. Geraldine picking up a loaded piece of pizza in her fingers. Her gaze met Jacob's, and his expression made it obvious he was thinking the same.

She stared fixedly at the floor. "It's time I got up." She reached for the railing.

"Just one moment." Richard grasped her hand, preventing her. "You didn't tell us how you came to fall."

"It was the top step. I noticed it was loose, but then I forgot when I started down…"

"Loose?" Richard glared at Jacob, as if it was his fault. "Why didn't you take care of that? Isn't that your job?"

Jacob's face froze into a mask, but Ms. Geraldine was the one to answer.

"No, it's not. I hired Jacob to refinish and repair the woodwork, not look for loose steps. It was fine the last time I went up." She moved, as if intending to go look.

Jacob stepped into her path. "I'll see to it. Let's get Rachel off the steps." He took her arm, but Richard had already put his arm around her waist. "Which is her room?"

Ms. Geraldine indicated her door, just down the hall. As she started to rise, it felt as if Richard and Jacob would pull her apart between them.

"If I can just hold on to an arm on each side, I'll be fine," she said, determined to take control of her own movements. "Denke, you're very kind."

Apparently getting the message, they each offered an arm, and she stood slowly. But it was fine. The dizziness had passed, and other than a little twinge here and there, she'd returned to normal, though she'd probably be a bit stiff and sore later.

"You relax now." Ms. Geraldine opened the bedroom door and glanced in as if to make sure all was in order. "Come along, Lorna. We'll go downstairs. If you want to be helpful, you can make me a cup of tea. I can use one after all this excitement. And one for Rachel, as well."

Lorna opened her mouth to protest, but at a look from her husband, she closed it again.

"It's just as well Holly was outside when it happened," Ms. Geraldine added. "She'd be upset. She's very fond of Rachel, you know."

Lorna didn't seem to appreciate that, but she paced along beside her aunt-in-law as they made their way to the staircase.

"Now for Rachel." Richard gave her a reassuring smile. "Time for you to have a rest."

Touched by his sympathy, Rachel smiled back. With her two escorts, she moved slowly to her room.

But when they made for the bed, Rachel shook her head. "I'd rather sit in the rocker, please. It will be more comfortable."

They reversed course and deposited her in the curved-back rocking chair. "Now you just shout if you need anything," Richard instructed. He patted her arm and turned to leave.

Once his footsteps had faded down the stairs, Jacob sat down on the edge of the bed, facing her. "Now that your admirers have left, suppose you tell me more about how you came to fall."

Rachel wasn't sure whether to appreciate his concern or be offended at his caustic tone. Or embarrassed at being alone in the bedroom with him. "I did, didn't I?"

"You just said the step was loose. How did you happen to go up there?"

She shrugged, wishing he'd go away. Her head had started to ache.

"Ms. Geraldine asked me to bring down something she wanted to give Ricky for his graduation. She told me exactly where it was, so it shouldn't have been hard to find." She remembered suddenly. "I didn't get it. I'll have to go..."

Jacob caught her arm and guided her back into the chair. "It can wait. Why did you fall?" His always limited patience seemed to be evaporating.

"I heard a car pulling in." He didn't need to know that she'd recognized Richard's voice. That comment about her admirers rankled. "I thought I should go to the door, so I hurried. And I forgot I'd noticed the step was wobbly. That's all."

"How wobbly?" he persisted.

"I noticed it wiggle a little when I went up. But maybe I put my weight on it differently when I started down. It just seemed to flip up when I stepped on it. Go and look if you're that interested."

And let me relax, she added silently.

"That's just what I'm going to do. Steps don't flip up under you with no reason." He appeared as if he'd say more, but after a long look at her, he clamped his mouth shut and headed for the door.

Rachel blew out a breath, relieved that he'd stopped asking her questions. Jacob never had been very useful when other people were sick or hurt, maybe because he didn't know what to do for them. She shook her head over his reaction and then wished she hadn't.

Whatever Jacob was thinking about that step, he'd have to deal with it. Right now all she wanted was to put her head back and close her eyes. She'd worry about Jacob's behavior later.

JACOB TURNED TOWARD the attic stairway and then stopped. There was no point in going without his toolbox. He headed downstairs and out the back door to get it.

When he went back upstairs with his toolbox a few minutes later, he knew what he intended to do. If there was something odd about these accidents on steps, he would find it. Not wax this time, but something.

When he reached the second floor, he spotted Holly, tiptoeing out of Rachel's room.

"What are you doing?" It had been obvious that Rachel needed rest, not visitors.

Holly gave him a defensive look. "I took Rachel a cup of tea because she has a headache. Aunt Geraldine said I could, and anyway, I know just how Rachel likes it."

He was forced to smile. "Not too strong, with one and a half spoons of sugar, yah?"

The defensiveness was swallowed up by the child's grin. "Right."

Rachel's words about trying to understand Holly sounded in his mind. "That's wonderful kind of you."

She looked startled and then gave a quick nod, glancing at the toolbox he held. "What are you going to do?"

"Figure out what made Rachel fall." He moved toward the attic steps, and Holly trailed him. "And fix it so it doesn't happen to anyone else."

"Can I come, too?"

He suspected she would whatever he said. Besides, maybe he owed it to Rachel to occupy the girl for a time, at least. If Holly was with him, she wouldn't be bugging Rachel.

"Okay, come ahead. As long as you don't mess with my tools, I don't mind."

"I won't do that," she said scornfully. "I'm not a little kid."

"All right, then." He opened the attic door and stood studying the stairs.

"Aren't you going up? She tripped at the top, didn't she?" Holly nudged him.

"I'm looking." He remembered Daad's comment about approaching a job. "Before you start to fix something, you always want to look it over and be sure you know what you're doing." He gestured toward the steps. "Take a look. What do you see?"

"Nothing," she said. Then, sensing that wasn't the right answer, she looked more closely. "The steps look fine, don't they? All except the top one."

"Right. So let's take a closer look." With the girl behind him, peering over his shoulder, he worked his way from the bottom to the top. Despite their age, the stairs had held up well. It was dry in the attic—that would help. The treads felt as solid as they probably had the day they were put in, at least a hundred years ago or more.

To his surprise, Holly didn't keep peppering him with questions. She moved along behind him, watching everything. When they reached the top, he let her clamber past the broken step so that she could kneel on the attic floor and look down at the step. He lifted the loose tread slowly.

He frowned, studying it without speaking, and then set his toolbox on the attic floor and opened it.

"Why did you say that?" Holly asked, her voice right in his ear. "About not fooling with your tools, I mean?"

It took a minute to realize what the girl meant. "They're important to me. I can't do my job without them." He'd prove he had patience if it killed him. "One of my little cousins kept messing with them when I was fixing his mother's jelly cabinet. He wouldn't listen. A real little schnickelfritz, that's what he was."

He could see the question forming on her face and hurried to answer. "That means a little kid who's always full of mischief. And he sure was. He ended up pinching his fingers with the pliers and screaming."

"Oh." She seemed to absorb that. "You have a lot of cousins?"

"Probably a hundred or so," he said, picturing the size of a Beiler family picnic.

"That's a lot." She fell silent, maybe counting up cousins. "I never knew any of mine until I came here."

"You never visited them?" He bent over the step, trying to decide if that scar on the wood was as fresh as it looked.

"Not since I can remember. Never visited, never even talked about relatives. My mom's always too busy for stuff like that."

Even though he was occupied by what he'd found on

the step, he couldn't miss what he heard. That was longing in the kid's voice. Longing for something she'd never had? Rachel would say so. It seemed like Julianne had led a rootless life once she left home.

He glanced at the child's face, trying to think of the right thing to say. "Now you have a chance to get to know them, don't you?"

She shrugged but looked thoughtful. Maybe he'd planted an idea that would make the kid more satisfied to be staying here. Life would be easier for all of them if so.

And if what he was thinking about the step wasn't so. He ran his fingers along the mark. Made by a chisel, he'd guess, but he could be wrong. Still, it hadn't been there long.

"That looks like somebody already worked on the step." Holly was breathing down his neck. She reached around him to put a fingertip on the mark. "Maybe somebody tried to fix it."

She was quick, he'd say that for her. It might also mean somebody had tried to break it, not fix it. He couldn't forget the wax on the staircase.

"Maybe so." He tried to sound noncommittal. "Have you been up here before now?"

He'd been too abrupt—he could see the sulky look come down on her face.

"Are you saying I did this? I wouldn't hurt Rachel. I like her. I'm not mad at her."

Did she know someone who was mad at Rachel? Or did she mean him? He stiffened and then had to remind himself he wouldn't hear the truth by accusing her.

"I thought we might figure out when the stair got loose, that's all. I was up here when I first started work on the house, just having a look around. The steps were sound then. But that's a good three or four weeks ago."

"I get it." She considered. "I came up—I guess it was that first day we were here. They told me to go explore while they talked," she added, her voice colorless. "It was okay then, because I stepped on it up and down."

Jacob counted back the days, but it didn't help as much as it might. So far as he knew, nobody else had had an opportunity to come up to the attic since then, but he wasn't around all the time. And someone bent on trouble would take care not to be seen.

Someone like Holly. Her reaction didn't prove she'd done anything wrong, but he hadn't forgotten her desire to get out of here. Maybe she'd think if Ms. Geraldine or Rachel got hurt, they'd have to let her leave.

If he knew Holly better, he might be able to tell if she was covering up, but Holly was a mystery to everyone here. She could have picked up a taste for manipulating people from Julianne.

Holly, seeming to lose interest in the project, prowled around the attic, poking into things and making occasional sarcastic comments about the things she found. An old-fashioned dress dummy seemed to fascinate her, and she pulled it out of the clutter of objects.

"Was this supposed to go in a store window?" She poked it in what might have been its ribs. "Funny looking."

"I think ladies used it to fit their dresses on when they made them. It looks like it adjusts to get bigger or smaller. But what do I know? I never used one."

Holly giggled. "You'd look pretty silly." She poked the dummy again. "If this was supposed to be Aunt Geraldine, it's too fat for her. She's skinny. Or did she used to be fat?"

He considered. "As far back as I remember, Ms. Geraldine always looked about the way she does now. Maybe it was her sister's. Or her mother's."

"She has a sister? I never met her."

He almost said she should be glad but restrained himself. "Gerald's mother. She's the youngest of the family. You'll probably meet her while you're here. She stops around once every week or two."

When she wanted something for her precious Gerald. She'd been here twice since he'd been hired, and he'd had to find work outside the range of that whining voice. He didn't know how Ms. Geraldine put up with it. But she probably had more patience than he did. Most anyone did.

"Seems funny."

Jacob wasn't sure whether she meant Ms. Geraldine's kin or the fact that she didn't know any of them. *Funny* might be the word for either of them.

But it sure wasn't for the damage to the attic step. That had happened recently. He couldn't prove it had been done deliberately, but he had his suspicions.

If so, had it been intended for Rachel? Or Ms. Geraldine? He could think of reasons why someone might go after either one of them when it came to the Withers family. It was time he and Rachel had a talk about this situation.

RACHEL WAS UP and moving in plenty of time to fix supper, but Ms. Geraldine refused to let her.

"Certainly not."

Rachel found her in the kitchen with Holly, having a glass of lemonade and one of the oatmeal-chocolate chippers she'd made. "Holly and I have decided we'll have pizza pie for supper."

"Just pizza," Holly put in. "You don't need to say *pie*."

Ms. Geraldine nodded as if making a note of that. "She tells me we can call and have it delivered, ready to eat."

"Aunt Geraldine hasn't ever had pizza." Holly shook her head at someone so deprived.

"Then I guess it's a gut time to start, ain't so?" Rachel glanced at the clock. "We won't have to call for another hour or so to order it."

"I got the pizza place menu on my phone, so I'm going to show Aunt Geraldine what the choices are," Holly said, sounding important, and Rachel had to try hard not to laugh.

After her rebellious start, Holly seemed to be settling down. Could they believe that there wouldn't be any more trouble with her? That might be going too far, given how changeable girls could be at her age, but at least they could hope.

"Let's go in the study, where we can be more comfortable."

The study was the small room behind the parlor. It was much less formal than the parlor, even boasting a television set, which Rachel supposed Ms. Geraldine seldom watched but probably Rachel would. *Holly*

Ms. Geraldine still leaned more heavily than usual on her cane. Was that the result of rushing upstairs in the aftermath of Rachel's fall? It seemed likely.

She wasn't to blame, so it was silly to feel guilty. She certain sure hadn't wanted to fall. But she still felt sorry for causing such an upset.

Watching Holly walking slowly alongside her great-aunt cheered her, though. They were such an odd pair—generations apart, and the one so tall and thin, the other shorter and lively, filled with energy and youth. No matter how different, they were tied by blood, whether Holly realized it or not. You could never entirely dismiss that relationship, even if you barely knew each other. Even if she hadn't seen one of her cousins in a long time, they'd still pick up right where they'd left off.

The thought brought Rachel's mind to her father, and how long it had been since they'd been together. Her friends thought him demanding and selfish, but even if he had been, she was fond of him. After all, she'd taken care of all of them after Mammi died.

Now things would be different, with a new wife to cater to him. If she did. She didn't know Evelyn well enough to be sure.

The family had so little warning that Daad was even considering re-marrying. Apparently he'd been writing to Evelyn ever since they met at a family event out in Ohio. If she'd known at the time, Rachel felt she'd have been better prepared for the news. As it was, things had happened so fast that she hadn't been able to respond.

Remembering that day, Rachel felt her stomach twist just as it did then. She should have talked to Daad about it, despite his reluctance to say anything about what he felt. She hadn't even wished him well—he hadn't given her a chance. Maybe, when he came back, she'd be able to find the words to make things better between them.

Left alone in the kitchen, Rachel decided to see if there were enough vegetables for a salad to go with the pizza. And she ought to have something in reserve to heat up in case Ms. Geraldine discovered she really couldn't eat pizza.

She was checking the refrigerator for salad ingredients when she saw Jacob coming in and dropped the head of lettuce she'd pulled out.

"Ach, clumsy," she scolded herself. She started to bend over to pick it up, but a wave of dizziness hit her. She grabbed the edge of the table. She'd hold on to something while she bent down.

But Jacob had already crossed the kitchen. He picked up the lettuce and straightened to hand it to her.

The sight of Jacob brought back the comments he'd made earlier about her accident. She'd thought she'd worry about his questions later, and it was later now.

"Aren't you supposed to be resting?" Jacob sounded disapproving, as if he'd like to order her back to her rocking chair.

"I've rested enough." She put the lettuce back in the fridge and took out the pitcher of lemonade, holding it up. "Like some?"

Jacob frowned at her for another moment and then nodded. "Maybe this is just as well," he muttered, pulling out a chair and sitting down at the table. "Komm. Sit down."

Rachel went on pouring the lemonade. Jacob seemed to have lost his manners today. She put the glasses on the table and stood, staring at him.

It didn't take long for him to get the import of the look. He gave a wry smile. "Yah, all right. Please sit down, Rachel. We have to talk."

Her lips twitched, and she sat across from him. "Why? Is something wrong?" She knew what he was wanted to say, but she'd let him bring it up.

"Apart from your bruises, you mean? Don't try to deny it," he added, maybe sensing she was about to do just that. "I can tell by the way you're moving. Your side, is it?"

"I guess I landed on it," she admitted, rubbing her ribs and discovering they were too tender for that. "But it's not bad," she said quickly. "I'll be fine by tomorrow. Did you get the stair fixed so no one else has an accident?"

"I did." He hesitated, and his expression tightened. "But I don't think it was an accident. Or at least, I'm not sure of that."

She could only stare at him. His words should be a surprise, but they weren't. That was obviously what he'd been hinting at earlier.

And maybe she'd been thinking the same this whole time, even while telling herself she should just be more careful. Her mind wanted to deny it, but her emotions said he was right.

She went with her mind, clinging to the easier answer. "That's ferhoodled. Why would anyone mess with the attic stairs? There's no point to tampering with them. For one thing, they're hardly ever used."

Jacob shook his head, and his hand tightened on the glass until his knuckles were white and she feared he'd break it.

"You went up today. Ms. Geraldine is always thinking of something she needs from the attic. Anybody who's around her much could know that. Sometimes she sends somebody, like she sent you. But if nobody is available, she goes up herself."

"How do you know, if you weren't here?"

"Because I caught her at it. She decided she had to look for some curtains she thought might be nice in the room I was working on. Instead of waiting to ask me to get them, she trotted upstairs herself while I was out in the stable working." He gave a wry smile. "She didn't like it when I told her she shouldn't have. You know what she's like. Independent and stubborn along with it."

You would know, she thought, but didn't say.

Rachel couldn't avoid his meaning. She wanted to. She wanted to just go on doing her job and avoid trouble. But she couldn't.

"You think someone wanted her to fall. The way she did that first day. That's it, isn't it?"

"Well, look at it, Rachel." He was starting to get impatient, the way he always had when she didn't agree with him. "We've never figured out how that wax got on the stairs."

"The cleaners…" she began.

"Maybe the cleaners did it, but maybe not. There's no way of knowing, and if we asked them, they certain sure wouldn't admit it."

She nodded. That was evident. Most people didn't want to admit they'd done something wrong.

"And now this," Jacob said, emphasizing the words. "If someone did it deliberately, it must be aimed at Ms. Geraldine. Or at you."

"Me?" Now she was startled. "Why would anyone want to hurt me? No one dislikes me that much."

Did they? She'd led a quiet life, never hurting anyone. She glanced again at Jacob's hand wrapped around the glass. Except Jacob, who would say she'd hurt him.

"I've been thinking on it." His eyebrows formed a straight, dark line across this face. "Think about what would happen if either of you was hurt very badly. Seems like the results would be the same, whether it was you or Ms. Geraldine." He held up a hand to stop her protest. "Hear me out. If Ms. Geraldine were hurt—even just a broken bone—she'd probably have to go to a nursing home. That can be serious at her age. She'd be out of the house, at least for a long time if not permanently. You'd lose your job. Holly would have to go to her mother…"

"If you're saying Holly did this, I don't agree with you." Surely the child wouldn't do something so malicious. They'd been getting along better, and even if they hadn't, she honestly didn't think Holly had it in her to plan something that could really hurt someone.

"I don't know who did it," he admitted. "I'm just saying

it's possible. I talked to Holly after your fall. She sounded genuinely sorry you got hurt, but she was hiding something. I don't know what, but something."

Even if she accepted Jacob's idea that the accident—accidents—were deliberate, she wouldn't believe that Holly would do something like that. Rachel was shaking her head when Jacob's hand closed warmly over hers.

"Wake up, Rachel. You may feel that kid has had a raw deal when it comes to parents, but she could have done it. She hasn't had anyone but Julianne to teach her what's right and what's wrong. With either you or Ms. Geraldine out of the way, she'd be sent back to her mother, ain't so?"

She couldn't argue with that, but she still didn't believe it. Jacob must have read her conviction in her face. He patted her hand and released it.

"Okay, I don't really think she would either, but she could have. Or if not Holly, there's someone else who's eager to get Ms. Geraldine out of the house. Lorna and—"

She didn't want to hear this. "I can't picture Lorna up in that dusty attic pulling a tread loose. Her clothes would be ruined, and I don't suppose she knows which end of the hammer is which."

Jacob's face relaxed for a moment in a half smile. "I have to agree with you there. But she's not the only one in her family who might have an interest."

"Ricky? He might be spoiled, but surely he wouldn't do such a thing," she said.

"Maybe. But he's not the only possibility."

"Richard? I can't believe that." An image slipped into her head of Richard as a teenager. Even then he'd been responsible. And kind. He'd always had a good word for her, even when everyone else was ignoring her.

"I see I hit a soft spot, didn't I?" Jacob's voice had hardened. "But Richard of all people would have a reason. Everyone knows he's next in line for the property, and that's his business. He'd probably make a fortune if he could develop this land for housing or some other sort of business."

She drew back away from him, rejecting the words with a quick gesture. "That's ferhoodled. A man like Richard wouldn't do such a thing."

She started to rise, but his hand clamped down on hers again. "Admit it, Rachel. You always did have a little crush on him, didn't you?"

"I did not." Her voice rose a little. "He was always nice to me when I was a little girl, that's all. And he certain sure has a gut reputation in the community. You've no call to hint something like that about him."

"He has a better reason than anybody—"

"No, he doesn't." She stopped to think. What was she saying? "Anyway, we've no proof that your suspicion is true. Accidents do happen, you know."

Jacob shrugged, his expression easing. "Yah, they do. And you might be right." His hand gentled on hers. "But I wonder." His lips twitched. "And I also wonder why I'm the only person you ever lose your temper with."

Leaving her at a loss for words, he headed out.

CHAPTER EIGHT

RACHEL TRIED TO go back to her salad making after Jacob left, but the things he'd said kept revolving in her mind. He'd certain sure given her plenty to think about, so why was she focusing only on his comment that she got mad at him? That was plain foolish.

Wasn't it? Well, that wasn't exactly what he'd said. He'd commented that he was the only one she lost her temper with, which was nonsense. Maybe she had become braver about expressing her own opinion. After all, she'd grown into an independent woman now. She'd been pushed into it, but all the same. Besides, if he didn't annoy her so often, it wouldn't happen.

Satisfied, Rachel began tearing lettuce for the salad. She'd noticed that Holly avoided greens, so she also cut some carrot sticks. But her knife soon slowed as she thought through Jacob's comments about her fall not being an accident.

She hadn't been surprised when he said it. She had to admit it. Apparently she'd already accepted the possibility in the back of her mind even if she hadn't let herself dwell on it. If someone really had rigged the step with the hope that Ms. Geraldine would fall—well, she couldn't believe that any of Ms. Geraldine's family members would be so cruel. If the elderly woman had gone all the way down the stairs, she might easily have broken her hip. Or worse.

No, it wasn't conceivable. She shouldn't let herself speculate about it, not ever.

She realized quickly that it was impossible not to think about something once she'd told herself not to. Fortunately Holly came bustling into the kitchen, holding her phone like a flag.

"We're ready. Can we order the pizza now? Do you want plain pizza or something on it?"

Hoping to hold on to Holly's good mood, she said, "I like most any kind. What do you and your great-aunt think?"

Holly wanted mushrooms and pepperoni, and apparently Ms. Geraldine had said she'd try it. A little doubtful that the older woman would really eat pepperoni, she suggested half plain and half mushroom and pepperoni. Holly was eager to call, so Rachel listened while she placed the order. She gave them the phone number and hung up, turning with a satisfied look.

"All taken care of. It'll be here in about half an hour. They seemed surprised when I said the Withers house."

"That's probably because no one ever ordered a pizza from here before," Ms. Geraldine suggested.

Holly shook her head as if in disbelief. "You want me to set the table out here?"

Rachel didn't speak. It wasn't her decision, after all.

"Yes, do that," Ms. Geraldine said. "We'll be informal tonight. It's silly to eat pizza with a tablecloth and the good china." She hesitated. "I think I'll go sit down until it comes. You can get the money from the drawer where I keep it, Rachel."

Rachel nodded and began tossing the salad.

"Do Amish people eat pizza?" Holly sounded as if she were interested but doubtful.

"For sure," Rachel said. "Sometimes it's ordered from

the shop, but often homemade. People exchange recipes a lot, and my mamm used to make the best crust, so everyone wanted hers. She put just a little sugar in it."

"I never heard of making your own." Holly sounded doubtful. "Do you throw it in the air, like they show on TV?"

Rachel had to laugh at the thought. "Well, no, I never have. But my cousin Jessie tried it once."

"What happened? Is it really better if you do that?"

She grinned. "We never found out, because it got stuck on the ceiling."

Holly giggled at the image but sobered after a moment. "You sure have a lot of relatives, don't you?"

"Most Amish people do, because we have big families." She wasn't sure whether Holly was envious or not. "You met some more of your relatives today, ain't so?"

"Uncle Richard and Aunt Lorna. They said I should call them that." She didn't sound enthusiastic. But then, at her age meeting more adults wasn't very exciting.

"They're Ricky's parents," Rachel pointed out. "So they're really your mother's cousins, but you should call people what they want you to."

She shrugged, uninterested. "Uncle Richard didn't seem to know that Ricky had been here. I thought that was funny."

"I suppose since he's been away at school, Ricky's gotten used to doing things on his own."

"Yeah." She pouted. "I wish I could."

That was probably a good subject to avoid. "I'm sorry my accident interrupted their visit. It was embarrassing to have everyone in the house come running."

"I don't think Aunt Geraldine cared if they were interrupted. They were talking to her about something that made her mad."

"They were? How do you know? I thought you were outside." That startled her so much she responded before telling herself she shouldn't encourage Holly to gossip.

"I came in because I wanted to know who'd come in the car. But when I heard their voices, I went back out again."

Holly had probably been hoping that the car contained her mother.

"I'm sorry if they made her angry," Rachel said.

"It was something about Aunt Geraldine moving. She really told them off about it." Holly grinned at the memory. "Then I decided to go outside. I guess it was right after that that you fell, because I didn't hear it."

Rachel nodded absently. Despite her efforts to dismiss it, here was proof that Richard and Lorna still wanted Ms. Geraldine out of the house, either for her benefit or their own. They must have plunged right into the subject, because she'd decided to come down when she'd heard their voices. She'd like to believe they were only concerned about Ms. Geraldine, but still... Jacob's words rankled in her mind.

Suppose Rachel had been hurt seriously enough that she wouldn't be able to continue work. Unless Ms. Geraldine could find someone willing and able to live in and help her, they'd have a good argument against her living alone. And if Ms. Geraldine had fallen—

No. No matter what, she couldn't believe that Richard would injure his aunt just to gain control of her property.

"I hear something coming," Holly said, hurrying to the door. "Maybe it's the pizza."

But Rachel could already see from the window that the vehicle wasn't a car. Sammy and his wife, Sarah, waved at her from the buggy, and the basket by Sarah's feet surely contained their infant daughter.

Holly was turning away from the door, looking disappointed that it wasn't the pizza delivery. Rachel caught her hand. "Komm. Meet my brother and his wife."

She tugged a reluctant Holly out the back door with her. "Sammy. And Sarah. And surely this is baby Anna Beth." She leaned over the basket. Anna Beth, just two months old, slept deeply, her little arms thrown back over her head, her face turned to the side.

"Ach, she's grown just since last week," Rachel said, smiling tenderly at the tiny face.

"She falls asleep as soon as the buggy starts to move," Sarah said, obviously doting on her little daughter. She patted the infant and then stepped down from the buggy. "And who is this?"

"This is Holly, Ms. Geraldine's great-niece." She took Holly's hand to draw her forward. "Holly, here is my bruder Sammy, and his wife, Sarah, and in the basket is my little niece, Anna Beth."

Holly barely acknowledged the adults, but she leaned over the basket, clearly enthralled by the baby. She touched the basket and glanced up at Rachel. "Can I touch her?" she whispered.

Smiling, Rachel glanced at Sarah, who nodded. "Gently, so she doesn't wake up, yah?"

Holly put one finger on the palm of the baby's hand. The tiny fingers twitched and closed around hers, and she looked up, awestruck. "She likes me."

"Yah, she does." Sarah smiled at her. "You haven't been around babies very much, ain't so?"

It didn't take the shake of her head to give them the answer. "How old is she?"

"A little over two months." Sarah moved closer, obviously prepared for a talk on her favorite subject.

Sammy touched Rachel's hand and nodded toward the porch. "Komm."

He must have something private to say to her, and Rachel's chest tightened as she followed him. "What is it? What's wrong?"

"Nothing." But she could see the concern in his eyes. "Why would anything be wrong?"

"I don't know, but you're standing there shifting from one foot to the other like you're about to ask a girl to ride home with you for the first time. Out with it."

His familiar grin came back. "Never could kid you, ain't so?"

"So stop doing it, and spill out whatever you're troubled about."

Sammy nodded, studying his shoes. "We had a note from Daad, that's all. He says they'll be home next week. No trouble, yah?"

Rachel shook her head, but her stomach flipped over. She struggled to speak calmly. "No, for sure it's not. We knew they'd be back soon."

"Right." Relief filled his voice, as he took her words at face value. "That's all. I thought you'd want to know ahead of time. And if you ever want to stay with us—"

"No, I won't want that." She patted his shoulder fondly. "I'm on my own now, and I like it that way."

But her stomach still felt queasy, and she didn't know how she was going to stomach pizza tonight with the thought of seeing Daad in her mind. Maybe she wasn't as independent as she kept saying she was.

BY THE TIME she was ready for bed, Rachel was exhausted and her ribs had turned purple on one side. She touched them lightly with her fingertips, winced and smoothed her

nightgown down. She'd best try to sleep on the other side
tonight.

Confident she'd sleep soundly, Rachel was surprised to
find herself lying awake with the events of the day running
through her mind. Making an effort to shove them away,
she focused on the full moon that sent a bright patch of
moonlight across the bottom of the bed—so bright, in fact,
that she could probably read by it if she wanted.

The moon hung just over the top of the ridge, seeming close enough to touch. Once in a while a wispy cloud
drifted across its face like a veil. Smiling at the fanciful
idea, she began to relax.

The pizza party had been a success, that was certain
sure. Whether Ms. Geraldine really liked the meal she
couldn't say, but if she hadn't, she'd put on a good front.
Strange, how Ms. Geraldine had taken to Holly, especially considering her attitude toward the rest of her family. Maybe she recognized in Holly a stubbornness to match
her own. With a smile on her lips, she drifted to sleep.

A pleasant dream about walking in the spring woods slid
slowly into something darker. The woods grew frightening, and she sensed an alien presence. Something…some-
one…was following her. She could hear the creaking of
their footsteps.

Creaking? Footsteps in the woods didn't creak.

And then Rachel was wide awake, clutching the quilt,
straining every nerve to hear and to identify. She stared
into darkness—the moon had moved higher in the sky now,
and it no longer shone into her window. Was that what had
wakened her? The change in the light?

No. She felt sure it had been a sound. Quietly she slipped
out of bed and pulled on her robe and slippers. Easing the

door open, she stood still, listening intently. Nothing now, but she had the overpowering sense that something was wrong.

She moved slowly along the hall, stopping to listen outside each door… She may as well go back to bed. Nothing was—

She heard it again, more clearly this time, maybe because she was closer to the stairs. The noises came from down there. A scraping sound, followed by a crack as if something had broken. She hesitated, considering. She could wake Ms. Geraldine, but if it was nothing…

Shaking her head, Rachel went quickly and quietly back to her room and got the flashlight from the bedside stand. At least she could go downstairs and try to determine what was causing the noise. It might be something as simple as a loose shutter or a branch scraping against the side of the house. The wind had come up—she could hear it whispering around the house.

With her hand against the wall, Rachel moved silently down the stairs, putting her foot to the wall side of each step to avoid creaks. She wasn't making noise, but she could still hear something, and when she rounded the corner at the landing, she could see something, too. A light came from the dining room, sending a narrow path across the hall floor.

Rachel froze. Someone with a flashlight? It wasn't bright enough to be the overhead fixture—at least, she didn't think so. Hardly breathing, she listened. Nothing. Was she wrong?

The light shut off with no sound to tell her that someone had snapped a switch. Silence. It lasted so long that she became convinced she was mistaken. No one was there. If there had been, he'd gone, and she couldn't stand here on the steps all night.

Even as she turned, the light reappeared, and her breath caught. Fear washed over her, and just as suddenly was replaced by anger. She would not stand here shivering. She'd find out what was going on.

Still silent, Rachel forced herself to move deliberately. Down to the bottom of the stairs, forward along the wall, in a moment she'd be able to see into the dining room...

She stumbled, bumping into the edge of a small table, which creaked in return. Holding her breath, she straightened.

The light went off again.

Before she could panic, it came back. Just as suddenly, she realized what it must be and her tension dissolved. It was the moon, high enough now to have reached this side of the house, casting light and then going dark as the clouds moved.

She wanted to laugh at herself, but something kept her quiet. That explained the light, but not the noises. She couldn't go back to bed until she felt sure everything was safe.

A couple of quick steps took her to the dining room door. The full moon shone brightly in the long window on the side wall. It reflected from the polished surface of the table and touched the vase of lilacs that stood in the center. No one was in the room but her, but the noise continued.

It took another minute, but then Rachel understood. The wind had come up, as she'd thought, and the window opposite her was rattling. Without letting herself have second thoughts, she hurried to it and grasped the sash. Yes, just steadying it stopped the noise. The last of the fear ebbed away, leaving her feeling unbelievably tired and longing for her bed.

She couldn't go until she'd fastened it in some way. Running her fingers along the sash, she tried to think what she could push into it to stop the rattle for tonight, at least. Jacob would fix it tomorrow.

With the thought, Jacob's face appeared in her mind, first stern and severe and then lightening suddenly so that his lips quirked and laughter made his eyes sparkle. Yah, Jacob would handle it. She'd tell him first thing. Her fingers grasped the lock at the top of the sash—grasped and tightened. The window was unlocked. But she had checked to be sure it was locked before she went to bed, mindful of the door she'd found unlocked.

She snapped the latch into place, locking the window and then wiggling it to be sure it was secure. Maybe the wind had made it work loose. Maybe. But she'd still have Jacob check it first thing tomorrow.

JACOB HAD JUST become engrossed in a new strip of badly damaged baseboard the next day, when he heard a step and a shadow crossed the ray of sunlight from the stable door. Even before he looked up, he knew it was Rachel. It may have been years, but he still had that instinctive recognition of her presence.

He finished the cutting he'd been doing before putting down his tools to greet her. "Rachel. What brings you out so early in the morning?"

"Nothing very exciting," she said, but he thought she looked as if there were something on her mind.

"But…" He stopped, raising an eyebrow. "What do you need me to do?"

Rachel smiled. "Ach, Jacob, you know me too well. There is one little thing you could check in the house."

"Well…" He looked down at the workbench, as if assessing how much work he had on hand. He'd found that a good way of ensuring clients respected his time, and he'd done it automatically.

"Too busy?"

He chuckled. "You caught me. I just like to be sure my customers don't interrupt me twenty times a day. But I don't need that with you." He dusted his hands off and rounded the workbench, moving into the patch of sunlight. "What can I do for you?"

"Check the dining room window," she said promptly, as if she'd known all along he'd come now—which she probably did. "The lock seems to be a little loose."

He paused in the act of tossing some tools into his bag. "I thought I checked all of the windows when I was assessing what had to be done. But maybe it worked its way loose." He joined her. "Let's have a look."

They started toward the house, and she bent to lift a daffodil that had been flattened by last night's wind. "Poor thing. I'll cut it for the house if it doesn't perk up."

He didn't want to talk about daffodils. "I saw Sammy and Sarah stopped by yesterday. Bringing some more of your belongings, were they?"

"Ach, yah. Every time I think I have everything I need, something else comes up. Sarah noticed I'd left the crib quilt I'd started behind, so she brought it over."

"For their little one? You're late, aren't you? I distinctly remember seeing a boppli in the buggy."

"I would be late if I were doing that," she said, her voice a little tart as if annoyed that he'd think she could be so remiss as not to have a crib quilt ready on time. "This one will be for Cathie Forster, but don't you say I told you."

"Silent as a stone, that's me," he said lightly. So Cathie and Michael were starting a family to go along with Michael's daughter, Allie. Good for them.

They crossed the porch and went on through the kitchen toward the hall.

"I'm wonderful happy for them." Rachel's face glowed with pleasure at the thought of her friend's joy.

"Yah." He dismissed the thought of the family he and Rachel might have had. "Anything new with Sammy and Sarah, other than getting up in the night with the boppli?"

"No. Well, not exactly." They had reached the dining room. Rachel didn't bother to lower her voice, so he guessed Ms. Geraldine was not within earshot to be disturbed.

"What exactly, then?" It was easy to tell when Rachel was evading something. She wasn't very good at it.

"Sammy thought I should know that Daad and his wife will be back from their trip next week. That's all."

"They were bound to come back sometime, ain't so?" He tried to sound as if he didn't realize that it had ruffled Rachel's peace.

"Yah, for sure. Sammy just thought I'd want to be…well, prepared to see them."

Usually the mention of her father annoyed him with its reminder, but he was more concerned with how it affected Rachel at the moment.

"Are you prepared? What exactly does Sammy say about it?" If she mentioned going home, he was prepared to argue the point.

Ignoring the question for the moment, Rachel led him to the side window. "It's this one. I tried to secure it, but it was rattling."

He set down the bag of tools and jiggled the window. "Not too much wrong with it, but I'll tighten the latch. So what exactly is Sammy worried about?" He wasn't going to let her get away with not answering.

Rachel's lips twitched. "He asked me again to move in with them. Maybe it's just as well that Sarah didn't hear him. I'm sure she'd dislike it as much as I would."

"Sarah seems like the accommodating sort. She wouldn't raise a fuss, would she?"

"That would make it even worse. I wouldn't be able to help acting like the big sister again, and she'd hate to say anything. No, I'm happy as I am." She gave the window a little pat, as if to show affection for the rambling old house.

He studied the latch needlessly. "What if your daad asked you to come back home?"

"He won't," she said. She paused for a moment, and then went on. "Even if he did, I wouldn't do it. I like it here. I'm independent, and that's how I want it."

He was tempted to ask if she couldn't have gotten her independence a little sooner but decided he didn't want to start a fight. At least she was confiding in him, and they were talking like the old friends that they had been once. Maybe they were becoming that again.

Putting down his screwdriver, he switched the latch from locked to unlocked a few times, trying to rattle it each way.

"There, not a whisper out of it." He glanced around. "I wouldn't think you'd even notice it unless it was really windy."

She put her hand on the window and tried it for herself. "It was really windy last night. It must have gotten going sometime after midnight. Didn't you notice the flowers?"

Jacob stopped putting his tools away and straightened

in order to meet her gaze. "And what were you doing down here after midnight?"

Shrugging, she evaded his eyes. "Nothing. I mean, I woke up and thought I heard a noise, so I got up to see what it was. I was concerned about Ms. Geraldine."

He could feel his face getting more rigid as she spoke. "That doesn't explain why you were down here. Wasn't Ms. Geraldine in bed?"

Where you should have been, he thought. And then he pictured Rachel snug under her quilt, her hair spread loose across her pillow. And veered away quickly from the image.

"Well, yes. But I could still hear something rattling. You know how it is when the house is quiet at night. You hear every sound. So I went down to check."

"By yourself." He didn't wait for her to affirm it. "Haven't you more sense than to go investigating noises alone? What if it had been somebody trying to break in?"

"If it had, I'd have gone straight to the telephone and called the police, of course." She sounded defensive. "There's a phone in Ms. Geraldine's room, one in the study, one in the kitchen…"

"While you were going there, someone might have attacked you. Burglars don't like to let anyone see them. Don't you know that?" He could hear the irritability in his voice but he couldn't stop it, any more than he could stop caring what happened to her.

Rachel's eyes flashed. "I appreciate your concern, Jacob, but I'm a grown woman and I don't need scolding from you or anyone else."

"Yah, I know, you're independent." He slapped the tool bag closed. "If you had found your independence a few years earlier, things would be different. I guess it took being told to leave to get you out of that house."

He'd gone too far, he knew, and regretted it the instant the words were out of his mouth. But she was so exasperating. So gentle and mild on the surface and with a core of granite when it came to doing what she thought was right.

"That might be true." Rachel had paled. "But it's not your place to say so." She swung around and was out of the room before he had a chance to say another word.

CHAPTER NINE

RACHEL CONTINUED TO fume about Jacob's lecturing off and on throughout the day, until she finally convinced herself that hearing advice she didn't want was part of having friends and relatives who'd known her from childhood. They'd always feel free to tell you what you were doing wrong. But not all of them were as rude as Jacob about it.

She realized, as the day went on, that Holly was starting to follow her around the house. Boredom, she diagnosed, but Holly didn't seem to like any of her suggestions, most of which involved helping with household chores. That didn't come as any surprise, and she guessed that no one had ever expected her to do something helpful before.

As she headed toward the kitchen to fetch Ms. Geraldine's afternoon tea, Holly trailed along, pouting a bit.

"Afternoon tea," she grumbled. "How boring. Who has afternoon tea anymore? It's like something from a book."

"Plenty of people take a coffee break in the afternoon," she pointed out. "And I've noticed you like something to drink and a snack about this time. Ms. Geraldine prefers tea."

"Old-fashioned," Holly muttered, making a face.

"Older people have a right to their own tastes, don't you think?" Rachel tried to stop her lips from twitching. "If you like—"

She lost the words as she swung open the kitchen door

and found a strange man standing at the counter. Thoughts of the burglars Jacob had mentioned flew through her mind. But after a moment of frozen stares, the man gave an uneasy laugh.

"Sorry. I didn't mean to scare you." He looked from her to Holly and back again as if he didn't know who to address. "I'm Ms. Geraldine's nephew. I just dropped by to see her."

If Rachel was speechless, Holly wasn't. She took a belligerent step toward him. "She's not in the kitchen drawer," she said tartly, sounding like her great-aunt.

He—Gerald, Rachel supposed—flushed a little and pushed the drawer shut. "I remembered Aunt Geraldine always kept some cash there, and I wanted to get change for a twenty."

Rachel didn't know what, if anything, she could do about his rummaging around the kitchen, but she'd best take charge before Holly started a battle.

"I think you must be Gerald." At his nod, she glanced at Holly. "Holly, this is another cousin of yours. Gerald Arnold."

"So you're Holly." He eyed her as if he considered her a foe. "I heard you were here. Visiting." He looked at Rachel and seemed to make an effort to pull in his stomach. "And you're the new housekeeper, I guess."

"Rachel." She supplied her name. It was clear that Gerald didn't remember her, but then, she wouldn't have known him either. He'd never been a match for looks to his cousins, and he seemed to have gone downhill as he got older. His stomach nudged over his belt, and the sports shirt he wore looked as if it needed a wash. The sandy hair she remembered had noticeably receded, and he couldn't be all that old. In his thirties, maybe.

"Guess I'll go and see my aunt. She in the parlor?"

Rachel nodded, wondering whether Ms. Geraldine would welcome this particular visitor.

Gerald circled them on his way to the door, keeping an eye on Holly as if he expected her to block him. But after a glance at Rachel, Holly shrugged.

No sooner had the door swung shut than Holly turned on her. "Why didn't you stop him? Aunt Geraldine wouldn't want to see him. She doesn't like him. She says he's a loser."

Rachel gave her the look she'd used on her little brothers. "Ms. Geraldine never used that word."

"No, but that's what she meant," Holly said darkly. "I don't like him."

"Like him or not, he's your relative." Rachel put the kettle on. "If Ms. Geraldine tells me to keep someone out, I will, but not otherwise."

Holly grinned. "You don't like him either. I can tell. He's the kind of guy Julianne warned me to look out for. He's…" She stopped, looking as if she were censoring her language.

Rachel grinned back. "I know what you mean. And I've heard the words before. But you shouldn't call your mother by her first name."

"She doesn't care." Holly opened the refrigerator door and stood surveying the contents. "Don't we have any soda?"

"You can ask your aunt to put it on the grocery list," she suggested. "But I'd wait until after your cousin leaves."

"Don't keep calling him that. Seems like a person ought to be able to pick their relatives."

"Well, they can't. So why don't you get some cider and a couple of cookies and stop asking for things until I get your aunt's tea ready?"

Holly didn't deign to answer that, but she busied herself with the cookie jar while Rachel swished hot water in the teapot. What she'd said to Holly had been correct, but she had to admit she didn't think any more of the grown-up Gerald than she had of the teenager. He'd been the type to play tricks on anyone who couldn't get back at him.

The damaged attic stair slid into her mind as if it had been waiting, and she tried to dismiss it. Granted it was the kind of thing he used to pull on her, but he couldn't have known she'd be the one caught by it. And anyway, he hadn't been around.

After a moment's hesitation, Rachel put a second cup on the tray before she poured boiling water into the teapot. "I hope you didn't take the last of the cookies," she said, reaching for the jar.

"Nope. But it probably wouldn't hurt if you were to make some more. Especially those snickerdoodle ones." Holly sounded very offhand, but Rachel wasn't fooled. She'd developed a passion for the crisp cookies after her first taste.

"I'll do that." With the tray ready, she carried it through to the hallway, where she could hear voices from the parlor. Well, one voice. Ms. Geraldine's, sounding annoyed and saying something about a job.

Maybe it was a good time to interrupt. Balancing the tray on the edge of the hall table, she swung the door open, picked up the tray and ventured in. Ms. Geraldine was seated in her usual chair, with her needlework on her lap. Gerald stood opposite her, hands in his pockets, looking like an Amish scholar called before the teacher's desk.

At a gesture from Ms. Geraldine, Rachel set the tray on the table and separated the cups for pouring.

"That's all right, Rachel." Ms. Geraldine glanced at the second cup. "I don't need that. My nephew isn't staying." She glared at him, and Gerald wilted.

"Yes, well, it was good to see you, Aunt Geraldine. I'll

just be on my way." He backed out of the room, as if afraid to take his eyes off her.

Rachel blinked. Clearly she wasn't the only one to find Ms. Geraldine intimidating. Wary of becoming the target of her temper, Rachel slipped away in her turn.

She hadn't reached the door yet when Ms. Geraldine spoke.

"Rachel, if Gerald shows up again, come and tell me before you let him come in. Will you do that?"

"Yah, of course." As long as Ms. Geraldine said so, she'd obey orders, no matter how Gerald felt about it.

Holly was right—it seemed her employer didn't think too highly of this particular nephew.

When she got to the kitchen, she found Holly putting the last of the cookies in a plastic bag.

"I see you're finding a snack."

Holly ignored that. "So? Did you tell Aunt Geraldine about finding Gerald with his hand in the cash drawer?"

"No, and I don't intend to. He explained that. And anyway, it's not a cash drawer. It's just the place where Ms. Geraldine keeps a little money in case I need to pay for anything. Like when we got the pizza."

"All I can say is, I'd check the drawer if I were you." Holly paused at the screen door, the cookies in one hand and a bottle of cider in the other. "There might not be as much money left there as you think."

JACOB, PAUSING ON the porch to let Holly get past, heard her final words. Seeing him, Holly tossed her head toward Rachel.

"Maybe you can convince her," she said and headed for the grape arbor, her favorite spot for gabbing on her cell phone.

He lingered where he was for a few more moments not sure what had been happening. The only way to find out was to go in. He had to, anyway, if he were going to mend fences with Rachel.

Not that he'd been wrong, he told himself. She had acted foolishly, and he'd been so fearful for her that he just might have spoken his mind too strongly. But he wanted to go back to being friends again.

He pulled open the screen door and stepped into the kitchen. Rachel was alone there. As near as he could tell, she was staring at the counter blankly.

"Rachel? Was ist letz? You look like you're in a daze. Or maybe you're ignoring me." He kept his tone light. No reason to make matters any worse if he could help it.

Rachel blinked and turned to him with a smile. "Don't be ferhoodled. You're my friend, even if you are too bossy sometimes."

"Yah, sorry." He avoided saying he'd been right. "That's how it is when you're…well, old friends."

He was glad he'd been restrained when her smile widened and it seemed she glowed with warmth. "Very old," she commented, laughing a little.

"So what was Holly going on about? I heard her say something about checking the money. What money?"

"Ach, Holly was jumping to conclusions, I think." She touched a drawer handle, then pulled her hand back. "It's just that Ms. Geraldine keeps some cash in here, just in case I should need to pay for anything."

He frowned, puzzled. "Did Holly think you'd been helping yourself, or what?"

"Of course not. It's Gerald. We came into the kitchen and found him here, and he had the drawer open."

He gave a low whistle. "I don't blame Holly. It's not a

big jump to get to the conclusion that he'd been helping himself."

"He explained." She didn't really sound convinced. "He said he needed to change a larger bill, and he knew his aunt kept some small bills in here."

"So Holly was speculating that if you checked, you'd find some money missing." He filled out the rest of the thought. "Have you checked?"

She shook her head. "I didn't want to do it in front of Holly. She really can't go around accusing her cousin of theft."

"No, but if you're responsible for the money, you should check on it, anyway."

Rachel opened the drawer. "The trouble is, I don't really know how much should be there. I certain sure haven't used much, if any, except for the pizza."

The envelope she took out of the drawer wasn't very thick. She opened it, pulled out the bills and counted them out on the countertop. "Twenties, tens, a couple of fives and what? Ten ones."

"Write it down," he advised.

"But I don't know how much was there," she protested.

She sounded as if she suspected some was missing but wouldn't venture to say it.

"You're responsible for it, anyway. If you make a note of it now, at least you'll be sure if any more…well, any money…disappears."

Rachel nodded, made notes on a sheet of paper and added it to the envelope with the money. When she closed the drawer again, she made an effort to smile. "That's done."

She was still worried—he could read that easily on her face.

"You're trying to decide whether or not to tell Ms. Geraldine, aren't you?"

"I don't want to cause trouble between them. But…is it my duty to tell her?"

"You're the expert on duty, not me," he couldn't help saying. "If you're not sure money is missing…"

Looking relieved, she nodded. "Yah, you're right. I guess I was upset at finding him here in the kitchen when I thought no one was in the house." She glanced toward the door to the back stairs. "I couldn't help but wonder…"

"You're wondering if he rigged the attic step, ain't so?"

"It's…it's foolish, I guess. I was just thinking that it was sort of like the tricks he used to play on the younger ones when he was a teenager." She shook her head fiercely. "I'm ferhoodled. He's a grown man now. Anyway he'd have no reason to trick me. He didn't even seem to know who I was."

"You might not have been the target," he reminded her. "It could have been done even before you were hired."

"Not much before," she said quickly. "You said you'd been up the stairs not all that long ago."

"True." He mused about it. Not that he'd put it past Gerald to be playing tricks, but… "He might easily think he had something to gain."

"You mean if he's mentioned in Ms. Geraldine's will…" she began, and then let the thought trail away. A little shiver went through her. "I don't like thinking this way about people."

Without hesitating, he clasped her hand, wanting to chase away the fear or apprehension or whatever it was. "You don't have to stay here, you know."

"It's not that. I don't want to leave." She raised troubled eyes to his. "Everything seems different here."

He almost asked what she meant, but realized he knew. "Different from when you were a child. Since you're a grown-up now, ain't so? You see Ms. Geraldine and the rest of them through adult eyes."

Nodding, she attempted a smile. "Some of it is gut. Like Ms. Geraldine. I used to be so intimidated by her. And really afraid of that portrait of her father."

Jacob chuckled at her expression. "Yah, he's a scary-looking old boy, all right. But Ms. Geraldine—well, she's used to having things the way she wants them, and I sure wouldn't want to cross her, but at least she listens to folks. And if you're right, she'll come around to it. Maybe not right away, but eventually."

Her hand still rested in his—not clasping it but seeming to be comfortable there. It felt familiar, to be holding hands with her.

"Seems like between being scared of Ms. Geraldine and teased by the rest of them, maybe it wasn't for the best that your mammi brought you here."

She blinked, startled. "It's not that. I liked coming. Mammi talked to me about things and made me feel like a real grown-up when I came with her. And Julianne was nice to me sometimes." She considered. "She wasn't ever nasty, like Gerald, but maybe she didn't want to be bothered. Other times she'd let me watch her putting her lipstick on and fixing her hair in some different way."

"Trying to attract the boys even then?" he asked, remembering Julianne's attitude the day he'd met her.

"I guess she was. Not that there were many to attract except her cousins." She chuckled. "Maybe she was practicing and she wanted an audience. Anyway, I guess I have a soft spot for Julianne, in spite of…"

"Her failings as a mother?" he finished for her.

"I shouldn't judge her or any of them. It's just funny to see how they all turned out. Except for William."

"What happened to him? A big success or gone to the dogs?" He couldn't recall Ms. Geraldine ever talking about him.

"William was Julianne's brother. Ms. Geraldine's favorite, I think. She said something about him quarreling with everyone and going off to… I don't know exactly what happened to him. She was disappointed in him, I know. She wanted him to do one thing, and he wanted to do something else, I think."

"Speaking as an old bachelor, I don't have an opinion on that one." He wasn't really trying to remind her. It just came out that way.

Fortunately she didn't jump to any conclusions. "You're a son, though. And I don't remember hearing about your daad pushing you to do something other than carpentry."

"No. I was fortunate that way. Daad's always let us youngers find our own way." If he ever should become a father, which didn't seem very likely, he could do no better than to model himself on his own daad.

"Your daad is a fine man." She carefully didn't make any comparison to her own, but he could sense something behind the words.

He found himself thinking what it must have been like for her all those years, with her father pressuring her to do what suited him best. It'd be hard for the young girl she'd been then to go against him.

His fingers moved caressingly on the back of her hand. "I'm sorry," he murmured, not even sure what he was sorry about.

Rachel's gaze met his, and her eyes widened, seeming to grow darker. Her fingers closed on his hand palm to palm. It was so quiet it seemed he could hear the beating of his heart and the way her breath quickened.

He couldn't be sure how long the moment lasted until a sound somewhere outside startled him out of immobility. He took a hurried step back. Neither of them would want to be caught that way. Maybe they both needed time to think before they said another thing to each other.

BY THE TIME Rachel was cleaning up after the evening meal, she had managed to rationalize those moments between her and Jacob. With her hands in the warm, sudsy dishwater, the uncomfortable feelings seeped away. It had probably been her imagination entirely. And anyway, even if it wasn't, it was just a momentary lapse—a second in which the feelings they used to have popped up to shake them. That was all it was.

A small voice spoke up in the back of her mind. What if it wasn't? What if all that wasn't in the past? She forced herself to consider it. Even if she felt something for Jacob, that didn't mean that he felt the same. And while on the surface the barrier between them was gone, it hadn't disappeared from their hearts. She would still consider her duty to others, not just him, and he would still insist on his way. It would be foolish to attempt it and risk a broken heart all over again.

The door swung, heralding Holly's entrance. "Are you still doing dishes? Why aren't you using the machine?"

"I am," she protested. Only because Ms. Geraldine insisted. "But some things don't get clean in the dishwasher, so I do them by hand." She put the last casserole dish in the drainer and dried her hands on the towel. "Now I'm done. What do you need?"

"Not me. Aunt Geraldine. She's going to show me pictures of my mother when she was about my age, and she thought you might want to see, too. She says you might be in some because you were around that summer, so come and look."

It would probably be just as well for her to go along. She guessed Holly expected to find this activity boring in the extreme. "Okay. Let's go and see."

In the parlor, Ms. Geraldine had set up the photo party with herself on the sofa and several large, heavy albums on the coffee table in front of her.

"Good, here you are." Ms. Geraldine patted the sofa on either side of her. "Sit here, and you'll both be able to see."

Holly rolled her eyes, and Rachel frowned at her while they took their places. Luckily Ms. Geraldine didn't seem to notice. She pulled one of the huge albums onto her lap. "I think this is the right one." She started leafing through it. "The first ones are of my family."

She stopped at a page covered with old-fashioned black-and-white images, and Rachel saw Holly stifling a grin. "Who's that?"

Holly put her finger on a woman in a high-necked, puff-sleeved dress posing in what was obviously a photo studio. Standing next to her was an erect, portly gentleman in dark suit and tie, his face adorned with a small mustache.

"My aunt and uncle." Ms. Geraldine leaned forward to look more closely. "He was considered a fine figure of a man in his day."

Holly sputtered, unable to control it, and Rachel suppressed her own giggle. Fortunately, Ms. Geraldine didn't seem insulted.

"Just you wait until you look at pictures of yourself twenty years from now. You'll feel the same way. All your clothes will look silly to you then, and you'll wonder how you could ever have worn them."

"I couldn't possibly be as bad as that," Holly said firmly.

She glanced at the two-page spread of formal studio prints from the last century. "Why do they all look so angry? Didn't they want to have their pictures taken?"

"It's not anger. In those days, having a picture taken was a serious business. People didn't have cameras, and they'd go to a studio for something special. They wouldn't smile on such an occasion." Seeing that Holly wasn't convinced, she added, "Besides, you had to hold the pose for a long time then. I don't suppose you could do that if you were smiling."

Holly wasn't impressed. "Where are the pictures of my mother?"

"I'm getting to them." Ms. Geraldine leafed on past a dozen pages and stopped. "Look, there's the whole group—all of my nieces and nephews."

Holly leaned forward to look closely at the picture she indicated, her ponytail swinging. "That's Mom." She put her finger on a lineup of kids standing in front of the grape arbor. "She hasn't changed a lot, has she? I'll bet she was always the pretty one." That might be an edge of envy in her voice.

"You're very like her, you know," Ms. Geraldine said.

Holly just sniffed and shook her head, but Rachel thought she was pleased at the comparison.

"And there's one with you in it, Rachel. Do you remember that time?"

Rachel nodded, smiling at the photo that showed Gerald chasing Julianne, and Rachel watching them from the safety of a branch of a nearby apple tree. "How could I forget? Gerald had a worm, and he threatened to throw it on Julianne's dress. Besides, I'd never had my picture taken before. And not many after that either."

"Why not?" Holly stared at her in amazement. She was

used to having photos, most of them selfies, as she called them, done a dozen times a day.

"I'd forgotten," Ms. Geraldine said. "I did ask your mother, and she said she didn't mind at your age."

"No, she'd be all right with that. Just not after joining the church."

"I don't know what you're talking about," Holly complained. "What was the big deal? Why would anyone mind having their picture taken?"

It would seem doubly strange to Holly, who hadn't been around Amish people. "Our church doesn't think members should have photos taken because of the Bible saying not to make graven images. It's all right for children, because they haven't joined the church and promised to follow its rules yet."

"Weird," Holly commented, dismissing the idea.

"People have different beliefs," Ms. Geraldine said firmly. "It's important to respect them even if you don't agree with them. Apparently your mother missed out on teaching you that."

Rachel wished she hadn't brought Julianne into it. Holly might criticize her mother, but she didn't like anyone else to do it.

"It's all right, Holly," she said quickly. "It didn't bother me."

Holly sent a resentful glance at her great-aunt and mumbled something that might or might not have been an apology. Rachel thought she could see regret for a moment on Ms. Geraldine's face, but knew her pride wouldn't let her back down.

"That's a nice photo," she said, pointing to another one. It showed William standing on the cliff overlooking the quarry with the sky behind him. He was laughing, and the wind blew his fair hair back from his face. "Very like him." In fact, it was her exact memory of William as he'd been then, laughing and playful, without a care in the world. What did he look like now?

"That's my uncle Will, right?" Holly seemed to have forgotten she was miffed. "He looks like Mom."

"Yes, they always looked very much alike." Ms. Geraldine was making an effort to be pleasant, she thought. "Sometimes people took them for twins. Julianne laughed at that, but it made William angry since he was older."

Her face settled into deep lines, and Rachel knew she was thinking about him, maybe regretting the past. She was silent, respecting her feelings.

"Well, boy-and-girl twins aren't ever identical, I know that. We learned it in science class." Holly wasn't intimidated—she probably didn't even notice her aunt's expression. "What happened to him? My mother never says anything about him. Why haven't I ever met him?"

"He left," Ms. Geraldine said tightly. "He didn't like the plans that had been made for him. He wanted to travel the world, so he did. He left us a note and went."

"But where is he now?" Holly persisted.

"I don't know." The strain of controlling her feelings made Ms. Geraldine's voice tight. "Still traveling, as far as I know."

Ms. Geraldine was probably regretting bringing out the photo albums at all. Once again, Rachel found herself trying to distract them. "That's a great picture of your mother, Holly. You really do look a lot like she did then."

"I do?"

She sounded as if she didn't believe it, and Rachel wished she knew whether she felt pleasure or regret. Julianne was posing, leaning against a picnic table that had been set up under the apple tree on the edge of the lawn. They must have had a picnic lunch, because the boys were still eating.

"That's your mother." Ms. Geraldine said suddenly. "There, in the corner of the picture. She must have been caught by accident."

Rachel would know that back anywhere. Mammi was turned away, carrying a tray toward the rear door. She wore the deep blue dress that was her favorite, and the white apron seemed to shine against it.

Ms. Geraldine reached for the photo. "You probably don't have any photos. If you want it—"

"No. Thank you." She smiled. "I don't need a photograph to remember her. She's still alive in my mind."

Their eyes met, and Ms. Geraldine nodded. "Yes, that happens with people we love." The depth of feeling in those few words gripped Rachel, making her wonder who the elderly woman was thinking of.

CHAPTER TEN

BY THE TIME lunch was over the next day, Rachel was so tired of hearing Holly say she was bored that she was ready to take desperate measures. The only trouble was that she couldn't think of any that would have an effect on the child. If either of her younger brothers had ever said such a thing, Rachel would have given them a list of jobs to do. But they'd known better.

Besides which, farm children, and especially Amish farm children, didn't have time to be bored. There was always something to do on a farm. Unfortunately she didn't have the authority to make Holly do anything.

How much of her bad mood was really boredom and how much the short lecture Ms. Geraldine had delivered the previous day, when she'd said something about what her mother hadn't taught her? It had been mild as corrections went, but she'd already seen that Holly was very sensitive when it came to her mother.

Ms. Geraldine came into the kitchen wearing a frown. "We must do something about Holly. She's unbearable today." She paused and then shook her head. "No, I'm the one who should do something. It's hardly your concern. But I don't know what to do."

How often in her privileged life had Ms. Geraldine had to admit such a thing? Not often, she'd guess. But it wasn't fair to put all the burden on her.

"I volunteered to help with Holly, so I am involved. But I'm not sure either." She thought again of her own family. "I can't very well tell her to clean out the stalls or feed the chickens."

A smile cracked Ms. Geraldine's face. "You sound like your mother saying that. She always said, when my nephews were unusually trying, that what they needed was some hard work." She considered. "She was probably right at that. It might have made a difference in how they turned out."

Just about anything she said would be likely to come out like a criticism of Ms. Geraldine's family, so it was probably best not to.

"I was thinking about going down into town to pick up some groceries. In the buggy, that is. Maybe Holly would find that a welcome distraction. She's probably never ridden in a buggy before."

"The grocer delivers, so you don't need to do that. And if there's something you want that we didn't get, it makes more sense for me to take the car and go shopping. You don't have to do that along with everything else you're doing."

Rachel could think of a dozen reasons why that wasn't the best answer, but she couldn't mention Ms. Geraldine's difficulty in getting around. It came and went, probably according to the weather, but she didn't ever admit it. She'd resent it and more than likely insist on doing too much just to prove she was fine.

"I thought taking the buggy would be unique enough to interest her. I might even let her take the reins a little on our way back up the hill. Not down on Main Street where there's traffic, of course."

She didn't push, just waited for Ms. Geraldine's decision. She was far too determined to stay in control to welcome anyone, including Rachel, telling her what was best. But as Jacob had pointed out, she would listen and sometimes agree.

Finally Ms. Geraldine sank into a chair at the kitchen table. "I suppose you're right." Her face relaxed a little. "Holly would probably like the novelty of going in the buggy. And I'd rather take a little rest this afternoon instead of walking around the grocery store. You can tell Hal Winters to put it on my bill. He'll expect that."

She glanced up at the ceiling, probably picturing her great-niece shut in her room busy with her phone. "Go ahead and call her."

Registering the silent hope that Holly would respond to her idea, Rachel opened the door to the back stairs and called up to them, "Holly? Holly?"

"What?"

Rachel hung on to her patience for a moment. "Come down here, please."

She heard footsteps, and then Holly appeared at the head of the steps. "What do you want?"

Controlling herself, Rachel waited, looking at her. Finally Holly gave an elaborate sigh and trudged down the steps, making more noise than ten girls her age, Rachel would think.

When they reached the kitchen, Ms. Geraldine had gone. Rachel could hardly blame her. It was asking a lot to expect a woman her age to cope with an annoying preteen girl.

Rachel picked up the grocery list she'd been keeping. "I'm going to take the buggy and drive downtown to get some things at the grocery store that I like to pick out myself. I thought you might like to come with me."

And get yourself out of your great-aunt's sight and hearing for a while, she added silently.

Rachel thought she saw a spark of interest in Holly's eyes, but she still wore the pout. "Why would I want to do that?"

"You could ride in a buggy. I don't suppose any of your

friends have done that. And it'll give you a chance to look around town. You haven't really seen it yet."

She held the pout for a moment longer, and then it dissolved and she nodded. "Can I pick out some soda?"

Rachel weighed the benefits of interesting her against the empty calories of soda and finally nodded. She'd have to ration it, that was all.

"Okay." Holly darted to the stairs. "I'll be ready by the time you bring the buggy up."

No hint that she might consider helping, but Rachel had already seen how little seemed to be expected of her. She could imagine Jacob's reaction if she spoke that way to him. On second thought, she didn't want to imagine it.

After telling Ms. Geraldine they were leaving, Rachel hurried out the back door. They'd best get going if she were to be back in time to start the chicken potpie she'd planned for supper. She headed for the stable, realizing she hoped Jacob wasn't there. She hadn't seen him to talk to since yesterday, and she still didn't know how to respond after what had happened between them. Well, maybe he was working upstairs.

He wasn't. As soon as she entered the stable, she saw him at the workbench, bending over the length of baseboard he was creating to match the rest of it in the room. He straightened and looked at her without speaking.

Nodding, she headed for the mare's stall. Bessie tossed her head and whickered, obviously happy to see her and even happier when Rachel led her to the buggy and backed her between the poles.

"You want to go somewhere, don't you, sweet girl? You must be as bored as Holly is."

"Is that what's wrong with her?" Jacob took the other side of the harness and helped lower it into place. "I'd give her something to keep her busy."

"You sound as if you've had a go-around with her already today." She carefully didn't meet his eyes while they worked in tandem buckling the mare into the harness.

"She tried following me around asking silly questions." He looked so irritable that she immediately thought it was because of what had happened between them. But she didn't know what to do about it. "I put an end to that, saying I'd make her sweep the workshop if she didn't get out of here."

She understood. When Jacob was occupied with his work, he didn't have time for anyone. Still, she could have wished he'd be a little more patient.

"Couldn't you have told her a little about what you were doing?"

His frown was intimidating. "That's not what I'm being paid for."

"A little kindness doesn't cost you anything," she pointed out, wondering again what had happened to the sweet boy she'd known. He might have been exasperated at such a thing, but he'd have made an effort to help.

"I suppose not," he grumbled.

She climbed up to the buggy seat without waiting for him to help her. She didn't think she wanted to feel his touch right now.

Frowning, he reached toward her hand. "Rachel—"

"I have to get going," she said quickly and slapped the lines, glad when Bessie moved out obediently. She'd never been nervous of Jacob's reaction in her life, but this seemed different, and she didn't want to cope with it right now.

RACHEL PAUSED IN the grocery store aisle to double-check her list. The store wasn't crowded at this time of day, since most folks did their shopping early or stopped by after work. Winters' Market was popular with older people in town because it was easy to walk to, and with the Amish because they liked to deal with people they knew.

Hal Winters was the third generation to have a market on Main Street, and he didn't seem worried about competition from the giant supermarket on the edge of town. He knew his customers too well to fear losing them.

Satisfied she had everything she needed, Rachel looked about for Holly. She'd agreed that Holly could browse around town on her own as long as she was back at 3:30 p.m. It was that now, but there was no sign of her. Perhaps she was waiting outside.

She smiled, thinking of Holly's fascination with the horse and buggy. She'd spent the short time to the store asking so many questions about buggies and horses and driving that Rachel felt dizzy. She began to understand Jacob's exasperation with Holly's questioning.

Still, how else did anyone learn? Holly's insatiable curiosity was a good thing, she'd think. After all, she'd never experienced this kind of life before. It was better for her to be interested than bored, anyway. Jacob, of course, was silent by nature. But that didn't mean he should be impatient with the child.

Fifteen minutes later, Rachel was the one who was impatient. Holly was late. Moreover, she wasn't in sight anywhere along the street, and Rachel's groceries were beginning to react to the warmth of the day. Shaking her head, Rachel went back inside and asked Hal to set her bags in the refrigerator, finding it necessary to explain that she'd have to go look for her charge. Hal, always sympathetic to valued customers like Ms. Geraldine, nodded, offering to deliver the groceries once he'd closed if she wanted.

Rachel appreciated the offer, but certainly hoped it wouldn't be necessary. With Hal's offer to keep an eye out for the girl if she showed up, Rachel set off to find her. She tried to control her exasperation. Holly would turn up soon, that was certain sure.

Rachel walked quickly down Main Street, eliminating possibilities as she went. Holly would hardly be in the bank or the Building and Loan Association. In fact, she couldn't think of many businesses that would attract an eleven-year-old who was probably used to upscale malls.

The coffee shop was nearly empty, but a few teens stood talking in front of the ice cream shop. Remembering Holly's affection for ice cream, she felt sure that was where she'd be, but the shop was nearly empty. Rachel talked with the teenager behind the counter, describing Holly's appearance as best she could. Nothing. She had the feeling the boy was only waiting for his shift to end, and a few questions weren't worth bothering about.

She'd stepped outside when one of the cluster of teens spoke to her. "Did I hear you asking about a kid with her hair in a ponytail, by herself?"

"Yah, I did. Have you seen her?"

The boy had a grin and freckles that reminded her of one of her cousins. "I think I saw the kid you want, going into Twin Screen. I noticed because she looked like my little sister."

"Thank you so much." She smiled her thanks and hurried across the street.

The small movie theater was nearly deserted this afternoon. From what she'd heard, people went to the big cinema center over toward Fisherdale if they wanted that sort of entertainment.

The teenage boy in the ticket booth had to be lured away from his cell phone to answer her questions. Yes, he'd seen a girl who was probably the one she described. Yes, he guessed she could go in to look for her, so long as she didn't sit down and watch the movie.

That was an easy answer. Judging by the posters, it wasn't something she'd ever consider watching even if the Amish did go to the movies, which they didn't, at least not once they were past rumspringa. She couldn't vouch for anything some of the more daring teens might try if they thought they could get away with it.

The inside of the theater was dark, and most of the seats were empty. She moved down the aisle, avoiding a glance at the screen, and paused to have a look at each silhouette. She earned a glare from one couple and an invitation to sit down from an elderly man.

Holly sat near the front, staring fixedly at the screen. She jumped when Rachel touched her arm. "What?"

Rachel suppressed a number of things she'd like to say. "It's past time to leave. We have to get the groceries home. Come along."

"I want to see the end. Can't you wait till it's over?"

"No." Her grip tightened on Holly's arm "Komm. Now." Tugging her along, she led her to the aisle and out of the theater, not letting go until they were on the street.

"I don't see what the fuss is about." Holly rubbed her arm pointedly while keeping up with Rachel's quick strides. "I was just watching a movie."

Where to begin? She made an extra effort to hold on to her exasperation. "You were supposed to meet me at 3:30. You were not supposed to go into a movie theater, or ignore the time, or watch something I'm quite sure wasn't suitable."

"My mother would have let me." The pout was back in full force. "She says I can decide for myself what movies I want to see."

Rachel could hardly believe that even from Julianne, but now was not the time to get into an argument about what Julianne would or wouldn't allow. "Your mother isn't here, is she? You were in my care this afternoon. I didn't give you permission to go to the movie."

That didn't end it as far as Holly was concerned, of course. She continued to grumble the entire time they picked up the groceries and loaded them. Aware of interested stares, Rachel tried to keep her embarrassment under control as she thanked Hal. But she didn't feel her flush subsiding until they were loaded up and on their way back.

It wasn't a long trip home, although the mare naturally went more slowly going up the hill. Holly complained most of the time. But even Holly eventually found it difficult to go on moaning to someone who didn't answer. She finally ran out of things to say, and a sidelong glance told Rachel that she was staring morosely at Bessie's flickering tail.

They turned into the driveway at last, and Holly stirred. "Aren't you ever going to say anything?"

"What do you want me to say?"

Rachel had by this time progressed through annoyance with Holly, to regret that she'd suggested this trip, to the desire to give Julianne what her Mamm would have called a good talking-to, to pity for a child who didn't seem to belong anywhere.

But expressing that pity wouldn't get them anywhere, and if she had to look after the child for another week or the rest of the summer, they had to find a way to make this work.

"You could yell at me." Holly's voice had become small.

"I don't want to yell." Not now, anyway. "I'd just like you to understand." She took a breath, searching for the right words. "I thought we were becoming friends, so I trusted you. But I don't know how to be friends with someone I can't trust."

Silence. When Holly finally spoke, the words were barely above a whisper. "I'm sorry."

She waited until she'd pulled up at the back porch and looked at the woebegone figure next to her. "All right. We'll start again. Now let's get the groceries inside."

Her experiment might have failed in a way, but Rachel felt something might also have been gained. At least Holly seemed to have some inkling that what she did affected other people. That would be a step forward.

JACOB HAD BEEN about ready to go looking for Rachel and Holly when he saw Rachel's buggy turn into the driveway. It was about time. She was plenty later than anticipated, making him sure something had gone wrong. Ms. Geraldine must think so, as well, because she'd been looking out the window for the past half hour.

Rachel passed the parking area by the front and pulled up at the back door, and they both got down. He had a good look at their faces, and it confirmed what he'd anticipated. Holly had done something wrong—something to make her look both mutinous and dejected and to give Rachel's sweet face an unusual amount of stiffness.

He took a step forward, thinking he'd offer to take Bessie to the stable, but then stopped. If he did that, he wouldn't have a chance to talk to Rachel, and he needed to. He'd tried before she left, but she hadn't given him the chance. That might have been just because she was in a rush, but he didn't think so.

Maybe it was just as well, though he hated to admit it. He hadn't known what he should say. Those moments when they'd looked at each other, he'd been caught by the feelings in Rachel's eyes. He'd been sure something had shown in his eyes, too. But what? He didn't know.

He leaned against the stable door, watching as Rachel and Holly unloaded groceries and carried them into the kitchen. Once they'd apparently taken everything in, all was quiet. Bessie stood, cropping at the grass along the edge of the drive. Jacob observed, seeing movement beyond the windows, wondering what was being said. He'd no doubt at all that Ms. Geraldine wanted answers. Rachel wouldn't reappear until she'd given them.

In any event, the conference didn't last as long as he'd expected. Rachel came out, hurrying a little, swung herself up and drove Bessie toward the stable. Bessie, he was sure, would have come on her own—she knew where her feed bag was.

As they neared him, Jacob moved forward, catching the headstall and leading Bessie to the spot where the two buggies, his and hers, were stored. Rachel nodded and slid down, then began to remove the harness without saying anything. Jacob let the silence stand for a few moments before he spoke.

"Well?"

Rachel looked at him reluctantly. "Well, what?"

"You know what I mean. What did Holly do now to get into trouble?"

Her lips tightened. "What makes you think Holly did something? I could have been delayed for any number of reasons."

"Wasn't it Holly?" He raised his eyebrows in a question, still certain sure of the answer.

"Yah. But it wasn't anything big. We just...we must have misunderstood what time we were supposed..." She let that trail off.

"She disappeared on you, ain't so?" He lifted the harness off Bessie's back and carried it to the hook. "You were upset." He glanced at her. "You still are."

Rachel led the mare to her stall and poured oats into the feed bag. "Not now." She seemed to make up her mind to talk to him. "You know how scary it is when you're supposed to be keeping an eye on someone and you lose them. As I recall, your little bruders were good at that."

"Yah, they were. Especially the time Joey climbed out of his crib and got out of his room." He couldn't help smiling, but he shook his head. "Joey was two. Holly is what? Thirteen?"

"Eleven," she corrected. "But still old enough to know better. I suppose I shouldn't have let her go off on her own, but there wouldn't have been much sense in taking her to town if I didn't let her see anything." She was arguing with herself as she leaned against the stall, looking tired, and that just increased his annoyance with Holly. "I should have realized…"

"Don't go blaming yourself for what's not your fault." A wave of tenderness swept over him at the expression on her face, and he longed to comfort her. Carefully he put his hand over hers where it rested on the stall bar, ready to withdraw if she showed signs it wasn't welcome.

But Rachel didn't move. If anything, she seemed to relax a little. "I thought we were really getting along well. Goodness knows that child needs a friend, especially with a mother who runs away from responsibility."

"And you run toward it." He stopped, suspecting he'd just said the wrong thing.

"You know what I mean." At least she didn't flare up at him. "I offered to take Holly with me to town. I thought she'd probably just walk down Main Street and back while

I shopped, maybe look into a store or two or buy an ice cream."

"What did she do?" It must have been something bad for Rachel to look the way she did.

"I found her in the movie theater."

He had to suppress a laugh. Rachel looked as if she were confessing she'd found the kid in a tavern.

"That's nothing to look so upset about." He squeezed her fingers. "We don't go to movies. At least…" A few rumspringa incidents of pushing the boundaries passed through his mind. "But she's Englisch. For all you know, she might go to the movies every week."

"Not a movie like that," she muttered. "Not that I looked at the screen, but I couldn't help seeing the posters. And hearing some of the language."

Again he had trouble keeping a straight face. What Holly had done wasn't funny, but Rachel had led a sheltered life, even for an Amish girl. More, a restricted life, with her mamm dying when she did and all the responsibility shifting to Rachel's young shoulders. She hadn't had the time or the opportunity to explore even as much as most kids did during their rumspringa. By the time she was fifteen, her Mammi was sick, and Rachel both couldn't and wouldn't leave her.

"What did Holly say when you got her out of there? I don't suppose she admitted she was wrong?"

"She insisted her mother would have let her watch that. I couldn't imagine, but for all I know, that might be true, poor child. I don't think Julianne pays much attention to her. Certainly not enough for a girl starting to grow into a young woman."

"I guess not."

He knew that expression. He'd seen it on Rachel's face

before, when her sympathy was caught by someone or something and she'd had to hurry to help. It had been true when she was six or seven, and it had never changed. The realization made him wonder why he'd ever expected anything different when her mother passed away.

Rachel patted Bessie and turned away. "I should get supper started."

"Wait a minute." He stopped her with a hand on her wrist. "I want to know what's being done about it. Ms. Geraldine ought to realize that you and she can't deal with a child like that. It's not fair to expect it of you or of herself."

Rachel yanked her hand free, eyes flashing. "I can so. I did."

"Did you scold her, at least?"

"No." She glared at him. "Did you ever change what you did because of being scolded?"

"Maybe not, but if that happened, Daad took a hand, and I couldn't sit down for a couple of days."

"I can't do that to Holly, and neither can Ms. Geraldine, even if we wanted to. Which we don't. So we have to find another way of dealing with her."

"Maybe so, but you shouldn't be dealing with her at all. Julianne shouldn't have left her here, and Ms. Geraldine should have told her so. And you certain sure shouldn't have said you'd help. If you had any sense—" He stopped, knowing he was going too far.

"You know exactly what everyone should do, ain't so, Jacob? You always did think so. If you hadn't been so bossy about what I should do back then—" Now it was her turn to stop abruptly, cutting off the words that he could see hovering on her lips.

"Are you blaming me? I wasn't the one who called off

our wedding. Or don't you remember that?" He couldn't believe what he was hearing.

"You gave me a choice, remember? I could either go with you and build a home of our own, or you didn't want to get married at all."

He wanted to deny it. It didn't sound very good when it was put in such bald terms. "That was what I thought marriage was supposed to be. Didn't you?"

"Did you ever try to find another solution? Or talk it over? No, you just decided you knew what was right and everybody else was wrong."

"And you were so obsessed with doing what your daad told you was your duty that you didn't give us a chance. You put him first."

The color came up in her face. "It wasn't just him. It was the boys, too. He said I couldn't desert them after they'd lost Mammi, and he was right. I couldn't."

That stung, demanding his attention, but he was too worked up to stop and think about whether it was true or not.

"You think you're independent now, don't you? But you just traded doing what your daad said for doing what Miss Geraldine says. Being independent means making up your own mind what's right."

"Don't you mean accepting your opinion as to what's right? You're just as stubborn and convinced you're right as you ever were." She spun and headed for the door. "If being independent means doing what I think is right, then that's exactly what I'm doing."

She stalked off toward the house, leaving him staring after her and convinced he'd said every single wrong thing anyone could think of to say.

CHAPTER ELEVEN

RACHEL WAS MOVING so fast she was nearly running when she rushed through the back door into the kitchen. She fetched up against the sink, breathing fast, and gripped it with both hands, telling herself to stop. To think, to take a deep breath, to wipe away all traces of that—what? Quarrel? She guessed she couldn't call it anything else.

What was wrong with her? She'd never spoken to anyone that way before in her life. Never lost control that much or come away feeling so shaken.

Shaken was the word—her hands were actually trembling. She stared at them for a moment, then turned the cold faucet on and thrust both hands into the stream of water. It helped, and she pressed wet palms to her cheeks, hoping she wasn't as flushed as she felt. But one glimpse of herself in the chrome side of the kettle showed her red cheeks and eyes that looked ready to shed angry tears.

Turning away from the sight, she dashed more cold water on her face, then held her hands under the cold stream until she seemed to feel the fiery glow subside. Finally she straightened, drying her hands on the soft dish towel and then pressing it against her damp face. With a quick movement, she shut off the running water. She had to get busy and fix something for supper. She couldn't expect Ms. Geraldine and Holly to go hungry just because she'd let Jacob infuriate her.

Before she had time to think where to start, Ms. Geraldine came through the swinging door to the kitchen. She stood there for a moment, studying Rachel, who began to feel she was flushing again. What was more, her hands were still trembling.

She pressed them hard against her skirt and tried to master a smile for Ms. Geraldine. "Is there something you'd like me to do?" With sudden realization, she reached for the kettle. "You haven't had your tea. I'm sorry. I'll fix it right now."

Ms. Geraldine's steady gaze seemed to intensify. "I'll have it here, if you don't mind. And fix one for yourself, too." She sat down at the table.

It was a relief to have something to do with her hands, and by the time she set two mugs of tea on the table, she'd begun to regain her composure. It was ferhoodled to let Jacob upset her so much, but maybe it would be a good thing in the end. He'd aired his grievances, so he might be able to start behaving like the friend he'd once been.

She hesitated and then sat down across from Ms. Geraldine, adding a spoonful of sugar to her tea.

"I'm not one to pry," Ms. Geraldine said, emphasizing the words. "But I can see you're upset. Is it Holly?"

Startled, Rachel shook her head. She hadn't even thought of Holly in the past half hour.

"Good." Ms. Geraldine took a sip of her tea cautiously, as if not used to drinking from a heavy mug instead of her usual china cup.

"I'm sorry." Rachel started to rise. "I'll get your regular cup and saucer—"

"Sit down, Rachel." She didn't exactly speak sharply, but there was something in her tone that said it was best to obey.

Rachel slid back into her chair.

"Now." Her employer looked at her firmly. "I'm not

going to ask for an account of all the things you and Holly didn't tell me about why you were so late." Her lips quirked just enough to tell Rachel she wasn't angry. "I'm just glad she admitted it was her fault."

Breathing easier, Rachel nodded. "Yah, I am, too. I think…well, I hope that some good may come of it. She did seem genuinely sorry once she realized how much trouble she caused and especially how worried I was about her. Maybe…well, maybe her life is just different from anything I can imagine."

Ms. Geraldine shook her head slowly. "Julianne bears a lot of the responsibility, I'm afraid. I hate to say this about one of my own kin, but she hasn't brought that child up the way she should."

"It can't be easy on her own," Rachel pointed out. "I noticed that Holly never mentions her father."

"No. As far as I can tell, he's even more irresponsible than Julianne is. He disappeared a long time ago, and if he ever paid a dollar toward Holly's support, I'd be surprised to hear it."

"I can hardly believe a man could just walk away like that from his own child." She tried to imagine a man who wouldn't care at all. Maybe it wasn't so surprising that Julianne was the way she was.

"Julianne just hasn't grown up enough." Ms. Geraldine sounded as concerned as she'd ever heard her. "She needs family around to help her. If she'd move back here, settle down, she could give up the rackety life she leads, and it would be better for both of them."

Rachel nodded slowly, trying to visualize Julianne settling down in River Haven. It wasn't easy. But she certain sure needed some support.

"I had the feeling…" She paused, not sure she should say what she was thinking.

"Go on. What do you feel about her?"

She took a breath. "It seemed as if Holly wasn't used to having someone notice and care when she wasn't where she was supposed to be."

Ms. Geraldine stared down into her tea for a moment. "I'm very much afraid that's true." She sighed, looking as if she carried a burden too heavy for her. "I suppose all we can do is try to make up for it while we can. But I have no right involving you in my family problems."

She looked so distressed, so different from the composed, dignified woman she normally was, that Rachel was stricken to the heart.

"Ms. Geraldine, I care about Holly, too. I want to help her. Really. It's not a burden to me. She's a sweet child under all that boredom she puts on."

Ms. Geraldine studied her for a long moment and then gave a short nod. "I think you do. Well, we'll do the best we can for her."

She rose, pushing the mug away. "I said I'm not one to pry, and I'm not. But I can see you've been quarreling with Jacob."

Appalled that her employer knew, Rachel stammered an attempted apology. "Jacob is…is an old friend, but I certain sure shouldn't be talking to him when I'm working. Or arguing. But he can make me so angry—" She stopped, wishing she'd stopped even sooner.

Ms. Geraldine nodded as she turned toward the door. "People you care about can make you too angry to think about what you're doing sometimes. I've learned that to my sorrow."

Abruptly she clamped her lips closed and, head erect, walked out of the kitchen.

Rachel looked after her, turning those words over in her mind. She'd like to argue, like to say that she didn't care that much what Jacob thought. But she couldn't, because it was true.

Surely, after all this time, she should have gotten over feeling that his opinion was so important to her. She wasn't a teenager in love any longer. But she had to acknowledge the truth of what Ms. Geraldine said. If she didn't care about Jacob, she wouldn't get so furious with him.

She wanted to believe that Jacob was totally and completely wrong. That his selfish attitude was the sole cause of their breakup. But she couldn't in all honesty deny that there was a grain of truth in what he'd said. No more than a grain, she told herself.

But even a grain of something could get uncomfortable in her shoe on a long walk, and Jacob's accusations had just enough truth to prick her conscience. She was likely to do what other people thought was important. Or right.

Right. That was a word that meant a lot to Jacob. He thought he was right, and he didn't seem to see the contradiction in what he believed. He said she was too easily swayed by what other people thought, but at the same time he wanted her to do what he thought. She could almost laugh about it, if it didn't hurt so much.

Maybe she did let herself be influenced by others, but how could she help it? When you had family, you owed them your loyalty and your love. You didn't walk away when they were in need.

But you couldn't please everyone, and she didn't want to view the rest of her life as one long period of doing what other people thought she should.

JACOB HAD BEEN replaying his conversation with Rachel in his mind all the way home. Conversation? More accurate to call it what it was—a fight. He'd aired all the things he'd been holding back for ten years. He hadn't even realized those thoughts were in his mind until he heard them coming out of his mouth.

Ten years. He'd been holding that disappointment in the back of his mind for a long time.

Jumping down once he'd reached the barn, he patted the gelding and began unharnessing him, but his thoughts kept going around and around the same thing. Was it really reasonable to have held on to that hurt for such a long time? He suspected if he asked the bishop or any one of the ministers, he'd get a sharp answer. Maybe that was why he'd never said a word about it.

Shoving the thoughts aside with determination, he let the gelding into the nearest field. Once there, Blackie shook himself, found a patch of grass that apparently looked comfortable and rolled. Jacob had to grin—the horse looked like one of his bruders shaking off the hay after baling.

The action had served to divert his attention, allowing him to lock away any questions in his mind for consideration later. He carried the harness inside to hang up and heard his father hailing him. Daad was on the far side of the field, apparently doing something to a fence post. Waving his acknowledgment, Jacob slung the harness into place and headed toward his father.

Daad wiggled the fence post in its hole when he approached. "Looks like someone ran into the post and knocked it loose."

"Yah." Jacob grabbed it and straightened it. "Anybody get out?"

"The foal wandered off, not knowing where the fence

was supposed to be. Then discovered he was too far from his mammi and panicked."

Jacob glanced at the foal, safely returned to the pasture and trailing his mother like a little shadow. "Maybe that taught him a lesson. Want me to do it?"

Daad grinned, hefting the sledgehammer. "You want to hold while I pound?"

"Or you could hold while I pound," he retorted, grinning back. Then he went down on one knee and took a firm grasp of the post.

Daad hefted the sledgehammer seemingly without effort and brought it down on the center of the post. A few loud blows and it was done. Together they began reattaching the wire fencing.

"You came home a bit early today. I hope Rachel hasn't had any more accidents. Has there been some trouble there?"

Daad gave him a look that was more than normal curiosity, as if he sensed all wasn't well. He probably did. He and Mammi saw more things than their kids ever wanted them to. And the older he got, the more embarrassed he felt under their watchful eyes.

He wasn't sure what he wanted to say. "She seemed to feel okay today. Went off to town to get groceries." He hesitated. "You know what I told you about that fall of hers—it was kind of funny."

"Yah? Funny how?" Dad's raised eyebrows invited him to say more.

"I'd been up those steps a couple of weeks ago." Absently he pulled the wire taut. "They were as sound as could be. Not that I was checking them especially, but I couldn't have missed it. That's the kind of thing I notice. Well, you know, Daad."

Daad nodded, acknowledging the truth that a man noticed anything related to his own specialty—animals or crops or construction, whatever you knew, you noticed.

"When I checked it after she fell…" He hesitated, seeing again Rachel lying head down on those steep stairs, not moving. "It looked to me as if it had been loosened so that it was only held in place by one shaky nail. Anybody stepping solidly on it would be bound to take a tumble."

Daad considered that for a long moment, not questioning it. "Did you talk to anyone about it?"

"Rachel." He shrugged. "Who else could I talk to? Anybody else might have done it. Well, not Ms. Geraldine, but Rachel thought we shouldn't upset her."

"Why? I mean, what would anybody there have against Rachel?"

Daad responded the way Jacob thought he would. All of them knew they could count on Daad for a considered response. Daad wasn't one to jump to conclusions. That made his advice valuable.

"No way of knowing. It could have been the kid I told you about, Holly. She wants to go home, and she might figure if she caused enough trouble, that would happen." Today's escapade slipped into his mind. Holly's disappearance might have had the same motive.

"That would only help her if she told them she'd done it, wouldn't it?"

"I guess so. Not that I really think she did it. She seems to like Rachel. Well, why wouldn't she? Rachel pays her more attention than anybody." Did that sound like he was jealous of a child? He sure hoped not.

"Who else would have any reason to play tricks like that?" Daad's tone didn't contain anything but a desire to know.

"Well, anyone who wanted to see Ms. Geraldine give

up living in her house. She couldn't go on there by herself without Rachel."

They'd started walking back toward the house together, and Daad let a few more yards go by before he spoke. "Seems like not very much to convince you something's wrong. That's what you're feeling, yah?"

He nodded. "Not very convincing, you mean. So maybe I should forget it." But he didn't think he could.

"I wouldn't say that." Daad stopped, putting a hand on Jacob's shoulder. "You're feeling something is wrong there, ain't so? You've always had good instincts, Jacob. No harm that I can see in keeping your eyes open. We wouldn't want anyone hurting either Ms. Geraldine or Rachel."

Jacob didn't realize how tense he'd been until he'd heard what Daad had to say. He'd been doubting himself, he realized. But like Daad said, no harm in keeping his eyes open. If someone did mean to cause trouble, they'd have to deal with him.

Before he could express his thanks, a small whirlwind hurtled toward them from the back porch, launching itself at him. "Jacob! Spin me, spin me. Please?"

He couldn't help grinning. Sally, at six the baby of the family, was everybody's darling. "Manners, Sally," Daad reminded her.

She batted her big blue eyes at him. "I said *please*, didn't I?"

"So you did." Jacob grabbed her under the arms and swung her around in a circle until he was dizzy, even if she wasn't. "There." He set her down firmly. "Now here's Mammi coming to call us to supper."

Clutching his hand and swinging it, Sally tagged along with them as they went in the back door, then stopped at the sink inside the mudroom to wash up for the meal.

Stampeding feet behind them announced Matthew and

James, elbowing each other to get to the sink first. Matthew was a grown man but Daad always said he acted like a fifteen-year-old whenever he was with James.

"We got here first," Sally told him, drying her hands.

"Scoot out of the way or I'll put my dirty hands on you." James wiggled his hands, definitely dirty, at his sister, and she squealed.

That was home, Jacob thought. If you wanted peace and quiet, you wouldn't find it here at suppertime.

He opened the door to the kitchen, giving Sally a gentle shove. Mammi turned toward them, obviously counting heads to be sure everyone was there before she dished up, while Anna filled glasses and Mattie held the serving dishes.

That was a typical supper at their house. In no time, it seemed, they were all in their places around the long table. The moments of silent prayer were followed by clinks and clatters as the dishes started around.

Home. He listened to the chatter begin as everyone had filled their plates. Most of them were right here on the farm all day long, except for Anna, who worked at the dry goods store in town, and him. But they were still never at a loss for something to say to each other.

Did Rachel miss this—the give-and-take of family life—now that she was spending her mealtimes in that big, nearly empty house instead of with family around?

Of course with her mamm gone for so long and the boys both married, things were a little different. But he couldn't believe they were much quieter with her brothers in and out handling the dairy herd.

As if she'd been reading his thoughts, his sister Mattie nudged him. "I said, how does Rachel like it there? You're seeing a lot of her, ain't so?"

There was way too much meaning in the words. Mattie was just about old enough to remember when he'd been going to marry Rachel.

"Fine," he said, cutting it off short.

"That's no answer." Mattie's face was alive with mischief, and he had the urge to drop her applesauce in her lap. When had she gotten so sassy?

"It's all you're going to get," he snapped, watching her eyes flash just about the way Rachel's had.

"Mattie, enough." Mamm's voice was quiet, but it was firm. Mattie subsided.

Jacob glared at his plate. Couldn't he get away from the subject of Rachel even in his own home? For just an instant he saw her face in front of his eyes, and it was flushed with anger. She'd said he was bossy, said he was always thinking he was right.

He looked around the table. If he asked, his sisters would no doubt agree with her. Well, he wasn't going to ask. And he wasn't going to brood about Rachel either.

THE NEXT DAY Rachel found that keeping herself busy both saved her from seeing Jacob and, to some extent, from dwelling on him. By afternoon, she was running out of things to do, so she started a batch of whoopie pies. They were a little more work than the usual cookies she kept around for a hungry preteen but worth it.

Besides, Holly had been curious about the treat ever since Ricky mentioned it the day he'd dropped in. Or maybe she was just interested in Ricky. A bond between cousins seemed normal to her, given the swarm of cousins she had, but Holly was lacking in family. She just hoped Ricky would remember he'd promised Holly he'd show her where the berries grew in the woods.

Maybe she was spoiling the child, but Holly had been

muted and cooperative since her adventures in town, and she'd like to reward that behavior.

As if she'd smelled the whoopie pies, which was impossible since they hadn't gone in the oven yet, Holly clattered in the back door. Somehow kids seemed to have an extra sense where sweet treats were concerned.

"What are you making?" She reached for the bowl, and Rachel blocked her with her elbow.

"Wash your hands first, and then you can have a taste."

Holly made a face, but quickly disappeared in the direction of the powder room. Unlike Rachel's brothers at that age, Holly was rather particular about being clean, and the amount of time she spent in the bathroom washing her hair reminded Rachel of watching Julianne spend endless time fixing her hair in front of the mirror.

When Holly returned, Rachel was mounding the rich chocolate batter in tablespoonfuls on a cookie sheet. She nodded to the bowl. "Have a taste."

Holly put in a tentative finger, licked off the batter and went back for more. "That's yummy. What is it?"

"It will be whoopie pies if you leave enough batter." Rachel smiled, watching Holly's blissful expression.

"That's the treat Ricky wanted." Her eyes lit expressively. "Is he coming?"

"I don't know for sure, but your great-aunt thought he might stop by this afternoon since it's Saturday. So we should have his favorite treat just in case, ain't so?"

"Definitely." She gave the batter another yearning look before glancing down at her shorts. "I better put something better on. I mean, if there's a chance of company, not just because…"

Rachel's lips twitched. "Of course."

Holly fled toward the stairs. No sooner had she gone

than a car pulled into the driveway. Ricky? Rachel leaned over to the window to check, but the driver was a woman.

Rachel stopped to wash the chocolate off her hands, trying to hear which way the woman was headed—the front or the back. Then the back door swung open, and she spun toward it. "May I help you?"

The middle-aged woman who'd walked in was bulging in a pair of bright red pants and a print top, her graying hair tightly curled. She eyed Rachel, her dark eyes somehow unfriendly.

"You're Rachel, I suppose. I've heard of you." She didn't look as if it had been anything good, and Rachel wasn't sure how to answer. She didn't need to, because the woman went on almost immediately. "Where is my sister? Geraldine," she added in a slightly louder tone, as if Rachel were unable to hear.

This, then, was Gerald's mother, Freda. She'd be the youngest of the siblings.

"I'm sorry. I didn't realize you were part of the family." That explained the woman walking right in the back door, she supposed. Freda was raised here, so no doubt she considered it home. "Ms. Geraldine is sitting out on the side porch. This way." She started to lead the way, only to have Freda step in front of her.

"I know where the side porch is," she said sharply. "You don't need to come."

Ignoring that, Rachel followed her toward the porch. She'd had her instructions from Ms. Geraldine, and they'd included not allowing anyone to interrupt her without announcing them. She couldn't restrain Ms. Geraldine's sister, but at least she'd accompany her.

She managed to hold the door for her, getting Ms. Geraldine's attention. "Your sister."

"She knows who I am," Freda said irritably and turned

to her sister. "This girl takes too much on herself. I don't need an escort in my own home."

"Rachel is doing what I asked." Ms. Geraldine rose, nodding a dismissal to Rachel. "How are you, Freda?"

"How do you suppose I am? I'm so worried about my poor Gerald." Her voice was a penetrating whine. "You shouldn't be so tightfisted with Papa's money, Geraldine. After all, Gerald is—"

Rachel closed the door on the rest of it, wondering how Ms. Geraldine could handle listening to that voice for very long. Jacob had said he'd had to escape the house when Freda was here, she remembered.

Well, that wasn't an escape she could take. Her work kept her in the house, even if there were a dozen women whining to Ms. Geraldine.

Laughing at herself, Rachel returned to the kitchen. She put the whoopie pies into the oven and began making the light, creamy filling. With Ms. Geraldine's electric mixer, it would take half the time it usually did.

By this time, Holly had returned, wearing a pair of jeans and a T-shirt that looked very much like the outfit she'd had on before. Holly perched on a stool, watching her run the mixer with a moody expression. She'd probably heard the car and hoped it was Ricky.

"I guess she's my aunt or cousin or whatever," Holly muttered, jerking her head toward the side porch.

"Something like that." Rachel tried to follow the tangle of relationships and gave up. "You'd probably be safe to call her a cousin."

Holly shuddered elaborately. "With that voice, I'd rather not be within earshot at all. When I came down, she was asking Aunt Geraldine for money, saying somebody's will wasn't fair."

"You shouldn't listen," she said automatically, trying not to speculate about what that meant.

"I couldn't help hearing it. Not with that voice. Whine, whine—"

She stopped at the sound of the front door slamming. They looked at each other, and then Holly grinned. "I'll bet that means Aunt Geraldine turned her down."

"You shouldn't…" Rachel began.

"Yeah, I know. But I bet you're wondering, too."

"Well, she's gone now, so let's forget about it and finish these whoopie pies. Do you want to put in filling?"

It wasn't until the treats were finished and the bowls licked clean that Holly gave up and went to the back door. "I think I'll go back to the arbor and read," she said casually.

Rachel nodded, reflecting that the arbor made an excellent spot from which to watch the driveway.

With Holly occupied, Rachel went to see if Ms. Geraldine wanted anything. She found her still on the side porch, frowning at the album she held open in her lap. More pictures, Rachel realized.

"May I bring you anything, Ms. Geraldine?"

She shook her head, preoccupied, and then seemed to change her mind. "I suppose you heard some of that. My sister's voice goes up when she's disappointed."

"Very…very little," she said, not sure what Ms. Geraldine was after.

Her employer shook her head. "Today was much the same as the rest of Freda's complaints." She sounded more resigned than irritated. "She's been chewing on a grudge for years, thinking our father should have divided his wealth between his two surviving children. She conveniently forgets that Father settled a substantial amount on her when she got married."

"I'm sure he did what he felt was fair."

It was intended to soothe, rather than because she knew anything about it. Usually in an Amish family there wasn't that much to leave. And if there was, everyone had gotten used to the division by the time it came. Someone would have the farm, often a younger son because by the time he was old enough, the father might be ready to retire to the daadi haus. But this wasn't about an Amish family.

"My father knew whatever he gave Freda, she'd fritter away, or that husband of hers would have gambled. He's gone now, thank goodness, but Gerald is just like him." She shook her head. "Always looking for the easy way, no matter what it is."

Ms. Geraldine seemed to rouse herself. "You could do something for me. Bring me the album with the red cover from the desk in my room."

"Yah, of course." She hurried out, glad to get away from hearing things she feared Ms. Geraldine might later regret saying to her.

She headed up the stairs, rounded the bend at the landing and stopped dead. Freda was just coming down. Rachel stared at her. Hadn't they heard her go out the front door?

Freda gave a high-pitched laugh. "Sorry I surprised you. I was just… I came up to use the bathroom before I leave." She edged past Rachel and hurried down the steps.

There seemed nothing to say, but Rachel stood and watched until she'd closed the front door behind her. Then she glanced upstairs. No reason why Freda shouldn't use the bathroom, of course. But she had to know that there was a powder room right below the stairs in the hall. So why come up here?

CHAPTER TWELVE

HOLLY'S VOICE, raised in excitement, pulled Rachel out of her distraction. It sounded as if Ricky had arrived.

When she reached the kitchen, Holly and Ms. Geraldine were welcoming Ricky, who grinned at her over Holly's head. "Sorry it took me so long to get back here. I got caught up in a lot of stuff."

Amused, Rachel thought he sounded like her younger brothers when they'd been up to something they didn't want to tell her about.

"As long as you're here, you'll stay for dinner." Ms. Geraldine sounded considerably more welcoming then she'd been with her sister earlier. Understandable, since at least Ricky was smiling as if happy to be there.

"I'd like to, Aunt Geraldine." Ricky assumed an expression of regret. "But I'm meeting…" He seemed to change what he was about to say. "I'm meeting a guy about a summer job. I figure I should earn some money for college this fall."

"Hmm." It was hard to tell whether she was convinced or not. "Glad you stopped by, anyway."

"Sure." He skated right over the doubt in her tone. "I told Holly I'd show her the best spots for wild strawberries, and they'll be getting ripe before long."

Holly had been drooping on hearing he couldn't stay

long, but she perked up right away at that. "Super. Let's go." She caught his arm.

Ms. Geraldine's expression softened when she looked at Holly. "You go ahead, then, but save a little time. I believe Rachel baked your favorites today."

"Whoopie pies?" For an instant he turned into a kid again. "You're the best, Rachel."

"We better hurry, then. Can I have something to put berries in?"

"They probably won't be ready yet..." Ricky began, but Rachel was already handing her a small pail. No doubt they'd still be green, but Holly would enjoy it more if she felt prepared.

"Okay, let's go." Holly grabbed his arm and pulled.

Ricky grinned and let himself be tugged toward the door. "Save those whoopie pies for me."

Once the door had banged behind them, Rachel stole a glance at her employer. Was she upset that they'd skipped out so fast?

But she was looking after them with an indulgent expression. "I'll have a little rest until they come back. Wouldn't do you any harm either."

Rachel shook her head, smiling. "Better if I keep moving."

Ms. Geraldine reached the door and glanced back at her. "Are you sure you won't go to your family tomorrow? It's Sunday, after all."

"I'd rather not." She had a lot of reasons, but not many she wanted to talk about. "They're going over to my cousins' place since it's an off Sunday when we don't have worship, and I don't care to go that far."

Besides, everyone would be talking about her father and new stepmother returning this week. Speculating about them and wanting to see her reaction to this surprise marriage. That was the downside of having such a large family. They couldn't help being interested in everything that went on, and they wouldn't be satisfied until they knew all about it.

Ms. Geraldine seemed to accept her reasoning, because she didn't press Rachel about it. Ms. Geraldine went off to the small room behind the parlor that she called her study. With comfortable recliners and a television, it had become a favorite spot for relaxing, especially with Holly here. Holly found the parlor too formal for comfort, and Rachel could hardly blame her. Ms. Geraldine would probably get out her needlework, settle in her favorite chair and go to sleep.

Rachel sat down, suddenly tired herself, and her thoughts slipped back to her family. Much as she'd enjoy seeing everyone, she'd wait. By next Sunday, Daad and Evelyn would be settled in and no longer the hot topic for the busybodies. At least she hoped not, and probably the newlyweds did, too.

Even better, she'd see them in the formal setting of church. It'd be much better to encounter them there, where the forms of a worship Sunday would make it easier. Anyway, she hoped it would.

It was more than an hour later when Rachel stepped out onto the back porch, her gaze focused on the path that led up the hill and into the woods.

"Looking for the kids?"

She hadn't seen Jacob coming around the house, and his voice made her catch her breath. "Yah, just hoping to see them coming back. Ms. Geraldine seems to be getting restless."

"Maybe she doesn't have enough to do," he suggested, but his lips quirked, turning it from a criticism to a comment.

"Well, she does want to spend some time with Ricky before he takes off again for whatever socializing he has in mind for tonight."

"Just like rumspringa, yah?" Jacob grinned. "I understand. I think I caught a glimpse of someone farther up there, where the hemlock thin out a bit. Looked as if they were on their way back down."

"That's good." She looked to the spot he'd indicated, but if they'd been coming down they wouldn't be visible by now.

Jacob came to lean against the porch post. "Looking for berries, were they?"

She smiled, relieved that Jacob seemed to be ignoring everything that had happened the last time they met. It was as if they'd returned to the careful friendliness they'd had before they got too close.

"It seems Ricky promised to show Holly—"

"The best places to find berries," Jacob finished for her. "I know. Holly only told me that four or five times."

"Well, she doesn't exactly have much to look forward to here." She closed her lips, determined not to allow her feelings about Julianne to slip out. "You can't be surprised she's excited about seeing another young person."

"You won't have to go looking for them." He nodded toward the path. "Here they come now."

Holly's cheeks were flushed with excitement when she reached them. "We found the wild strawberries," she announced. "There were some ripe ones already."

"And you ate them," Jacob suggested.

"Couldn't stop her," Ricky said. "Not that I tried. After

all, you couldn't have made anything with a handful of berries."

"Right. You wouldn't want them to go to waste." Rachel took the pail from Holly. "You'll be able to pick them again in a couple of days, yah?"

Holly nodded. With her cheeks flushed and her hair messed by the trek through the woods, Holly looked like the little girl she tried so hard to leave behind. "And we found where the wild black raspberries grow, so I can pick them when they're ready."

"There will be blackberries after the raspberries." Ms. Geraldine stood at the screen door. "Rachel, you know where they are, don't you? That gravelly place up toward the quarry?"

Memories flooded back from long-ago summers. She and Mammi picked the blackberries, with Ms. Geraldine supervising. Enough for Mammi to make blackberry pie, blackberry cobbler and blackberry jam. But she didn't suppose Ms. Geraldine would want her to do all that.

She came back from her memories at a suddenly sharp tone in Ms. Geraldine's voice. "A surveyor's stake? Are you sure?"

Holly looked uncertainly toward Ricky, who nodded. "Yes, ma'am. I've watched surveyors working before. That's what we saw. Up there, farther along past where the berries grow. It's like someone was marking the boundaries."

"Along that log drag on the far side below the quarry?" Jacob asked, apparently interpreting the vague gesture Ricky made.

Rachel had no idea where the boundary was nor how it was marked, but it was clear that the news had upset Ms. Geraldine. She was looking at Ricky, her eyes flashing, her mouth thin.

"Is this your father's doing?" She shot the words at Ricky.

The encounter had turned sour so fast that Rachel couldn't keep up with it. She ought to calm things down, but she hadn't an idea what was upsetting Ms. Geraldine so much.

Before she could speak, Jacob touched her hand to draw her attention. He shook his head very slightly, obviously advising her not to get involved.

Ricky, collecting his scattered wits, managed to answer. "No, I'm sure it's not. I mean… I guess I can't be sure, but he wouldn't do anything he hadn't cleared with you." He hesitated, as if looking at his last statement, and then fell silent.

"If he thinks he can go behind my back…"

Jacob interrupted her. "No sense in jumping to conclusions. Who owns the adjoining property? Pete Whittaker, isn't it? Maybe he's having his line surveyed."

Ms. Geraldine's flush faded slowly. "I suppose."

"I'll go up and have a look," he said quickly, before she could heat up again. "I know most of the surveyors around here, and they all use different markings. Then you can find out, if you need to know."

Rachel nodded. Jacob had averted a battle—another battle—between Ms. Geraldine and her family. At least for the moment.

"Let's go in and take care of those whoopie pies," she said, shooing them toward the door.

"Yes, that's right," Ms. Geraldine said. "I'm sorry I spoke so sharply. I wasn't thinking."

For an instant she thought Ricky might storm off, but he seemed to force himself to relax and followed his young cousin through the door Ms. Geraldine held open.

Jacob's hand on her wrist kept her from moving. "Try

and settle her down," he murmured. "I'll see what I can find out. Right?"

"Right." She smiled at him, relieved. She and Jacob were on the same side again. Friends again. That was all she wanted.

WHEN JACOB CAME back down from the woods, the first thing he noticed was that Ricky's car was gone. That could be good or bad, depending on what Ms. Geraldine's mood was. Still, he trusted Rachel's ability to calm people down and make peace. She'd done enough of it over the years with that father of hers.

It wasn't any of his business if Ms. Geraldine quarreled with her relatives, but he'd become fond of the prickly woman and he hated to see her at odds with people who ought to be closest to her. If that was what came of having so much money in the family, he could be glad his didn't suffer from that. And not much danger of that changing, he thought with an inward grin.

Rachel was in the kitchen, of course. That was her usual spot, and she'd made it hers with potted herbs on the windowsills and a rocker in the corner with a sewing basket next to it. She swung around at his entrance.

"Did you find anything?" She was quick with the question.

He'd barely had a chance to shake his head before Ms. Geraldine was calling from the other room.

"Is that Jacob? Bring him in here."

Shrugging, Rachel led the way to the small room where Ms. Geraldine spent much of her time now. They found her sitting in her favorite spot near the bookshelves, a book on the table beside her and needlework spread in her lap. As far as he could tell, she wasn't paying much attention to either of them.

"Well?" Ms. Geraldine zeroed in on him before Rachel had time to speak. "Was there really a surveyor's stake in my woods?"

He nodded. "Just where the kids said it was. Probably about at the line between your property and that stretch of woods of Pete Whittaker's, like I said. Maybe he's doing a survey for some reason."

"I called him," she said shortly. "He's not." Ms. Geraldine stared straight ahead, brooding. "That means it's someone else who wants to know the extent of my property."

He knew what she was thinking. Richard was the most likely, with his interest in real estate and developing. It seemed there was nothing he liked better than taking a prime piece of farmland or an unspoiled woodlot and putting houses or businesses on it.

"Ricky said his father wouldn't do that," Rachel ventured.

"Ricky wouldn't necessarily know." Ms. Geraldine said it, but he'd been thinking it. "But if it was Richard, he'll regret it."

"You'd best find out for sure, don't you think?" He agreed with Ms. Geraldine that Richard was the most obvious person. He might have a pretty good notion that he was going to inherit the property and be planning already.

He caught Rachel's eye and knew she wouldn't agree. She was ready to defend Richard, and Jacob couldn't help wondering why. Just because he'd been a little better to her as a kid than the rest of Ms. Geraldine's kin... Come to think of it, that wasn't saying much.

"Rachel is looking worried," Ms. Geraldine announced.

"I'm not going to start a battle with my nephew, but I'm going to learn the truth. Does that make you happy, Rachel?"

Rachel's cheeks grew pink, and for an instant he wanted to speak sharply to Ms. Geraldine. But then Rachel smiled.

"Yah, it does. I don't like family quarrels." She burned a deeper red at that, thinking about her daad, he guessed.

"No." Ms. Geraldine's face softened for a moment at that. "I guess not. So what did you find out from the surveyor's marker?" She shot the question at Jacob, and he had to stop paying attention to Rachel and focus.

"It's not anyone local, or I'd have recognized it. It'll be someone from a bigger town, like maybe Williamsport. I can ask around, if you want."

Ms. Geraldine nodded. "Do that." She frowned at the needlework in her lap for a moment. "All right. Go back to what you were doing. I want to think."

"Sure thing." He grabbed Rachel's elbow and hustled her out of the room.

"Wait a minute." When they reached the kitchen, she jerked her arm free. "I wasn't finished. What are you doing?"

"Keeping you from making her worse than she is," he said promptly. "She's on the verge of exploding already. Just let her simmer down." He took her arm again. "Komm. Let's go outside where we can talk."

She glared for another minute, and then gave in and nodded, and they walked out onto the porch. "Okay?" She sat down on the porch swing, but she didn't relax.

"Okay." He perched on the railing. "You didn't like it when I hustled you out of there, but you were about to defend Richard, and that would just get her back up."

"But…" She shook her head, more out of helplessness

than because she disagreed, he thought. "I just hate to see her alienate her family. They don't seem to get along very well as it is, and who else does she have?"

"I know."

His voice gentled. Despite what he saw as her own father's selfishness, Rachel still had a rosy view of families. And he guessed she was right, most of the time. Most families he knew might quarrel among themselves, like his brothers and sisters, but they stood together when anything else came up against them.

"Look, it is reasonable for her to think Richard would be at fault. You weren't here for the big battle they had over Richard's proposal to sell a sizable chunk of the property for development. I'd think you'd have heard her all the way over to your place."

"I didn't know," she admitted. "But surely he wouldn't go behind her back now and start a survey. She'd be bound to find out, and that wouldn't get him anywhere."

"You're probably right there," Jacob admitted. "He's got too much to lose. She might take managing her property back out of his hands. Or even leave it to someone else. But who else could have an interest in surveying the property lines?"

Rachel was silent for a moment, thinking. And worrying, he thought, about Ms. Geraldine. She was feeling a responsibility for the woman already, he could see.

"I don't know," she said finally. "But it's there. Have you seen anybody up in the woods while you've been working here? Anybody you didn't know?"

He shrugged. "Sometimes hikers wander through. Or hunters in season. None of that land is posted. Nobody that I've seen has ever come close to the house. Except Gerald."

"Gerald? What would he be doing in the woods?" She

didn't like that idea, and he remembered the incident with Gerald and the housekeeping money.

"I don't know. He just sometimes turns up when Ms. Geraldine doesn't expect him. Like that day Julianne was here. He was just sort of wandering around. As far as I could tell, he never intended to go into the house. That day he wanted to know what was going on."

Shaking her head, Rachel looked worried and at a loss. He shoved himself away from the railing and came to sit on the swing with her. "Don't worry so much. It's not really…"

He stopped, knowing there was no point in saying it wasn't their business. They'd both, in their separate ways, become fond of the woman, and if for Rachel that fondness took the shape of wanting to bring Ms. Geraldine close to her family, he couldn't fault that, even if he didn't think it would do much good.

"I just don't want to see her taken advantage of," he said finally. "There seem to be too many people who think old people are easy targets."

"I know," she said. "I hear about those things, too. Just think about that investment fraud that actually targeted church communities like ours."

"Yah." Every Amish person had heard about that scandal, preying on Amish families with its talk of an all-Amish investment group. "And just last fall there was a guy who kept Zeb Fisher talking outside while his partner went inside and stole from the jar where Alice kept her egg money."

She nodded.

"Well, then, you know older people need protecting sometimes."

"It should come from their families." Her gaze lifted to his, her eyes darkening with concern. "It seems so wrong to think that Ms. Geraldine's own family might be…well, trying to push her into doing things she doesn't want to."

"I know."

She looked so distressed that he couldn't help but take her hand, enveloping it warmly in his. She didn't draw it away, and they sat, hands clasped, in silence for a long moment.

This is the way it should be between us, he thought, and then his mind scrambled back from that idea. They were friends…or at least they were friendly to each other. That was all he wanted—all it was safe for him to want.

THAT SUNDAY, Rachel decided, was different from any she'd ever experienced. Naturally she was used to the fact that every other Sunday was the off day for worship. Sometimes she attended worship with a different group, especially if she happened to be visiting someone. But usually off Sundays were days of family gatherings.

Not that she was alone here. Ms. Geraldine was back from worship at her church, and Holly was glooming around the house, upset about something she wasn't yet ready to share. After finishing wiping down the bathroom mirror, Rachel stood for a moment at Holly's door, wondering if she ought to try to find out the trouble.

The clicking of Holly's phone reached her in the quiet, so she went on down the hall. Holly was most likely texting a friend her troubles.

As Rachel rounded the bannister at the top of the stairs, Ms. Geraldine's door opened, and she looked out.

"Rachel, will you come in for a moment?"

Nodding, she hurried into the large bedroom overlooking the front lawn. Ms. Geraldine was standing at the dressing table with the triple mirrors, similar to the one that was up in the attic. It had probably been a popular design at one time. Rachel smiled, thinking for a moment of Julianne primping herself in front of them, trying to see all sides of herself at once.

Having called her in, Ms. Geraldine didn't seem to know what to say to her. After a lengthy moment of silence, Rachel decided it was up to her.

"Is there something you'd like me to do in here, Ms. Geraldine?"

The woman shook her head as if to clear it. "Not exactly. I noticed this last night, but I'm not sure…" She let that trail off. Then she abruptly pulled open the top side drawer of the dressing table, frowning down at its contents. "Did you notice that this was open the last time you did the room?"

Frowning, too, Rachel stopped to think. "I…I don't think so. I mean, I didn't look at it specifically either last night or this morning when I made the bed, but I believe I'd have noticed if it was and closed it." She had a sudden thought. "Is something missing?"

"No, nothing like that." She turned to glance at Rachel. "I keep various papers in here, some old photographs and cards that I want to save. As far as I can tell, they're all here. But they're not arranged the way I keep them."

Was she imagining that Rachel had been prying? Her heart gave a thud. "I wouldn't know if they were. I've never seen inside the drawer." She hesitated, but surely it was best to face the situation squarely. "If you think that I would look…"

"No, I'm sure you wouldn't." Ms. Geraldine's rare smile warmed her face. "I know I can trust you, Rachel. But someone has been looking at these. I wonder if Holly—"

It was probably a natural question, and she didn't know the answer to it. "I don't think she would have. Unless…

well, unless she thought you'd had a letter from her mother that she didn't see. But even then, I think she would ask. I hope so, anyway."

The truth was that it was difficult to know what Holly might do if she felt decisions were being made about her.

"I haven't received anything like that. Julianne is not a very good letter writer," Ms. Geraldine added, her lips twisting a bit. "I don't like to think it of Holly but no one else has been upstairs…"

She stopped when Rachel's expression changed. "Has someone been up here? Other than Jacob, when he's working."

"Well, yah. When your sister stopped by," she said reluctantly, "I thought she'd gone, because I'd heard the front door, and it startled me when I ran into her coming down the stairs. But she…"

She couldn't say that surely Ms. Geraldine's own sister wouldn't do such a thing. Like Holly, Freda was an unknown quantity when it came to some things.

"I see." Ms. Geraldine didn't sound surprised. "I thought she'd gone straight out. I'm sure I heard the door, too. Did she say anything?"

Rachel considered. "She seemed a little embarrassed. She said she'd come upstairs to…well, to use the bathroom. I didn't think much about it, except…"

"Except that she knows perfectly well that there's a powder room down in the hall."

"Yah." She couldn't think of any other reason for Freda being upstairs. Ms. Geraldine knew her better than she did, and she didn't seem to find it surprising.

"Don't look so upset, Rachel. I do know my sister, after all." She closed the drawer. "The whole family knows I've been considering some changes to my will. I've no doubt she hoped to come across it. Accidentally, of course. She'd like to know how her precious Gerald will make out."

There seemed little that she could say. It was natural to understand your family members, but sad that Ms. Geraldine had such an opinion of her own sister. "I'm sorry. Maybe…" She hesitated. "Maybe you ought to just tell her?" She made it a question, knowing it wasn't really her concern.

"When the time is right." Ms. Geraldine smiled, but there was no humor in it. "When the time is right, they'll all know." She suddenly turned brisk. "No point in wondering about it. If you could convince Holly to get out of the house and get some exercise, it might improve her mood."

"I'll try." She certain sure understood Ms. Geraldine's feeling. When she had the pouts, Holly didn't exactly brighten the place up.

In any event, it wasn't hard. When she rapped on Holly's door and suggested a hike, Holly seemed ready to accept any offer of entertainment. Not that she didn't groan about it, but she did follow Rachel downstairs, still hanging on to her cell phone.

What would she think if they went into one of the areas around here where folks said there wasn't cell phone coverage? Not that she knew a lot about it, but Amish who had businesses used cell phones sometimes. And a good many Amish teenagers managed to get a cell phone, one way or another.

As they went through the kitchen, Rachel took a couple of water bottles from the refrigerator and handed one to Holly.

"I don't need that." Holly seemed determined to be disagreeable.

"Fine. Don't expect me to share mine when you get

thirsty." She reached out to return the bottle to the shelf. Grumbling, Holly grabbed it and they set out.

Other than walking through town, the only real choice for a hike was to head up into the woods again. So they set off along the now-familiar trail.

A few minutes of steady walking took them to a spot where the path divided. Rachel gestured to the left. "Have you gone up this way yet?"

Holly shook her head. "What's the difference? It's just more trees, right?"

"There's a stream that comes down the ridge over there. I'd guess it comes from the same spring that feeds the water in the quarry. It's a nice spot to cool off. We used to wade there sometimes when I was small."

Holly didn't manage a show of enthusiasm, but she did shrug and turn off onto the branch path.

The way up was steeper here. Rachel had forgotten that, but memory brought it back. Funny. She remembered running down this way and didn't remember why.

Then it came back to her. "Gerald."

Holly looked around, startled. "Where?"

"No, I don't see him. I was just remembering. He liked to play tricks...practical jokes, I guess you'd say, on younger children. He gave me such a scare one time, leading me up this way and then running off. I started back, but then he stalked me, pretending he was a bear." She smiled. "It sounds silly now, but then I was young enough to be easily frightened."

"Sounds like him." Holly didn't sound very impressed by her cousin Gerald. "He probably still likes practical jokes. He looks the type."

The insight impressed Rachel. Holly knew more about people than she'd expect. More than was normal, maybe,

for her age. She'd guess the sort of life she'd led with Julianne had contributed to it.

Then her mind started turning over what Holly had said.
Was it possible that Gerald would consider something like
tampering with the attic steps a practical joke? Surely he'd
realized that was dangerous. She was so busy considering
possibilities that they'd reached the stream before she realized it.

Holly was still inclined to mope, but once she'd been
persuaded to wade into the cold water, she cheered up a
little. Sitting on a convenient rock, Rachel removed her
shoes and dangled her feet in the water.

"Nice, isn't it?" Rachel looked up at the ash trees arch-
ing overhead. "It seems—"

She was going to say *peaceful*, but Holly burst into
speech. "My mother texted me. Can you believe it? She's
going to Reno. Honestly!"

The word expressed vast scorn, but she wasn't sure
whether it was because her mother was going there or for
some other reason. "Why? I thought she was heading to
California."

"She was, but she's probably on her way by now. She
says she wants to see all the casinos. Maybe trying to find
some rich guy to hang on to."

Rachel wanted to say that she shouldn't talk that way
about her mother, but how could she? Holly knew her
mother much better than Rachel did. For a moment she
felt regret for the pretty young girl who'd primped in front
of the mirror and sometimes remembered to be kind.

Holly clicked on her phone, apparently looking at the of-
fending text. "Nothing about coming back, or where she's
going to stay, or anything. Just that she met someone."

Rachel's heart sank. Julianne was welcome to meet all

the people she wanted, but she ought to give some thought to her daughter's feelings.

"I'm sorry," she said, because it was clearly bad news to Holly. "But maybe she won't stay long."

"Maybe." Holly sounded doubtful. "But there's no way of getting in touch with her when I don't know where she is if she doesn't answer her cell phone. And I don't suppose she even bothered to tell Aunt Geraldine."

Rachel doubted it, too. "You can always text her or leave a message," she pointed out. "And I'm sure in an emergency Ms. Geraldine would be able to find her."

Her mind ran up against a blank wall of ignorance. What could Ms. Geraldine do? Ask the police for help? She supposed it might be the only way.

That wasn't likely to make Holly feel any better, and she didn't know what would. She tried to shake off the chill that slid down her back. There wasn't any reason to feel so… well, frightened, just because Holly was upset.

She let her gaze wander around the clearing while she tried to think of something that might make Holly feel better. And then she realized why she felt so suddenly afraid. There was someone else in the woods. Someone was watching them. The feeling swept over her with a sense of certainty.

Rachel tried to reason with herself. She hadn't actually seen anyone. There'd been a sound, but there were always sounds in the woods. And that flicker of movement just beyond the range of her vision—well, there were often creatures moving in the woods. It might have been a bird, or a squirrel.

But she suddenly wanted to take Holly and get to a place of safety. She couldn't explain it, and she didn't even bother to try. She reached for her shoes and socks.

"I think your great-aunt needs to know about this. After all, it's her responsibility. And if she feels your mother ought to come home at some point…well, she's the only one who could make that happen."

Holly didn't say anything. She just waded out and retrieved her shoes. Maybe she felt the same uneasiness that Rachel did. Maybe not. In any event, they'd both be better off in the house.

CHAPTER THIRTEEN

RACHEL STIFLED A yawn as she polished the intricate carving on the tall bureau in Ms. Geraldine's bedroom the next morning. She might have known the bad dreams would return last night after what had happened in the woods.

She caught herself on that thought. Nothing had actually happened, had it? It had all been in her mind—hearing rustles that could be anything, catching glimpses of movement, of something that didn't belong. It was irrational to be so frightened when nothing had happened.

She'd actually been moving so fast when they came back down from the woods that Holly had been out of breath. She hadn't been able to help it. That sense of eyes watching them had been too strong to ignore.

Ferhoodled, that was what it had been. She could tell herself that in the clear light of morning. Holly certain sure hadn't noticed anything. She'd brought on her own bad dreams, she told herself.

She rubbed the walnut until it gleamed, wishing she could rub away the nightmares as easily. It had been the old, familiar dream of running down the hill, through the woods, knowing someone or something was after her, hearing it growing closer, not knowing who or what it was…

There's something I should remember. The thought came from nowhere, startling in its clarity. Something. And just as quickly the thought was gone. If there had been a flicker of recognition, it wasn't there now.

"Rachel!"

It sounded as if Holly was at the bottom of the stairs, shouting up. At least she was in a happier mood today. Unburdening herself, hearing reassurances from Rachel and from her great-aunt—all of that had served to wipe away the apprehension about her mother from her eyes.

Rachel walked to the top of the stairs and looked down. "I'm here. Don't shout, just tell me." How many times had she said that to her brothers? Needless to say, it had never done any good.

But Holly did lower her voice a fraction. "A buggy coming along the driveway. Maybe it's your brother. Do you think they brought the baby?"

"We'll find out, won't we?" She started down, holding the polish and cloth in one hand.

Holly didn't wait for her, and she was already outside by the time Rachel reached the kitchen. After putting the cleaning supplies away in the pantry, Rachel hurried out to join her.

Holly would be disappointed, she realized when she looked out. It was a wagon, not the family buggy. Both of her brothers had come, but there was no sign of Sarah and the baby. She raised her hand in a wave of greeting.

"What brings the two of you out this morning?" She hugged both of them, maybe holding on a little longer than was strictly necessary before she stepped back. "Holly, you remember Sammy. This is my other brother, Joshua."

Holly was already asking Sammy eagerly about Anna Beth, demanding details. Sammy met her gaze over Holly's head. Holly had clearly fallen in love with his baby girl. But who could help it? Little Anna Beth had no trouble clasping anyone's heart in one tiny hand.

"You didn't answer me. What brings you here today?" She looked up at Joshua, wondering if he could possibly have grown another inch since she'd seen him.

Josh looked down at her, putting his arm around her for a hug and then tapping the top of her head. "Who's the little bruder now?" He grinned.

She smacked his hand away laughing, remembering his eagerness to reach the point of being taller than she was. "You are," she said. "And you always will be, so don't get sassy."

He held up his hands in mock surrender. "Sammy needed some help in getting the chest from your room down the stairs." He glanced at the height of the Withers house, towering above them. "And up the stairs here, ain't so?"

"For sure." Sammy glanced at her from his conversation with Holly. "But first, Sarah wants to know if Holly would like to come back with us for a few hours. She can always use some help with the baby, and her sister Leah is coming over, too, with some rhubarb."

He obviously trusted her to make sense of that mixture of baby, Leah and rhubarb. Sarah knew how taken Holly was with the baby. And the point about her little sister Leah was not the rhubarb but the fact that Leah was just Holly's age.

"How thoughtful of Sarah," she said, gratitude in her voice. "What do you think, Holly? Would you like to go?"

She almost didn't have to ask the question, since Holly's answer was written on her face.

"Might as well." Holly tried unsuccessfully to sound as if it didn't matter.

"Best go and check with Ms. Geraldine, then. The boys won't be long getting the chest unloaded."

"Not long?" Josh gave a convincing groan. "Do you know how much that thing weighs?"

"Sounds like little Josh needs a hand."

She hadn't seen Jacob approaching, but somehow she'd known he was there. She had to smile at Josh's expression.

"Little Josh? Listen, I'm as tall…" He stopped, eyeing Jacob, who had at least an inch on him. "Never mind." He grinned. "We'll take any help we can get, right, Sammy?"

"Right." Sammy moved to the back of the wagon. "Everybody give a hand, and we'll do it in no time."

Rachel stepped back, ready to hold the door for them, and watched. Did Jacob realize that had been her dower chest? Daad had made it himself and given it to her for her sixteenth birthday, when she'd already begun filling it with things for her future home with Jacob.

She remembered so clearly her mother's expression when she gave Rachel a set of pillowcases for her dower chest. They'd laughed together about Rachel's own first attempts at needlework. But that was before Rachel had learned that the home and the marriage were not to be.

But Jacob's expression didn't change as they carried it onto the porch, so probably he didn't even think of it. She held the door open, not meeting his eyes. He should know, but he didn't react. As far as she could tell, it was just a burden to be shared.

With a certain amount of thumping and a few more groans from Josh, who had always been the dramatic one, the chest made its way up the back stairs and into her room. She followed, hoping Ms. Geraldine wouldn't be annoyed by the noise, but her employer was watching with every sign of approval.

"Very nice." She nodded approvingly, touching the close-fitting lid. "Your father's work?"

"Yah, it was. From Mammi and Daad for my sixteenth birthday." She held her breath, hoping Ms. Geraldine wouldn't lift the lid. Not that she cared, but the double-wedding-ring quilt that had been made for her wedding was on top. If Jacob didn't recognize anything else, he'd surely know that.

But she didn't. The boys clattered back downstairs while Ms. Geraldine detained her for a moment. "That's such a nice idea, having Holly go to your sister-in-law's today. I should have realized she needs to get out more. You don't think she'll be too much trouble to your sister-in-law?"

"Ach, no. Sarah is such a sweet person. She saw how taken Holly was with the baby."

"She's one who does something when she sees a need. Like you and your mother. Too many people just see it and turn away." For a moment she looked uncertain, and it was an expression Rachel didn't see on her face often. "I have a great deal to learn, I think, if I'm going to do right by Holly."

Rachel turned that over in her mind as she followed the others down the steps again. Did Ms. Geraldine mean that Holly would be here for an extended time? She seemed to have come to some decision since Holly had told her about the text from Julianne.

When Rachel got outside, Holly was already perched on the wagon seat between her brothers, obviously eager to get going. Sammy set the big gelding moving. Rachel waved, watching as they drove out onto the road. If only this distracted Holly from her fears about her mother…but probably nothing could do that.

"SHE'S FINE," JACOB SAID, recognizing the concern in Rachel's eyes and unreasonably annoyed. "Your bruders will take good care of her. Now tell me why you look like you've been dragged out of bed too soon."

"I do not." She flushed, smoothing her hair back under her kapp.

The denial just annoyed him more. Rachel should be taking better care of herself. Or somebody should.

"You have dark circles under your eyes. What is keeping you up at night? And don't tell me it's nothing."

He recognized the bossiness in his voice just about when the words came out. When was he going to learn to control his tongue? He tried again, softening his tone.

"Komm, Rachel. We know each other too well, yah? I just want to help."

"It was my own foolishness, imagining myself into bad dreams. I should know better." She turned away, avoiding his eyes.

He resisted the urge to catch hold of her before she could get away. "I don't think that knowing better changes anybody's dreams, ain't so? What were you imagining?"

She shot him a suspicious look, as if convinced he'd start lecturing at any moment. Then she nodded reluctantly. "Yah, all right. I had gone walking with Holly, up to that place with the flat rocks, where the stream makes a pool. You know it?"

"Sure." He'd been through the woods often enough to picture it. "Nice spot. What went wrong? Did Holly push you in?"

Her eyes crinkled with her smile. "I'd know what to do about that. She'd have gotten even wetter. No, it was something else." Her face sobered, her eyes darkening. "She was talking, telling me something about her mother."

"Nothing good, I guess."

Rachel shook her head. "It wasn't really that. It was just..." She stopped, and this time he did take her hand. But not to stop her. To reassure her.

She took a breath, seeming to settle herself. "I just felt as if someone else was there, watching us. Listening. I told you it was foolish." She started to pull her hand away, but he held on.

"Did you see anyone?"

"Not exactly. It was like something moved just at the corner of my eye." She shrugged. "Foolish, like I said. It could have been an animal or a bird."

It could. Probably it was. But it seemed to trouble her out of all proportion.

"Did you hear anything? Any sound a person might have made, for instance?" There were always sounds in the woods, if a person listened. "Not a bird calling, or something like that?"

"The birds were quiet," she said, a little impatience in her voice. "You think I don't know a bird when I hear one? It was as if someone moved, stepping carefully. Ferhoodled, like I said."

Jacob studied her face, considering, his fingers smoothing along her skin. "I'd think you would have heard birds up there."

"I don't know. All I know is that I was scared of nothing." She made an effort to laugh at herself, but it didn't work very well. "I came down the path with Holly, rushing her along as if there was a bear chasing us. She probably thought I was crazy."

He was too busy thinking about it to react, except for knowing there wasn't anything crazy about Rachel. Stubborn, yes, especially when it came to doing what she thought was right. But not crazy.

"That's what you dreamed, then? That you and Holly were running away from a bear?" He was on the verge of saying how silly that was, but he guessed she didn't need to hear it from him, of all people.

"Not exactly. I suppose it just reminded me of a time when I was small. Something scared me, and I remember running down the path, sure someone or something was after me. That's what I dreamed about, feeling it closer and closer." She shook her head. "It's a wonder I didn't wake up shouting. That would upset everyone, for sure."

"Did you ever find out if there was someone chasing you?"

She hesitated, and he wondered if she realized that she'd turned her hand so that it clasped his. "I don't... I'm not sure. There was one time when Gerald pretended he was an animal and chased me, but I don't think it was that. William found out what he was doing and knocked him down. They were always roughhousing. You know how boys are."

"Yah, I do." He felt a sudden urge to knock Gerald down himself. He released her hand slowly and stepped away. "I think I'll go for a walk."

"A walk? Where?" Rachel's eyes widened.

"Up to the pool. I don't know what Gerald or anybody else did years ago, but if someone was there yesterday, I might be able to find something to tell us so." He hesitated, then decided to tell her what he was thinking. "Yesterday we drove over to Onkel Harley's place in the afternoon. We went past that old logging road that's just before you get to the Fox Hill bridge. You know where I mean?"

She nodded. "I know. It leads up toward the quarry, doesn't it?"

"Yah, but it's not usable by car most of the way. Thing is, I noticed a car parked in the logging road. Empty, with no one inside."

"You mean someone could have parked there and walked up toward the quarry. Toward Ms. Geraldine's property."

"Someone could. I didn't know the car, so I can't say who it might have been. But somebody parked there wouldn't have a long walk to get to the pool. So that's another good reason for me to check it out."

"Besides my foolishness, you mean." A flush came into her face, and she looked as if she wished she'd kept quiet.

"Not so foolish at all." He smiled at her. "I need some exercise anyway. I'll see you later."

He set off, and when he reached the point where the path went into the woods, he glanced back. She was still standing there, staring after him.

Resisting the urge to look at her a little longer, he plunged into the woods, telling himself he was an idiot. He couldn't go around holding girls' hands as if he were still a teenager. Thing was, he wouldn't. It was only Rachel whose hand he wanted to hold.

Forcing himself to concentrate, Jacob kept his eye out for anything unusual along the path. If someone had been following, he'd have wanted to keep out of sight, though. Trouble was, it would be too easy to slip from one tree to the next, and the ground, covered with last year's leaves, wouldn't show anything he could pick out and be sure was made by man.

The clearing where the small pool was looked more promising. The ash trees weren't as thick, and the ground was damp enough to take marks. He found plenty. The pool was obviously popular with the creatures—he spotted deer, rabbit, squirrel and even the fat footprint of a bear in the soft earth near the pool.

It wasn't until he made a wider circle around the pool that he found what he was looking for. Someone had stood behind the large trunk of a willow that overhung the pool. Well, someone or something. Recently, judging by the marks, but he couldn't prove anything. He walked a little farther, his eyes on the ground, and there it was. No doubt about this, that was certain sure. He could even make out the tread on the shoes.

His momentary elation faded quickly. He couldn't be sure when it had been made, and he couldn't prove that it belonged to someone who'd spied on Rachel and Holly. But then, he wasn't the police. He didn't have to prove it. He could assure Rachel that she hadn't imagined things, and that was all.

Come to think of it, while that might convince her that she'd hadn't imagined it, it might also increase her worries. Maybe it would be better not to tell her.

Except that he couldn't lie to Rachel. She'd know in an instant that he wasn't telling her the whole story. And even if he could, he wouldn't. If the vague feeling in the back of his mind that they might start again came into being, he certain sure couldn't begin with a lie.

RACHEL STOOD FOR a moment at her bedroom window, looking out at the night. Clouds had moved in, and the air felt heavy, as if it would rain at any moment. Should she leave the window open, to catch any air that was moving? But that meant taking the risk that it would let rain in.

She stood looking down at the dark, shadow-filled side yard for another moment. Then with sudden decision, she closed the window firmly. Folding her quilt back, she slid under the sheet, hoping for a restful night, if that were possible after what Jacob had told her when he'd come back from the pool. He'd found the marks that told him someone had been there, circling where they sat and talked. Spying on them.

Footprints didn't prove that person had been there when she and Holly were, Jacob pointed out, but she found it hard to believe otherwise. Why else would someone be circling the clearing, except to peer at the pool?

There was no innocent explanation that she could come up with. Someone had hidden there, and what other reason could there be than to watch and listen?

But why? Why did someone care what she and Holly talked about? It was of interest only to themselves, she'd think.

Maybe he'd hidden because he didn't want to be seen there. Maybe he'd known he was trespassing. It could have been kids, she supposed, but she'd think kids would have giggled or otherwise given themselves away. Or a courting couple, looking for a spot to be alone. But in the middle of the day?

Still, it could have been, and there was no way of knowing. It kept going around and around in her mind, until she became convinced that she'd never get to sleep. And then, as if she'd pressed a switch, she fell into an uneasy slumber.

Rachel couldn't say how long it had been when she woke suddenly, lying there rigid and alert, staring at the ceiling. Afraid to move, she listened, her senses probing the sleeping house for the sound that had wakened her.

Just when she was convinced she'd been mistaken, the alien sound came again. Rattling, creaking and then a sharp crack resounded through the quiet house. Clutching her courage with both hands, Rachel slid out of bed. She stood on the braided rug, shivering, and listened for any reaction. Had she been heard? The bed had creaked, just a little, when she slid out.

No, she didn't think so. She swung a heavy sweater over her cotton nightdress and pulled it close. She had to check. She couldn't just cower in her room. What if the sound had been Ms. Geraldine, sick and in need of her?

That thought was enough to propel her to the door. She eased it open, one hand on the knob, the other flat above it, holding the door steady. Now she could tell where the noises came from. Not, thank goodness, from Ms. Geraldine's room, but from downstairs again. From the dining room, she felt sure.

Maybe the window was rattling again. But how could it, when she'd watched Jacob fix it?

She had to get closer, so she felt her way along the hall, her bare feet silent on the wide boards. And then her hand missed the wall, touching something soft and yielding. She gasped, and she heard an echoing gasp.

"Holly," she whispered. "What are you doing out here?" Holly stood just outside her bedroom door, the opening a darker rectangle behind her.

"Same as you. I heard it. Didn't you?" She sounded more excited than frightened, but maybe that was natural at her age. She was still more child than young woman.

"It's probably just a loose window." Rachel tried to sound reassuring in a whisper. "I'll check and see. You stay here. I'll tell you as soon as I know."

Holly didn't stay, of course. As Rachel moved, she felt Holly slipping along behind her, touching her now and then to be sure of where she was. She probably ought to tell her again to stay put, but it was good not being alone. Besides,

Holly wouldn't listen, and if they made noise, anyone downstairs would be long gone before they got down the steps.

By the time they reached the top of the stairs, Rachel's eyes had begun to grow accustomed to the darkness. She could make out the white of her own nightdress, the faint rectangular grayness that was the hall window, the shape of Holly close behind her.

Gripping the post at the top of the stairs, she strained her ears to listen, sorting out faint sounds. Nothing from Ms. Geraldine's room, thankfully.

Yah, the noise came from the dining room, as she'd thought. Now it was a faint shuffle, as if feet moved across the floor and then stumbled on the edge of the Oriental rug that lay under the dining table.

"I'm going down," she whispered.

"Me, too." Holly sounded determined, gripping the sleeve of her sweater. Two was better than one, wasn't it?

Maybe that was what they should do—scare him so that he'd flee. But if they did, they'd never know who it was. She shook her head. They couldn't let Ms. Geraldine wonder any longer if one of her own family was playing tricks. They had a chance to resolve the situation, and they had to take it.

Putting her lips close to Holly's ear, she whispered, "Stay against the wall so the stairs don't creak."

She felt the movement of Holly's hair against her shoulder as she nodded. Creeping down, step by step they went, with Rachel straining her ears for any sound from below. Something creaked and then scraped, as if one of the heavy drawers of the sideboard had been pulled open.

A thief, she thought. Ms. Geraldine kept the lined boxes of silver in those drawers. They must be valuable.

A faint gleam came filtering through the archway. A

candle? No, it must be a flashlight, maybe with something over it to block some of the light. They slipped along the wall, step by careful step. All they had to do was get close enough to see who it was. Then they could withdraw, make noise, shout, run for the phone. That would send him fleeing, but they'd know who it was.

But she'd reckoned without the small table that held a huge, curving vase filled with sprays of dried flowers. She must have brushed against one of the extending twigs. That was enough to set the whole vase wobbling and rock the table.

Rachel grabbed it in time to prevent a crash, but the damage was done. They heard a muffled sound from the room, then feet rushing for the window. Holly started forward, probably trying to get a glimpse of him before he could get out. She ran into Rachel as she tried to save the vase, and they both stumbled.

By the time they recovered, it would be too late. "Lights," Rachel gasped. "The switch…"

She meant the switch by the archway, but Holly sent a gleam of light from something in her hand. For a moment she wondered where Holly had found a flashlight, and then she realized it was a cell phone. She charged into the dining room, Holly right behind her. But even with the lights on, it was clearly no good. The window stood open, the curtains blowing in the welcoming breeze that had come up, the room empty.

They rushed together to the window but couldn't make out a thing. The shadows still lay deep in the yard. There might have been the faintest movement near the lilac hedge, but it was gone before she could be sure, and Ms. Geraldine was calling from upstairs.

"Rachel! Holly! What's happening? Are you all right? Where are you?"

Rachel hurried to the bottom of the stairs and looked up to where she could see Ms. Geraldine leaning over the bannister, looking down the well of the staircase.

"We're both here. We're fine. But I'm afraid someone broke in."

"I'll call 911." Holly, sounding more mature than her years, pressed the numbers on her phone, but as someone answered, she thrust it into Rachel's hand.

She'd never called the emergency number before, but somehow she managed to stammer through telling the person who answered the important points, like what, when, how and who. Except that she didn't know who, thanks to her clumsiness. That rankled.

She thought the woman's voice quickened when she heard the name of Withers.

"A patrol car will be with you in a few minutes. Are you sure the intruder is not still in the house?"

Rachel collected her thoughts. "I'm sure he's not. We heard him go out the window, or at least that's what it sounded like. By the time we got the light on, he was gone."

"Turn on all the outside lights you have and then don't touch anything. Keep everyone together, all right?"

"I will."

"The officers will be there soon. Try not to worry. I'll stay on the line until they arrive."

Even as the woman said that, Rachel could hear the distant wail of a siren.

"It's okay. We can hear them coming now."

She clicked off quickly over the woman's protests, concerned to see Ms. Geraldine coming down the steps in a robe, probably too quickly for safety. After handing the phone to Holly, she hurried up to take Ms. Geraldine's arm, steadying her. Somewhat to her surprise, the woman didn't pull away. Maybe this was too shocking for pride.

"Holly, will you flip the switches by the front door to turn all the lights on? The police said not to touch anything else."

Holly, pale but looking responsible, nodded and hurried to the switches. There were the back lights, too, but she didn't want to send Holly out of her sight, not alone, anyway.

"The back," Ms. Geraldine murmured. "We should get those."

"Yah, I'll do that now." She guided her employer to the hall bench. "Why don't you sit down, since we're not supposed to touch anything. Holly will stay with you."

Now Ms. Geraldine asserted herself, pulling her arm free. "I can look at the damage without touching it."

She stalked into the dining room. Rachel froze for an instant, torn between staying with her and getting the lights on. But as Holly came back from the front door, Rachel nodded toward Ms. Geraldine. Eyes big in her small face, Holly went to join her.

Rachel pushed the swinging door to the kitchen and groped for the switch, suddenly aware of how dark the back premises were at night. She frowned. Hadn't she left the low light on the range turned on? She usually did.

Her hand found the switch, and light flooded the darkness, revealing the ordinary, cheerful kitchen she was used to. She found the switches that controlled the outside lights and turned them on—the back porch, then the garage light and finally the pole lamp that illuminated the area back to the stable.

For an instant her eye caught a flicker of movement to

the left of the stable, but when she looked more closely, it was gone. Maybe an animal, frightened away by all the lights going on. She double-checked the locks on the door and then hurried to check the side door before going back to the others.

Ms. Geraldine was staring down at the opened drawers of the sideboard, her arms folded, apparently so she wouldn't touch anything. Holly, next to her, copied her position.

"Can you tell if anything's missing?" Rachel joined them.

Ms. Geraldine shook her head, her jaw set. "Not without touching anything. I can tell you one thing. When I learn who did this, he'll wish he'd never been born."

The siren wailed from the driveway, as if it accented her words.

CHAPTER FOURTEEN

By the time the police left, Holly was yawning uncontrollably and Ms. Geraldine's face had turned gray with fatigue.

"It's time for bed, ain't so?" Rachel tried to sound cheerful, but she had been more shaken by the break-in than she'd expected. It did something to her to know that an intruder had been creeping through the house.

She was exaggerating. The thief hadn't been able to do much creeping, since he'd made enough noise to wake them. She double-checked the locks and then moved to take Ms. Geraldine's arm.

"Is there anything you want before you go up?"

Ms. Geraldine shook her head. "Just to rest." Her earlier defiance had disappeared, leaving her looking more than her age. "You'll sleep in tomorrow, both of you. Don't you bother with breakfast, Rachel. We'll get something when we come down."

Rachel couldn't imagine sleeping in, since she'd never done so in her life, but now was not the time to argue the point. "We'll be fine," she said soothingly. "Ain't so, Holly?"

Holly's response was interrupted by a huge yawn. She nodded and trailed toward the stairs, still in what Rachel supposed were her pajamas, although it looked more like shorts and a T-shirt.

Rachel urged her employer to the stairs, and they started up. They'd gotten to the second step when headlights reflected in the front windows and a car pulled to a stop in the front. A few seconds later someone pounded the knocker.

Ms. Geraldine exchanged glances with her. "Maybe they've forgotten something. Will you get it?"

Leaving her clinging to the rail, Rachel hurried to the door, eager to stop that pounding. She flipped the lock and yanked it open to be confronted by Lorna Withers, fist raised to the knocker. Richard was rounding the car behind her.

It was Richard who spoke. "Rachel. Is my aunt all right? We heard the police were here. You should have called me."

Ms. Geraldine spoke from the stairs. "How did you hear? Is gossip all over town already?"

"No, of course not," Richard said, his voice soothing. He came in with an apologetic look at Rachel, and Lorna followed close behind.

"The police dispatcher is the daughter of a friend," he went on. "Naturally, she thought I'd want to know."

"I don't see anything natural about it," Ms. Geraldine grumbled. "People who work for the police should keep their mouths shut. Aren't police calls supposed to be private?"

Richard advanced to her. "Now, Aunt Geraldine, I'm sure she meant it for the best. You're sure you're all right? All of you?" His gaze swept from Holly to Rachel.

"We're fine," Rachel said quickly, wishing they'd leave and let her get everyone to bed. "We were just about to—"

Lorna cut in without looking at her. "An intruder actually in the house. It's terrible! This place isn't safe at all." She glanced around as if she expected someone to lunge out at her. "Now tell me exactly what happened, Aunt Geraldine."

That was obviously the last thing she wanted to do. Rachel expected Richard to intervene. Surely he could see, if Lorna didn't, how exhausted his aunt was. But Richard, having seen the upheaval in the dining room, had wandered in there.

After a moment, with Lorna still talking to Ms. Geraldine and ignoring the others, Rachel followed him.

"The police told us not to touch anything until they've cleared the scene." She managed a smile. "Whatever that means. They're coming back in the morning." She glanced pointedly at the time shown on the ornate clock on the sideboard, but he didn't seem to notice.

Instead, shoving his hands into his pockets, she supposed to keep himself from touching anything, he prowled around the room, frowning. In front of the window, he paused.

"This is where he got in? There should be locks on these windows."

"Jacob will be here in the morning. I'm sure he'll take care of it." She looked at the clock again. It was past two o'clock in the morning.

"Jacob?" He looked as if he'd forgotten for a moment. "Oh, yes, the carpenter. Is he still working here? I should think he'd be done by now."

Rachel decided it was best not to attempt to answer. Was he implying that Jacob was dragging out his job in order to charge more? She happened to know that Jacob charged for the job, not by the hour. She shrugged, telling herself there was no use in getting upset about what sounded like a slur on Jacob. It wasn't her concern, was it?

Since he didn't seem to be taking any of her hints, she'd have to speak up. "I'm afraid we're all too tired to talk much tonight. I'd like to get your aunt settled, if you don't mind."

Recalled from studying the drawers that lay on the floor, Richard nodded absently. "Yes, fine. You do that." Then, seeming to understand what she was driving at, gave her an apologetic smile. "Sorry. It's just that I can't help wondering what they were after. I don't think Aunt Geraldine keeps anything very valuable in this room."

Rachel decided not to enter into the speculation, instead walking back to the hallway. With a last look over his shoulder, Richard came, as well.

Lorna had been, it seemed, talking about how unsafe it was for an elderly woman to live in an isolated house by herself.

"I am not alone," Ms. Geraldine said sharply. She had sunk down to sit on the stairs, as if determined to emphasize that she was ready to go up. Or maybe too tired to move. "Rachel and Holly are here. They take good care of me."

"Against a burglar, you need more protection than one woman and a child. Now, at Green Pines, you would have—"

"I don't want to hear about it." Ms. Geraldine's tongue was still tart, despite the lateness of the hour.

"But…" Lorna began, but Richard spoke.

"Quite right. As Rachel said, it's time everyone was in bed. Come along, Lorna."

His wife looked as if she wanted to argue the point, but finally she shrugged and moved toward him. "I suppose you're right. But your aunt needs protection. I told you that. Probably every lowlife in the county knows that there's a wealthy old lady living alone here."

Ms. Geraldine's head went up, her nostrils flaring as if she were about to deliver a shattering opinion of Lorna, but Richard grabbed his wife's elbow and propelled her to the door.

Rachel, jerked into awareness, went to hold the door, suppressing the desire to slam it on Lorna. Her mamm would have said that Lorna must have been standing behind the door when they gave out the common sense. What a thing to say to someone in Ms. Geraldine's situation.

Richard pushed his wife outside and stood for a moment, holding the door and looking down at Rachel. "Thank you so much, Rachel." His quiet smile was for herself alone. "You're taking care of things beautifully. I'll stop by or call tomorrow to make sure my aunt is all right."

Rachel nodded, pleased but too tired to find anything to say. He didn't seem to mind that. He just pressed her hand lightly, stepped out and closed the door.

Once again Rachel checked locks, flicked off porch lights and then turned them on again, thinking they'd all sleep better if there were lights around the entrances.

As she helped Ms. Geraldine up the stairs at last, Rachel was nearly stumbling with fatigue. How glad she'd be to crawl back into her bed. But would she be able to sleep? Or better yet, sleep without dreams?

JACOB STRODE TOWARD the kitchen of the Withers house the next morning, his stomach churning. *They're all right*, he reminded himself. Nobody was hurt.

That was the news he'd heard this morning, anyway. If he'd known last night…

Well, he hadn't, and Rachel wouldn't have been able to contact him even if she'd wanted to. For the first time he regretted the distance between the house and the phone shanty.

Not that she'd have been likely to call him in the middle of the night anyway. He strode across the porch and into the kitchen. She didn't owe him that consideration.

Rachel spun away from the sink, alarm in her face.

"Sorry, sorry. It's just me." He held out his hand to reassure her.

"I'm all right." She made an effort to laugh at herself. "Silly, isn't it? I didn't even realize I was still nervous."

"It's no wonder." He crossed the space between them in a few quick strides and clasped her hand. "You're sure you're all right?"

"Ach, I'm fine. Nobody was hurt. Just tired from being up so late." A shadow crossed her face. "I tried to get Ms. Geraldine to let us bring her breakfast in bed, but she wouldn't hear of it."

"No, I don't guess she would." Each word she spoke reassured him. She was all right. They all were. "So what were you doing, chasing down burglars?" He nearly choked trying to keep from scolding her. She should have…

Rachel shook her head, and he knew some of what he didn't say must have shown on his face. "We didn't do much chasing. We—Holly and I—were trying to see who it was, but he got away before we could."

"He?"

She shrugged. "I guess I'm jumping to conclusions, but surely most burglars are men, aren't they? I guess the only thing I can say for sure is that there was just one person." She hesitated. "I guess someone else could have been waiting outside."

He was still holding her hand, and he let go reluctantly. "You turned on the outside lights?"

"Yah, but by then there was nothing to see. I thought…"

But he wasn't able to find out what she thought, since Ms. Geraldine, probably hearing voices, came in, with Holly right behind her.

Holly rushed toward him. "Did you hear we had a break-in last night? It was really exciting. The police came and everything."

"I know. I heard you and Rachel chased the burglar off." He couldn't help smiling at her enthusiasm. If she'd been

scared, she was over it now. Kids bounced back faster than
grown-ups.

"Well…" She seemed to be torn between the real version and a more exciting one. "I guess we scared him off,
but only because we made some noise."

"Just as well you did." He managed to grin at her. The
kid was growing on him. Still, he had more pressing things
to take care of. He turned to Ms. Geraldine.

"I picked up some window locks for the first-floor windows. Okay if I put them on? I guess it's locking the barn door
after the horse is gone, but we may as well do what we can."

Ms. Geraldine nodded, looking relieved. "Yes, do that.
But you won't be able to do the dining room until the police are finished. And, Rachel, will you take care of them
when they come? I'll be in my study if they need to speak
to me, but only if necessary."

"I'll see to it."

Nobody moved until she'd left the room, and then Holly
burst into speech. "Can I look around outside? Maybe I'll
see where they went before the police do. There might be
footprints where they ran away."

"I guess that's all right," Rachel said. "They said not to
touch anything in the dining room, but they didn't mention going outside."

"Just be sure you don't step on any footprints," Jacob added.

"I know better than that." Holly's tone was scornful, and
she hurried out the back.

"I suppose she watches police shows all the time on
television," Rachel said. "There was no way to keep her
out of it."

"Not unless you tied her to the bedpost." Jacob shrugged.
It never worked to try to keep anything from kids that age.
"We need to talk, but I'll get the latches and my tools first."

By the time he got back, the police were coming up the driveway, and he had to delay starting until they'd begun their work, measuring and photographing inside and out.

Since they were interested only in the dining room, he was able to get started on the kitchen windows. Rachel put on a pot of coffee.

"Can't that wait? I want to talk to you."

"I can make coffee and talk at the same time," she said. "Just like you can tinker with that latch. What is it? Haven't you heard enough about the break-in? I'm tired of talking about it. Now Holly—"

She was being deliberately aggravating, he supposed. "Not nearly enough to me. Like why you went downstairs instead of going straight to the phone."

She got the coffeemaker going and leaned against the sink while it started making noises, facing him. "You must know why. I wanted to see who it was. Holly and I were sure we were going to spot him. Then we'd run to the telephone."

"You think it was one of Ms. Geraldine's family." He couldn't argue with that, because the same thought was in his mind.

"I'd rather prove that it wasn't." Her forehead wrinkled. "But I'm afraid it's part of everything else."

He did, as well. "Yah. I'd be glad to be proved wrong. Did Ms. Geraldine ask Richard about the surveying?"

"She seemed satisfied when he said he didn't know anything about it. But still…"

"I did find out whose surveyor mark that was, but it didn't help much. It's an outfit in Williamsport, and they won't give out any information. At least, not to me." He glanced around for his screwdriver, and Rachel came and put it into his hand, absently watching him work.

"Ms. Geraldine thinks that her sister tried to find her will, or maybe any notes on her will, when she was here."

He considered. "Probably wants to know what her precious Gerald comes in for. But I can't picture Freda climbing in a window."

Rachel smiled, her face lightening. "Me neither."

"But Gerald, now…"

"You're talking about who broke in." Ms. Geraldine made one of her sudden appearances, her voice startling them. "I thought of that, but I don't believe Gerald is that desperate."

Jacob acknowledged that with a nod, and he kept his doubts to himself. "I don't like leaving you alone here at night. How would you feel about having me stay over at night for a while? I could sleep in that room over the garage. I'm here all day anyway."

He could feel that Rachel was ready to object, but fortunately Ms. Geraldine nodded before she could.

"That's not a bad idea. But you don't need to stay out there. You'd be more comfortable in the house."

He couldn't help glancing at Rachel and noticing the flush that came up in her face.

"I'd rather be in the garage. It's close enough to hear if anything's going on." He glanced again at Rachel, amused to see her blush subsiding. "Anyway, it wouldn't be… appropriate to stay in the house."

Ms. Geraldine's gaze went from him to Rachel, and then she nodded. "That will be fine. The room shouldn't be too bad, since the cleaning service was supposed to keep it clean, but I can't vouch for them. Their contract runs out the end of the month, and I've already told them I won't be renewing." Her sniff confirmed her opinion of the cleaners.

"I can take care…" Rachel began, and he shook his head.

"You have enough to do. I'll bring my sisters over to do it. They ought to know how by their age. It'll do them good." And get back at them for all their teasing, too.

Ms. Geraldine nodded, satisfied. "I suppose I'd better see if the police want anything else. When you have coffee ready, you might tell them."

"Yah, for sure." Rachel turned to the coffeemaker. "It's almost ready."

As soon as Ms. Geraldine was gone, Rachel turned on him. "It's not necessary for you to move in here. I can take care of Ms. Geraldine and Holly perfectly well."

"And the burglar as well, I guess." He caught her hand in his again. "Well, you're not going to. Like it or not, I'm staying. Looking out for you—all of you—is my business, too."

He gathered his tools and headed on to the next room, leaving her staring after him, probably wondering what he meant. Not surprising, since he was wondering himself.

RACHEL STOOD STARING into space for a moment after Jacob went out so abruptly. His words continued to echo in her mind. Looking out for her? Or looking out for the household? It could very well mean that. He'd been working here for some time, and it was obvious he'd become fond of Ms. Geraldine. And maybe even fond of Holly, after their rocky beginning.

He must have meant all of them. But if he were thinking especially of her…well, she wasn't sure how to respond. She couldn't deny that she had feelings for Jacob. That had become very evident to her, if not to him, since they'd been here together. Seeing him every day seemed to have awakened all the old feelings she'd had for him.

But she was an adult now, not the immature girl she'd been then. She looked at things differently. Did she really want to risk love and marriage now? Was that even what he was leading up to? And if so, how long would it be until Jacob reverted to being as bossy and dictatorial as…*her father*?

The words seemed to have been dredged up from someplace very deeply hidden. *Her father.* She groped, trying to find her way through the tangle of thoughts and emotions that clung to her like brambles. So that was why. That was what lay behind all the things she felt so strongly about, like not giving up her independence. She didn't want to step back into that trap.

Almost fearing the direction her thoughts were going, Rachel shook her head sharply and looked at the clock. She ought to go see if the police had finished yet. If they had, there would be plenty of cleaning up to do. Being too busy to think seemed like a very good move right now.

She worked on through the morning, still unable to rid herself of an awareness of Jacob, of where he was and what he was doing. But he didn't come near her again until he popped his head in to say he was going to pick up his sisters and would be back in an hour or so. She nodded, relieved to have his disturbing presence taken away.

They'd formed the habit of having a light lunch in the kitchen, since Ms. Geraldine was used to her heavier meal in the evening. Sometimes she'd have hers on a tray in the study, while Rachel and Holly ate in the kitchen and talked the whole time, although Holly did most of the talking.

Holly was endlessly curious about everything, and at the moment that curiosity was focused on the police. After a complete review of everything they'd done and said, some of which she probably hadn't been meant to overhear, she finished her lunch and headed off to look for clues, as she put it. She paused in the doorway.

"Just think if I found something they didn't. Something that showed who the burglar was. Wouldn't everyone be surprised?"

She couldn't deny that. "Just don't go out of sight of the house without telling me, all right?"

Holly objected, more out of habit than conviction, before she agreed and trotted off.

Rachel didn't really think there was anything for Holly to find. If the police hadn't, it was doubtful she would, but at least it kept her occupied.

With Holly safely taken care of, Rachel went to see if there was anything Ms. Geraldine needed. Ms. Geraldine had held up very well to the previous night's excitement, but she'd looked tired all morning. If she'd only take a nap this afternoon... Well, if she did, it would be her own idea. She wouldn't like to hear the suggestion from anyone else, that was certain sure.

Her employer was back in the small study, and Rachel noted immediately that she'd gotten the photo albums out again. The same album, in fact, with photos of the summer she should remember.

She did remember, she told herself. Or at least as much as could have been expected at her age then. She went closer. "Is there anything you want, Ms. Geraldine?"

"Do you remember this?" Ms. Geraldine turned the album so that Rachel could see. "The picnic up at the pool?"

The picture showed the very spot where she and Holly had sat and talked. And she'd felt as if they were being watched.

"Yah, I guess." She was a little uncertain, and she leaned over to look more closely. They'd all been there, including Ms. Geraldine, sitting on a flat rock, her skirt carefully arranged to cover her legs. "It was a happy day. Mammi had packed the picnic lunch for us, and Julianne said I should go along."

"Julianne," Ms. Geraldine repeated, tracing her face in the photo. It showed Julianne standing in the water, laughing up at her brother, who looked as if he were splashing her. "I wish I knew what happened to that child. To both of them, in fact." She moved her fingers to William's young face. "They had so much promise. And now Julianne is wandering around the country looking for a man to take care of her, and William ended up who knows where."

Tears glistened in Ms. Geraldine's eyes, and Rachel felt her throat grow tight. It wasn't hard to see that they had been her favorites, and they'd both let her down in their different ways.

"I should have done more," she said abruptly. "I let them down."

"Ms. Geraldine…" She tried to find the words to express what she felt. No one, not even a parent, could accept total responsibility for how a child turned out.

"I have another chance with Holly," she said, studying Rachel's face as if to be sure she understood. "I can make up for failing them. And that means I'm not going into any retirement community to fade away." Her voice gained strength on the last words. It was as if she challenged anyone to argue with her.

"I understand," Rachel said finally.

Ms. Geraldine nodded. "I know you do. Thank you, Rachel."

It seemed to be a dismissal, so Rachel left. Ms. Geraldine obviously wanted to be alone with her memories, even if they made her sad.

It wasn't long after that when Rachel saw Jacob's buggy coming along the driveway, with his sisters Anna and Martha squeezed on the seat with them. They both seemed eager, as if looking forward to an afternoon of cleaning someplace different.

Why not? They were used to cleaning at home, so it wasn't a challenge, but doing it in a new place, and Englisch at that, was probably an adventure. They were only a little older than Holly, and anything different would be fun to them.

They disappeared up the steps to the second level of the garage, carrying buckets and mops. In a few minutes Jacob came back down to take care of the gelding, turning him into the paddock and apparently going back to work.

What was she thinking? The girls would need bedding as well as towels, soap and other supplies from the house in order to finish setting up the bedroom and bath. She scurried around the house collecting them and then cut across the back lawn toward the garage.

As she climbed the stairs, Rachel could hear the girls chattering away, erupting into giggles now and then. She smiled at the sound. It reminded her of herself with her dearest friends, happy to be doing anything together.

Jacob's sisters were pretty, lively teenagers—at least these two were. She didn't know the baby, Sally, as well. Anna and Martha had always been friendly, just as Jacob's parents had been. It was only Jacob who'd tried so long to ignore her, and no one could blame him for that, she supposed.

She opened the door. "I can hear giggling, so it must be Martha and Anna, ain't so?"

"Rachel!" Martha reached her first. "Here, let me take that." She grabbed the sheets and pillowcases and handed the towels to Anna. Martha had her mother's soft brown hair and a pert face with golden brown eyes that always seemed to be smiling. And Anna was enough like her to be her twin.

Anna clutched the towels against her chest. "Now, Mamm says you're not to do anything. That's what we're here for, and you're busy enough with that big house to take care of. How's Ms. Geraldine? We heard about the break-in. A terrible thing. Who could believe…"

"Enough," Martha said. "You don't give a person a chance to answer." She smiled at Rachel. "She's always like that."

"That's fine. I like to see people enthusiastic. Ms. Geraldine seems a little tired today, but that's natural. We were up pretty late."

Anna's eyes widened. "It must have been scary. Weren't you scared?"

She considered. "It all happened so fast that I didn't have time to be, I guess. But I sure felt shaky afterward."

"We heard they didn't catch the guy yet," Martha put in. "So it's a gut thing for Jacob to sleep over here."

"He'll keep you safe. Even if—"

Footsteps on the stairs silenced her as Jacob appeared in the doorway. He gave his little sister a mock glare. "Even if what? What dumb thing were you about to say about your bruder?"

She sniffed. "I'm never dumb," she said, nose in the air. "Now, you—"

Jacob snatched up a pillow from the bed and tossed it at her. "You get to work, and let Rachel get back to the house, or I'll tell Mammi on you."

Both girls made faces at him, not noticeably impressed. "Denke, Rachel," Martha said.

"Don't pay any attention to Jacob," Anna added.

He opened his mouth to say something back and then reconsidered. Looking at Rachel, his eyes crinkled. "They'll keep you here all day with their chatter if you let them. I'll walk down with you. Something I wanted to say, anyway."

Rachel walked in front of him down the stairs, which seemed narrower with Jacob right behind her. At the bottom she stopped, glancing at him.

"You needed to talk to me about something?"

For an instant, Jacob seemed startled, as if he'd forgotten.

"Yah, right. I wanted to say you were right." He hesitated. "And I was wrong."

"About what?" She was suddenly breathless. Surely he wasn't going to admit… Her mind scurried back to their quarrel, the day she'd told him what she thought of him. A flush rose to her cheeks when she remembered how she'd lost control of herself.

"About Holly. What you said." He seemed to feel he had to explain, had to pick his words carefully. "She really is a good kid. Too bad she got shortchanged when it came to her parents."

"At least she has her aunt Geraldine now." A tear glistened in her eye as she remembered Ms. Geraldine's words.

"And you," he said softly. "She knows she can count on you." He stood studying her face for a moment. Before she could guess his intent, he bent forward and kissed her, very gently but very thoroughly, on the lips.

When he drew back, he was smiling, and she was breathless. "See you later," he said and went off to the stable, still smiling, as if pleased with himself.

CHAPTER FIFTEEN

By MIDMORNING THE next day, Rachel had tried for too long to reason away the thing she couldn't explain. Well, she still couldn't. Jacob had kissed her. He hadn't looked embarrassed, or apologetic, or anything other than a little pleased with himself.

And when she thought about that smile, she felt like throwing something. Her fingers tightened around the pitcher of lemonade. Carefully she put it down. Just because Jacob had suddenly lost his sense, that didn't mean she should.

The sound of a horse and buggy coming in the driveway set her stomach churning for a moment. She glanced out and recognized Sammy, and her stomach settled. She was getting ferhoodled, jumping like that at the sound of a buggy... and all because Daad and Evelyn were coming back this week. They probably weren't here yet, and when they did come, a visit to her wouldn't be the first thing they'd do.

She'd said she'd be moved out of the house when they returned, and she was. She was settled with a job and a place to live, and there was no reason to worry about seeing Daad again.

But she knew exactly what the problem was. She hadn't at the time, but a little time and distance had made her feelings about Daad more clear. His decision had been a shock. She'd been taken aback, and she hadn't responded

<u>at all</u>. She still didn't know what she should have said or what she had wanted to hear from him. But <u>there should have been some exchange of feelings when he was changing their lives so drastically.</u>

In a way, it resembled Ms. Geraldine's feelings about her missing nephew. He had changed his own life and those around him with nothing but a short note, and it wasn't enough. It had left Ms. Geraldine doubting herself and her relationship with him.

Going out the back, she reached the walk as Sammy's buggy pulled up. To her surprise, he wasn't alone. He'd brought Sarah's little sister with him.

"Leah, how nice to see you." Rachel smiled at Leah and glanced questioningly at Sammy, but before she could ask the obvious question, Holly rushed out to join them, letting the screen door slam.

"Hi, Leah. Hop down." She glanced at Rachel, slightly defiant. "I invited Leah to come. Okay?"

"For sure." Her smile wiped the defiance from Holly's eyes. "I'm always glad to see Leah. I just made a pitcher of lemonade. Why don't you two girls go and have some?"

"None for me?" Sammy teased, once the two girls had gone inside.

Rachel grinned back. It always did her good to see Sammy. "I'll bring you some. The girls probably don't want company—at least, not grown-up company."

"Don't bother. I'm not thirsty, and I'd best get back. Sarah is in a tizzy because…" He hesitated. "Daad and Evelyn are supposed to get here this afternoon."

"It's all right," she assured him. "You don't have to be careful when you mention them. So Sarah is fixing supper for them."

He nodded, and the mischief came back to his eyes.

"Nobody knows yet if Evelyn can cook, so Sarah thought we should have a meal ready."

She swatted his arm. "If she can't, she's the only Amish woman I ever met who couldn't. I wouldn't worry about Daad."

"I won't, but it certain sure feels funny. What am I going to call her?" He was suddenly worried.

Rachel had to laugh at him. "Just say Evelyn. It'll be all right. She probably feels as awkward as we do."

Sammy nodded, easily soothed, and with a faint surprise she realized that she'd spoken the truth. Evelyn was bound to feel uncomfortable to be meeting Daad's family for the first time. After Daad met her at a family funeral in Ohio, they'd exchanged letters, but she'd never come here. The move had to be strange for her.

Why hadn't she considered that before? The truth was, she'd been so busy thinking about herself that she hadn't troubled her mind about Daad's new wife.

"Okay if I come back around four to pick up Leah and drop her at her house?"

"Fine." She reached out to pat her brother's arm. "Just relax. It will be all right."

She'd said that so many times to Sammy. Despite his grin and his jokes, Sammy was the more sensitive of her two brothers, the most likely to worry about doing the right thing. "Go on, now." She stepped back and watched as he turned the buggy and drove off.

She could hear voices as she approached the kitchen. They probably didn't want to be interrupted, but she had work to do in the kitchen. In this big house, they could find another good spot for talking.

As she went in, Leah was telling her something about

the Amish school, and Holly was listening intently. Holly shot a questioning look at Rachel.

"If I stay here, could I go to the Amish school? It sounds great."

"I don't think… Well, I'm sure your mother and aunt would want you to go to the Englisch school. They'll have the classes you need."

Holly made a face, but she didn't fuss. Instead, she rushed on to a different subject. "Can we have something to put berries in if we find any?"

"Sure." She pulled out the miniature bucket that had been used for berries even when she was small. In fact, her mother had probably provided it for Ms. Geraldine's niece and nephews.

"If you get some ripe wild strawberries, be sure to bring a few back for your great-aunt. She loves strawberries."

Holly grinned. "Okay, we won't eat them all." She drained her glass and hopped up, heading for the door, but Leah paused. "Denke, Rachel. It was gut."

"You're welcome," Rachel said gravely, trusting that Holly would take the hint.

"Yeah, thanks, Rachel." Holly held the door open, and they hurried off toward the woods, the bucket swinging between them.

Jacob, watching from the stable door, waved at the girls and then sauntered toward Rachel. She stiffened. If he wanted to talk to her, he was going to give her an explanation. And an apology. And she would not think about how she'd melted into the kiss, light as it had been.

But even before Jacob had reached her, another vehicle pulled into the drive—the police car this time. It parked and Chief Jamison stepped out.

Everyone knew Chief Jamison, and just the sight of his

solid, dependable figure was enough to make a person feel safe—that and the kindness in his square, ruddy face.

"Yes, I'm back again," he said, apparently in answer to their expressions. "No news yet, but that doesn't mean we're going to drop it. We can't have people breaking into houses, not in River Haven."

"So you want to see Ms. Geraldine?" Rachel gestured toward the house, ready to take him inside.

"In a minute." He sat down on the porch steps, looking glad to be off his feet. "A couple of questions for you two, first."

Rachel nodded, and Jacob leaned against the porch post and prepared to listen.

"Now, Rachel, you were closest to the burglar, right? If anyone noticed anything, it would be you."

She shook her head hopelessly. "But I didn't. It all happened so fast, and it was dark."

Jacob moved, seeming about to speak, but the chief stopped him with a look. "Sure, it was dark, but you had been moving around in the dark for a few minutes, right? Your eyes got used to it, you were able to see more and more. You came down the steps okay."

She couldn't argue with his words. She and Holly had crept down the steps, careful not to make a sound, and they hadn't stumbled or fallen. She pictured the stairway, stretching out ahead of them, remembering how Holly pressed against her, shaking a little, but determined.

"That's right," Jacob said softly. "You can see it, can't you?"

His voice seemed to lead her on. "We came down the steps, not making any noise. I wanted Holly to stay in her room, but she wouldn't. We weren't sure at first where he was, but then we saw the glimmer of light from the dining room."

"Go on," the chief said, keeping his voice slow and quiet, the way Jacob had done. "You went along the hall."

She nodded. "I remember I peeked around the edge of the doorway. I thought maybe I could see who it was. But the light was so bright, and I couldn't see anything behind it but a shadow."

She heard Jacob's indrawn breath. Jamison spoke, a little louder. "You didn't say that before."

"Didn't I?" She tried to think. "I guess I didn't remember it until now. The light and the shadow."

"Not the face?"

She shook her head.

"The clothes?"

Her forehead wrinkled. "Something dark. Even his hands were covered."

"You couldn't see his face, but you could see the shadow. How big?"

She blinked, focusing on Chief Jamison. "Big?"

"Was he tall?" He stood. "As tall as me? Or Jacob?" Jacob straightened. "Heavy? Thin?"

She shook her head slowly, but even as she did, the shadow seemed to sharpen in her mind. "Not as tall as Jacob. And heavier."

"Anything else?"

She tried to focus harder on the shadow, but it was already slipping away. "No." She looked at them in surprise. "But I remembered more than I thought I did."

"Any guesses as to who it was?"

She shook her head, feeling helpless again. "I couldn't even guess."

Jacob stirred, almost as if he would guess, but Chief

Jamison didn't seem to notice. Maybe it was just clear to someone like her. Someone who...

"You did a good job, Rachel. Why did you think it was someone you knew?"

She gaped at him. "I...I didn't say that."

"No. But it's not the usual way of putting it. Most folks would want to see his face so they could recognize it if we caught someone. But you seemed to think you'd know."

She shook her head, but he was right. That was how she was thinking. "I guess I thought he must have been in the house before. He came in the dining room window, and it seemed he went right to the sideboard where the silver is."

"Mmm." He didn't seem to entirely buy that. But after a long moment he shrugged and turned to Jacob. "What about you, Jacob? I know you weren't here when it happened, but have you seen anything I should know about?"

Jolted, Rachel exchanged looks with Jacob, and they seemed to come to a silent agreement.

"Nothing I can be sure of," he said slowly. "But I... we...had the feeling there's been someone trespassing in the woods lately."

Jamison looked up toward the woods, seeming to measure the distance from the house. "What made you think so?"

"I guess I started it," Rachel said. "Holly and I were up there by the pond on the creek, and I heard movements and felt as if someone was watching us. Maybe even following us as we came back down. I didn't see anything, but then Jacob..." She turned it over to him.

"I'd caught a glimpse of someone in the woods a couple of times, so I went up to see if I could find anything. Around the pond I spotted some broken branches and scuffed footprints in the mud. No way of knowing when they'd been made, but it had to be recent."

Chief Jamison nodded slowly, his face grave. "Could be just a hiker or someone planning a little illegal hunting, but it might be someone looking for the best way in and out of the house. I'll send someone out here with a camera. You show him where." He was all business now. "Okay?"

They both nodded.

"Good. I'll go in to Ms. Geraldine now. You don't need to come with me." He hesitated, as if he had something else to ask, but then he shrugged. "We'll talk again later." He disappeared inside before she could register his meaning.

JACOB WATCHED RACHEL'S face as the police chief walked away. Her eyes were troubled. Well, there was plenty to trouble anyone, and hard to know the best way to handle it.

Rachel turned her attention to him. "Do you think we should have told Chief Jamison about the rest of it? The accidents? Our suspicions?"

He ran a hand over the back of his neck and wished he had a ready answer. What was wrong with him? He didn't usually have any trouble deciding on the right course of action.

"How do you think Ms. Geraldine would feel about it?" he asked, delaying an answer. "I haven't talked to her about it enough to know."

Rachel shook her head. "Me either. She hasn't wanted to, I guess that's why. And I haven't wanted to upset her."

"Seems like we're tiptoeing around her feelings because they're her family," he pointed out. "But she doesn't seem to have many illusions about them."

"N-no." She was probably thinking about Ms. Geraldine's caustic opinions of Julianne's mothering failures and Gerald's laziness.

"But anyway, we can't talk to the police or anyone about her business without her permission." She spoke with renewed energy, as if she was certain of that, at least.

"If someone from her own family is trying to cheat her or steal from her, they deserve what they get." He felt that strongly even if he wasn't sure of anything else. "She ought to speak to Jamison about it."

"Would you?" Rachel's expression was serious as she studied his face. "If your brother had set a booby trap for you, or your sister had taken some small change from your bureau, would you call the police?"

"That's different. They wouldn't." His initial irritation died down as he considered her words. "Okay, I see what you mean. I couldn't call the police, even if I thought they had. I guess I'd try to find out for myself. Maybe confront the person."

The worry in her blue eyes deepened. "That's what I'm afraid of." She blew out a breath. "At least we know Holly can't have anything to do with it. She could have monkeyed with the attic step, but not anything else. And I don't see her doing that."

Jacob forced a smile, not liking to see her so stressed. "I guess not. She's more likely to sulk. Or threaten to run away."

She was immediately diverted. "She seems happier now, don't you think? She and Leah were actually comparing notes about what they'd do when school started. She seemed to accept the idea that she might be here."

That startled him. He'd still been thinking of Holly's stay as a short-term thing. "Do you think that's likely? A woman Ms. Geraldine's age?"

She shrugged. "She'd need help."

"And I suppose you think that should be you." There she was, putting other people's needs in front of her own.

Or did he mean his? He shouldn't have allowed that edge in his voice.

Rachel seemed not to notice it. At any rate, she just shrugged. "It's my job, and I like it."

He nodded, hoping…well, he didn't know what. He just knew he didn't want to be on bad terms with her. "I guess all this is for Ms. Geraldine to decide. But I'd like to know who put that surveyor's stake up in the woods. And who has been trespassing up there."

"And who broke in," she added, smiling a little. "You want all the answers."

"I guess I don't like unanswered questions. I want to know where I am. Let's face it, we're both thinking it might have been Gerald."

"I…I wouldn't put it that strongly," she said quickly. "The things that point to him are all so minor."

"The fact that you caught him in the cash drawer." He tapped one finger. "The fact that he shows up around here without notice." He tapped another. "And he doesn't have a regular job." He had to admit, that wasn't much to hold against him.

Her forehead crinkled again. "There was that business with his mother."

"What business?" Something she hadn't told him, obviously.

"I guess I didn't mention it. I thought maybe I shouldn't."

Jacob managed to tamp down his anger that she'd kept something from him. "If we're going to look after Ms. Geraldine, we'd best share what we know."

"We?"

"Yah, we," he said, admitting it. "I was here before you were, remember? I care about the old lady, too."

Rachel's expression cleared. "Gut. It wasn't anything big, but when Gerald's mother, Freda, was here, I found her upstairs. That was after both Ms. Geraldine and I thought she'd left the house."

He turned it over in his mind. "Any idea where she'd been?"

"No. But when I told Ms. Geraldine, she wasn't surprised. She said Freda was probably looking for her will, because she'd mentioned that she had it here to revise it. Ms. Geraldine said Freda would want to know if Gerald was included in it. But that she kept it in a place Freda wouldn't find it."

He grimaced at the thought. "She'd probably be better off to let all of them know what she intends. Then maybe they'd stop bothering her."

Most Amish families talked about it openly—who would be interested in running the farm or business, who would need to live in the house or even build another house on the property. If you didn't have secrets, then nobody would sneak around trying to find out.

Rachel nodded. "I think maybe she's not sure what she wants to do. Maybe there's a lot of money." She said that hesitantly, and he suspected she didn't know what she meant by *a lot*.

"Getting to know Holly might have made her change her mind about things, I guess. And at another guess, I'd say the land itself is valuable enough that her kin might argue over it."

"That comes back to what the surveyor's stake is all about, doesn't it?" Seeming frustrated, Rachel shook her head. "We just don't know enough."

He made a sudden decision. "There's one thing I can find out. Nobody would put in just one marker. There have to be more, so I guess I'll go up and look for them. See just what they're marking off."

Feeling a spurt of energy at the prospect of something positive to do, he started to walk away and then stopped abruptly when Rachel grabbed his arm.

He looked at her hand and then up to her face. "What?"

"We haven't talked about it." A flush colored her cheeks. "Why did you do it?"

He couldn't try to pretend he didn't know what she was talking about. They both knew. It was under every word they spoke.

"It wasn't the first time I've kissed you."

"That's not a reason," she said, her voice tart. "Why?"

He wished he had an answer, but he didn't. At least not any answer he wanted to face. "Maybe there wasn't a reason. Maybe I just wondered if it would feel the same as I remembered."

Rachel's eyes looked as if they could shoot blue flames at him. When was he going to figure out how to relate to her? And what exactly did he feel for her?

"Until you find a reason, just keep your curiosity to yourself," she snapped and flounced off to the house.

No, that hadn't gone well.

WHEN CHIEF JAMISON reappeared in the kitchen, he looked frustrated. His jaw was clenched so tightly it seemed he wouldn't be able to talk. But it turned out he could.

"Of all the stubborn, determined women in the world, Geraldine Withers takes the prize." He glared at Rachel as if she were responsible. "What is it she's not telling me? I know there's something."

Rachel shook her head, smiling. "You know I can't talk behind Ms. Geraldine's back."

"Not even to someone who's known you since you were a baby?"

She pressed her lips together for a moment and then shook her head. "You know better than that."

"Yeah, I guess I do." He crossed the kitchen to the counter, where she rolled out potpie noodles. "Chicken potpie?"

"You recognize them." She drew a sharp knife across the flattened dough.

"My favorite Sunday supper," he said in explanation. "I'd better be on my way. And there's a patrolman on the way with a camera. Have Jacob show him the footprints."

It sounded as if Jacob had best return from the woods and stop snooping on his own. "I'll tell him."

"Good." He stood there frowning for another long moment and then shook his head. "Listen, Rachel. I know I can depend on you. If anything happens that worries you, I want to know about it. Call me. Any time."

He put a lot of emphasis on the words, looking her steadily in the eyes. "We don't want anything to happen to Ms. Geraldine."

"N-no." It startled her that he'd come so close to her own fear.

"Good girl." He patted her shoulder and was headed for the door when the two girls, flushed and running, burst in.

"Look what we brought back." Holly thrust the small pail under Rachel's nose.

Rachel inhaled. "Mmm, it smells so sweet." The little pail was a quarter full with the tiny red strawberries. "You brought back more than I expected."

"We wanted to leave some for Aunt Geraldine. And for you." She jiggled the pail. "Go on, have some."

She was so eager that Rachel couldn't disappoint her. Or Leah, either, who was watching her closely, anticipation on her face. She took a small handful, rinsed them under the faucet and popped them into her mouth, one at a time. Sweetness exploded on her tongue, and she savored every morsel.

"So delicious. Wild strawberries taste best, ain't so?"

Holly and Leah nodded, smiling with berry-stained lips. "That's so much fun," Holly said, and for a moment she looked like any carefree child. "Leah showed me all the places where the raspberries grow. She says when they're ripe they will be black, not red?" She looked at Rachel for confirmation.

"That's right. When they're really ripe, you just have to touch them with your fingers and they come right off into your hands. They're like little caps, so people call them blackcaps. You can make pie, or cobbler, or shortcake, or jam…"

"Or just eat them off the bramble," Leah put in, obviously anticipating.

"There's more coming than that. There must be millions of them. When they're ripe, can Leah come and pick them with me?"

"Sure thing." She felt a surge of gratitude to Sarah, who'd thought of getting the girls together. "So long as her mamm says it's all right." She glanced at the clock. "Look at the time. You'd better wash up. Sammy will be back soon to pick up Leah."

With only minor grumbling that the time had gone so quickly, they rushed off to the bathroom. Hearing their feet pounding up the stairs, she wondered how Ms. Geraldine was enduring the noise and energy that filled her house now. Perhaps it reminded her of those summers her niece and nephews had spent at the house.

When the buggy pulled in a few minutes later, Leah and Holly both appeared with clean, shining faces and hands, and Sammy grinned at them. "Have a gut time?"

"Great!" they both said at once, and then looked at each other and giggled.

"You can do it again soon." Rachel expected Sammy to pull out again at once, knowing he wouldn't want to be late for supper. Instead, he swung himself down and came to join her.

"Was ist letz? Is something wrong?" She looked at him with apprehension, knowing Daad and Evelyn would have turned up by now.

"Nothing," he said quickly. "Daad and Evelyn got home okay. Evelyn got on the good side of Sarah right away by praising the boppli, cooing at her and everything."

Rachel could see the pride in his face. Naturally everyone would praise his beautiful baby girl.

"She has good taste, then," she said, knowing that would make things easier.

"Yah. Anyway, I happened to hear her telling Daad that he should come over and see you." He hesitated. "Sounded like she was laying down the law to him." He looked suitably surprised. So far as either of them knew, no one had ever been able to do that.

She suppressed any apprehension she might feel. "That's fine. I'll look forward to seeing him," she said firmly.

Sammy looked at her as if making sure she meant it. Then he gave her a quick hug, and they were on their way.

As she turned to go inside, Rachel saw Jacob coming back down the path from the woods. Some part of her wanted to flee, but common sense said she had to know what he'd found.

"Did you find any more of the markers?" she asked even before he reached her.

"The markers?" For a moment his strong face seemed to freeze, but then he shook his head. "Sorry. I was thinking of something else. No, I didn't. It's a little tricky when you only have one and have to guess which way."

"But you found something else," she said, sure of it from the way his eyes lit with interest.

"Yah." He came closer, stepping up to the porch, maybe so he didn't have to look up at her. "I struck a line up toward the ridge, to the right of the quarry, thinking it might be that way."

She nodded, picturing it.

"Anyway, I came across what's left of the old road they used for access to the quarry when it was worked. Seems funny it wasn't overgrown years ago."

"The one where you said you saw a car on Sunday. I don't suppose I went that far very often, if ever."

His smile flickered, and she felt a responding lurch of her stomach. "No, your mammi wouldn't have let you, I guess. Anyway, the point is someone's been coming in and going out that way."

She could only stare at him. "You mean... Do you think it's the person who tried to break in? When the policeman comes, you should tell him."

Jacob put up a hand to dampen her excitement. "It's not as easy as that. Whoever it was has been in and out several times, pulling in and parking about as far as the road is passable. I could see the different places it was parked, and I'd guess it was the same car each time."

A shiver worked its way down her spine. "Someone has

been driving up that road and then coming onto Ms. Geraldine's property. He could have been up in the woods watching us any time."

He nodded. "It was the same car every time. I could tell by the tire marks. And it must have a slow leak. I found some oil dripped each place it was parked."

"Couldn't the police find out who it was? Couldn't they take pictures of the tracks or something?"

"I guess so. Thing is, I can make a pretty good guess myself at who it was. I've seen the car before, or one dripping that way, anyhow."

"Who?" Her lips were stiff, and she wasn't sure she wanted to know.

"When Ms. Geraldine's sister was here visiting, I noticed her car was leaking oil. I'd have told her, but I didn't see her before she left. It was…it must have been…Freda's car."

CHAPTER SIXTEEN

AFTER THE EXCITEMENT of the break-in and the police investigation, things settled down. Ms. Geraldine took Holly shopping for clothes one afternoon, and that seemed to be an eye-opening experience for her. Rachel was amused at how lively Ms. Geraldine had been after the shopping trip, and it had distracted her from complaining about the police's inability to find the burglar.

Holly put on a fashion show for them, modeling each of the outfits and looking flushed and happy. Looking from one face to the other, Rachel couldn't help but feel that being together was wonderful for both of them.

The next afternoon, Holly went to Sammy and Sarah's place, to help with the boppli, Holly said. She'd been picking up words and phrases of Pennsylvania Dutch, although she and Leah spoke English to each other. Ms. Geraldine seemed to welcome the quiet and retired to her favorite spot on the side porch.

As she finished the upstairs cleaning, Rachel paused to glance at the woodwork in the room Jacob had been restoring. He'd taken the final length of baseboard out to the workshop today, so he'd soon be ready to move on to the next space. Ms. Geraldine clearly understood the time it took for a craftsman to finish a job like this. Jacob was a perfectionist when it came to his craft, and perhaps in other things, as well.

Downstairs all was quiet. Ms. Geraldine might well be dozing in the porch glider after yesterday's excitement. She went through to the kitchen just as a car pulled into the driveway. She took a second glance. It was Freda's car, although Gerald was driving. A movement from the stable caught her eye.

Jacob was watching the car, eyes narrowed. He was probably planning to check to see if it was still leaking oil once Gerald was out of the way.

When he reached the back porch, Gerald looked through the screen door and raised both hands to show they were occupied. She held the door while he carried a plastic tray with several quarts of strawberries into the kitchen.

"How lovely." She gestured to the table. "If you'd like to put them down…"

"Show them to my aunt first. I brought them for her. Where is she?"

Gerald wasn't wasting time being polite to her, but she didn't expect it. "She's on the side porch. I'll get the doors for you."

Going ahead of him, she held the doors while he took his gift through to the screened porch. He lifted the tray to present it to Ms. Geraldine with a flourish.

"For you, Aunt Geraldine. I popped down to York County to a place that's selling already. Picked them myself."

Ms. Geraldine looked a little skeptical at that, making Rachel wonder if it was true. It must be hard not to know if your own nephew was telling the truth or not. Since Ms. Geraldine was inviting him to sit down, she retreated, wondering whether they should have told her about what Jacob had found. That wasn't easily answered either.

A look out the kitchen window told her that Jacob was

doing just what she'd expected—looking under the car for the telltale oil leak. She hurried out to him.

"Well?" She kept her voice low, although it wasn't likely she could be heard from the other side of the house.

"Yah. That's the one." He dusted himself off and brushed dirt from his hands. "What does he want?"

Rachel shrugged. "He told Ms. Geraldine he came to bring her some strawberries he picked himself for her. Three quarts of them."

"Was she impressed?" There was a hint of amusement in Jacob's eyes.

"She looked a little skeptical." She considered. "Do you suppose he realizes that he might be suspected of the break-in?"

"And came over to get on the good side of his aunt?" He completed the thought. "It's possible." He looked at the car again. "I think this was the car that was parked in the access road, but that doesn't really prove anything."

"It's Freda's car," she pointed out. "I don't think she could have been driving it." She tried to picture the fussy, middle-aged woman hiking over the ridge and failed.

"But apparently Gerald can use it when he wants." His eyes, serious, studied her face. "Are you ready to talk to Ms. Geraldine about it now?"

She hesitated, feeling the pressure of his gaze as strongly as if he held her in place. Finally she nodded. "I'll try."

Suspecting that he would push harder if she stayed, she hurried back into the house. And then she stood in the kitchen, looking toward the side porch as if she could see through the intervening walls, and wondered what they were talking about.

There was one way to get a hint, at least. Moving quickly, she pulled out a tray and set glasses on it, then reached for the pitcher of iced tea she'd made earlier. After adding ice to the glasses, she carried the tray through the house, then paused as she reached the porch door.

She listened, but if they were talking, their voices didn't carry through the door. Not that she would eavesdrop, she told herself. But she couldn't help what she might hear as she carried the tray out. Balancing it, she opened the door, holding it back with her elbow.

"...quarry just going to waste sitting there," Gerald was saying as she went through to the porch. He stopped, looking annoyed at the interruption.

"I thought you might like a cool drink." She set the tray down next to the berries, then poured tea over the ice in the glasses.

"A lovely idea, Rachel." Ms. Geraldine took a glass. "Gerald, you remember Rachel, don't you? She used to come with her mother during the summers when you were here."

Gerald's hand stopped for an instant while he reached for a glass. "Yeah, sure. I didn't realize... Nice to see you, Rachel." He didn't sound very pleased, and a glance at Ms. Geraldine showed her looking amused.

"Thank you, Rachel." Ms. Geraldine gestured toward the berries. "You can take those to the kitchen now. I'm sure we'll enjoy them," she added, with a gracious glance at her nephew.

Rachel had no excuse but to leave. And though she lingered at the door, she couldn't hear anything more about whatever Gerald thought his aunt should do with the quarry. Something that would benefit him? She wouldn't be surprised.

She had been surprised, though, that he didn't seem to have recognized her. She'd remembered each of them so clearly, even though they were adults now. How much did people really change?

Whatever Gerald had been talking to his aunt about, it didn't last much longer. They came through the house toward the kitchen, with Gerald still talking about some great opportunity. For him, she wondered again, or for his aunt?

Gerald came first, ushered by Ms. Geraldine, and he had a big smile for Rachel. "It's been a long time since we played together out in the yard, hasn't it? And to think that you're working here just like your mother did."

There didn't seem to be much she could say in response to that, so she smiled.

"It's been great to see you, Aunt Geraldine." He leaned over to put a kiss on her cheek. "Now, don't forget to think about it, will you? It doesn't matter to me, of course, but you could make quite a bit of money out of it."

"I'll consider the matter." She drew back, seeming to wrap herself in the cool exterior she generally presented. "Goodbye, Gerald."

She stood, motionless, until he'd pulled out of the driveway. Then she turned away.

Now was her opportunity, Rachel thought. If she were going to tell, it may as well be now.

"Ms. Geraldine, about your nephew..."

"Not now, Rachel." She moved toward the door. "I think I'll lie down until dinner."

So it wasn't an opportunity at all. Rachel felt deflated. But if she had spoken, how likely was Ms. Geraldine to suspect her own nephew?

JACOB TRIED TO concentrate on the length of baseboard on the bench in front of him, but his mind kept straying. Would

Rachel have talked to Ms. Geraldine yet? How would she react?

Maybe he shouldn't have pushed it. He'd felt, when he'd seen Gerald driving the car with the telltale leak, that it was necessary. If Gerald had broken into the house, how could they ignore it? Weren't they responsible?

Responsible. The word echoed in his mind. He was getting as bad as Rachel, who accepted responsibility for everyone who crossed her path needing help.

A little voice in the back of his mind chided him. Wasn't it the right thing? He couldn't ignore Ms. Geraldine's welfare any more than Rachel could.

Before he could follow that idea, Holly came in and headed straight for him. "Hi."

"Hi, yourself. I thought you were at Sammy's place."

"I was." Her face lit up. "Sarah let me change the baby and rock him. It was so great."

He had to smile, thinking that any boy her age would probably run in the opposite direction at the idea. "She's a pretty cute boppli, yah?"

Holly nodded, smiling, but then her face grew more serious. "Sarah seems like she's really happy. She said being a mammi is the best thing ever."

He nodded, but suspected they were heading into dangerous territory. If she wanted to talk about motherhood, she'd come to the wrong person.

But she seemed determined to go on. "Do you think mothers get...well, tired of being mothers? I mean, like, stop being worried about what their kids do?"

Panic swept over him. This was not a talk he wanted to have, now or ever. He sucked in a breath, trying to find the words he wanted to keep this from turning too personal.

"I...I don't know. I'm the wrong person to ask. I'm not going to be a mother."

"Well, you have a mother, don't you?" She was intent on putting him on the spot.

"Yah, for sure." He hesitated, wishing he were somewhere else.

"Would she stop being worried about her kids?" she demanded.

"No." He could hardly say anything else. "Sometimes my sisters wish she would, I think."

She shrugged, and it didn't take someone like Rachel to see what this was all about. Even he could tell that she was talking about her mother.

"I bet they wouldn't like it if she did," she muttered.

"Look..." He wasn't responsible for this kid. And there was that word again. He brushed it aside, but he couldn't stop thinking, who was?

"Look," he tried again. "Sometimes people take longer to grow up than other people. Your mother..."

She pulled back at that. "I'm not talking about my mother. I mean..." The silence grew, and she stared down at the workbench. "Okay, I guess I was."

He wished again that Rachel was there to take over. "I don't know your mother very well. But now you have your aunt Geraldine. I do know her, and I know she wouldn't ever let you down."

Again the silence lay between them. Finally she looked up, and tears shone in her eyes, tears that she hastily blinked away. "Yeah. You're right."

As they stood there on opposite sides of the workbench, Jacob's ears caught a sound from the driveway. "A buggy." He jerked his head toward the noise. "Wonder who that is."

Holly moved toward the door, and Jacob followed her.

Holly wouldn't know the newcomer, but he did. It was Rachel's father, and the woman who sat beside him was undoubtedly his new wife.

Holly took a step forward, but he stopped her with a hand on her sleeve. "Better not interrupt them." Rachel had come out of the house and stood looking up at them.

"Why not? Who is it?"

He'd have to tell her something, clearly. "That's Rachel's daad. He's been away with his new wife."

Holly glanced from the couple on the buggy to him. "That's her father? The one who broke up your wedding?"

"What... How did you hear that?" he demanded.

She shrugged. "I get around. I hear things."

From Leah, most likely.

"He didn't break up our wedding," he said firmly. He'd have to have a word with Sammy and Sarah.

"Well, what?"

She was persistent. He'd have to tell her something.

"We were talking about it, but then Rachel's mother died. Her father insisted it was Rachel's duty to stay home and raise her two younger brothers. So we just...didn't get married. That's all."

That wasn't all, not by a long way. The anger could still come up in him when he thought about it. Thought about his pain. His pleading, even. Rachel had stood firm. It was her duty.

"Seems like you gave up awful easy." She looked at him as if she were disappointed. "Couldn't you have found some way—moved in with them, maybe, or had the boys move in with you?"

He tried to ignore her, but it didn't seem to work. She was a kid. She didn't know anything about it.

"Look, I don't want to talk about it anymore. Just don't interrupt them."

Good advice, he figured. He wouldn't interrupt them either. Too bad he couldn't keep from watching them and wondering what they had to say to each other.

RACHEL HAD A spurt of nervousness when she saw Daad's buggy pull in. She fought it down, reminding herself that she was a grown woman. An independent woman. Holding herself erect, she walked out to greet them.

When she stopped by the driveway, noticing the woman who sat next to him. Evelyn. She must remember to call her that.

Daad looked stern and controlled as always, his lean face lined above his beard.

"Daad." She managed a smile. "I hope you had a gut trip. You and… Evelyn." She extended the smile to her.

Evelyn returned her smile, and Rachel focused on a pair of kind brown eyes in a serene face. She found herself relaxing a little. Evelyn looked like she'd take care of Daad. That was the only thing that should concern her now.

Evelyn nudged her father and nodded to her. "You can get down now. I'll turn the buggy and give you time to have a few words in private with your daughter."

Somewhat to Rachel's surprise, Daad climbed down without a murmur. Evelyn clucked to the horse and moved on toward the stable, where there was space enough to turn.

Gathering her scattered wits, Rachel gestured toward the back porch. "Would you like to sit on the porch?"

"I'll stand. I… We won't be here long." Before she had time to think that the words sounded ominous, he cleared his throat and went on. "After all, you're working. It wouldn't be right for us to take up Ms. Withers's time."

"That's fine. I'm not busy now." What did he have to say to her that wouldn't take long? Evelyn must think it was important to insist on leaving them alone.

"We thought… I thought we should come over to let you know we're back. We'd like to get together when you have some time off." He seemed to relax a little as he started talking. "How do you like it here? Your mammi always said Ms. Withers was a fine person to work for."

"Yah, she is. I'm liking it very much." She thought about mentioning the buggy and the mare she had here and decided to leave it. If Daad wanted them back, he'd say so.

"That's gut." Another awkward silence fell, and she wondered again why Evelyn thought they'd needed time alone for this conversation. "Did you and Evelyn get to visit everyone you wanted to?"

"Yah, yah. Everyone sent their greetings to you."

She nodded, seeing that Evelyn had turned and was coming back. She pulled up next to them.

"You look like you've had a lot of experience handling a buggy," Rachel said. Some married women got out of the habit.

"Ach, well, I had to. I've been on my own for a gut while. My son and daughter aren't too far, but far enough that I didn't want to walk."

"That's nice. Do they both have families?"

"Yah." Her face lit with grandmotherly pride. "Joshua and his wife have a two-year-old, and Mary Ann and her husband have two little ones, all just as cute as they can be. And now there's Sammy and Sarah's little one."

"She's a sweetheart, isn't she?" Rachel found her easy to talk with—easier than Daad, at the moment. She could see what had drawn Daad to her.

"Ach, yah. I just love babies. And Sarah is such a gut mother. You can see that in a minute, can't you?"

Rachel nodded, smiling.

"And the two boys," Evelyn went on. "You had quite a challenge to bring them up, young as you were yourself. You certain sure did a fine job with them."

Daad coughed slightly, and Evelyn looked at him. A message seemed to pass between them.

"You didn't say it yet." There was a decided firmness in her tone.

"I…" Daad turned to Rachel. "I realized…well, Evelyn pointed out how hard it must have been for you, giving up your wedding plans and all. Devoting yourself to the family. I guess I didn't thank you enough." He flushed, something that was unheard-of for him. "Anyway, denke, Rachel. I'm grateful for you." His voice was getting hoarse. "You're a wonderful gut daughter."

"Denke, Daadi." It came out in a whisper.

Evelyn nudged him again. "Hug your daughter," she said.

Daad, his face red, stepped toward her, reaching out. Hardly able to think, Rachel hugged him back, thinking how long it had been since she'd felt Daadi's arm around her.

Daad stepped back. "We've taken up enough of your time. We should get going." He climbed up quickly, trying to hide his embarrassment at showing so much emotion.

She wasn't much better, she realized. She turned to Evelyn, who held out her hand and clasped Rachel's for a moment. When she spoke, her voice was soft.

"I never knew your mamm, but she must have been a fine woman to raise a daughter like you." For an instant, her eyes shone with tears. "I can't be a mother to you, but I hope we can be friends."

Rachel felt answering tears in her eyes. "Denke," she said softly.

Daad picked up the lines and then nodded toward where Jacob stood with Holly in the stable doorway. "I'm sorrier than I can say that you two didn't marry when you wanted."

She shook her head, surprised at her own feelings. "It was for the best, Daad. If we had married then, it would have been a mistake."

She couldn't believe she'd said that, but she knew it was true. It would have been a mistake.

CHAPTER SEVENTEEN

THE NIGHT HAD been untroubled by any noises or bad dreams. Rachel was almost surprised to realize it. She'd have expected to feel churned up over the encounter with Daad and Evelyn. Instead, she felt not only calm but contented. If she had harbored any resentment toward her father or any fears about his new relationship, all that was gone as if it had never been.

Not only that, but the truth she'd spoken without planning to had left assurance in its wake. It *would* have been a mistake if she and Jacob had married then. They hadn't been mature enough, either of them, to make a lifetime commitment. She hadn't known how to balance her relationships and fulfill her commitments at that time. Maybe she didn't now, but at least she was aware of it. The hard years after Mammi's death had taught her a great deal about loving and caring for those she loved.

As for Jacob…well, he probably wouldn't admit it, but he hadn't been ready either. He'd been too quick to fly off the handle and too blind to options seeing only what he thought was right. She'd like to believe she had changed, and she'd give a great deal to feel sure that he had.

With breakfast served in the dining room, she could turn her attention to putting a meal on the table in the kitchen. She smiled, picturing Holly and Ms. Geraldine seated at the polished mahogany table, eating from the fine china.

Holly might roll her eyes at the formality, but it was probably good for her to learn the ways that Ms. Geraldine considered proper.

Holly's life would be different, of course. But what was important wasn't so much the learning as the time and experience with her great-aunt. Things like regular mealtimes with family formed ties that wouldn't easily be forgotten. The routine told Holly that she was a part of a family and a tradition, and not just a stray person without roots.

Now that Jacob was sleeping over the garage, he came to the house for meals, and she could see him crossing the yard now. She suppressed a smile. Like her father and brothers, Jacob was never late for a meal.

He stopped for a moment, looking off to the west. Leaning forward to see what had attracted his attention, she spotted the long line of dark clouds massing along the western horizon.

"Storm coming," he muttered, pulling out his chair. "Maybe it'll pass us by."

She nodded, but feeling the humidity in the air, she thought a storm might be a relief. It would clear the air, anyway.

No sooner had they settled at the table than Jacob looked at her with a question in his eyes. "Well? How did things go with your father? I could never get you alone last night to find out."

"Surprising," she said. "That's the word for it. He actually apologized to me. Said he hadn't ever been properly grateful to me for taking over after Mammi died."

Jacob blinked. "Are you sure that was your father?"

She had to laugh. "I know. I think that Evelyn has been gut for him. She doesn't hesitate to tell him what's what. And he listens."

"I'd never have believed it." Jacob shook his head. "It doesn't sound like your father to me."

"It shows that people can change, ain't so?" She hesitated, hoping he wouldn't think she was hinting that he could stand to change.

But he didn't seem to take offense, maybe because he was sure change wasn't needed in his case.

"If it makes things easier for you, then I'm glad." He didn't sound completely convinced, but she couldn't blame him for that. He took the last spoonful of scrambled eggs and then had a long drink of his coffee.

"More eggs?" she asked, gesturing toward the pan, but he shook his head.

There was a moment of silence between them, but she found it a comforting thing. Maybe she was just in such a contented mood about her father that she was seeing things that weren't there.

She watched a frown gather on Jacob's forehead. "Have you spoken to Ms. Geraldine yet about Gerald?"

"No. I couldn't. I don't know how she might react." She'd barely said it before the door behind her swung open.

"What should you tell me about Gerald?" Ms. Geraldine stood there, looking at them. Rachel rose to her feet, feeling a flush mounting her cheeks.

"I...I..."

"I'll tell you." Jacob stood. "I guess that's right since I'm the one to think you should know."

Ms. Geraldine gave a sound that might have been a snort. "Rachel doesn't want to hurt my feelings, but I don't have any illusions left about Gerald. Whatever it is, I'd rather know."

Jacob looked as if he wished he'd kept quiet, but he nodded. "I got to wondering if the person Holly and Rachel heard in the woods might have something to do with the break-in. He might have been spying, trying to figure out the best way to approach the house."

"And you think that was Gerald. Why?" She shot the question at him, and Rachel wondered uneasily if she was quite as hardened to Gerald's behavior as she wanted to believe.

Jacob looked at her gravely. "I searched around up there, and I found footprints from the person watching Rachel and Holly. They were pretty scuffed up, so that didn't help a lot." He paused, taking a breath. "So I decided to try and see where those other surveyor's stakes were, in case that had something to do with it. I ended up by that old road that led up to the quarry from the other side of the ridge."

Ms. Geraldine's forehead wrinkled, but she nodded. "I know it. I didn't think it was passable."

"It isn't very far, but where it petered out, I saw that a car had been parked, maybe more than once. Could have been anyone, I guess. There's no way to tell. But I noticed whatever car was parked there leaked oil. And when Gerald came driving his mother's car, I saw that it was leaking oil, too, leaving the same sort of spot where it was parked."

He came to an end, and for once didn't try to tell someone what to think. He left it up to Ms. Geraldine to make of it what she could. That was best, Rachel realized. Ms. Geraldine wouldn't want to be told.

They both waited, and Rachel wondered again how much Ms. Geraldine could believe about her nephew. Finally she nodded.

"It could have been for some other reason," she said. "But it might be. The break-in didn't succeed, which would be like Gerald."

A wave of sympathy swept over Rachel, and she longed

to do something to relieve Ms. Geraldine's mind. She took a step forward, reaching out.

Ms. Geraldine responded with a slight smile and a shake of her head. "Gerald was here yesterday, pushing some idea he has to reopen the quarry. He said he has a friend who wants to work it again if I'm willing to lease it." Her lips twisted wryly. "I'm sure there's something in it for Gerald, if so."

"That would account for the surveyor stake," Jacob said. "And maybe for his parking where he did. He might have been scouting out the quarry instead of looking to break into the house." He sounded reluctant to give up his theory.

"I suppose so." Ms. Geraldine seemed distracted, as if her mind was elsewhere. "I'll have to think about it. Thank you, Jacob."

The words seemed to be a dismissal. Jacob looked as if he'd say something else, maybe argue his point, but at a look from Rachel he turned and went out.

Still, Ms. Geraldine stood there, her thoughts far away.

Then she glanced at Rachel and waved to her chair. "Sit down. Finish your coffee." She sank into the seat across from Rachel. "And don't look so tragic." Her lips twitched in what might have been a smile.

Rachel sat, wondering whether it would do any good to say anything. After a lengthy silence, she ventured to speak. "I'm sorry."

Ms. Geraldine brushed the words away with a sweep of her hand. "It's best that I know." She shook her head. "Freda has always been foolish, even if she is my sister." She seemed to be talking as much to herself as to Rachel. "She was jealous because after my brother died, my father decided I should have control of the property since I wasn't married and my two sisters were. He settled money on them instead." She was silent for an instant, as if considering what she'd said about her family. "What's worse, Freda raised Gerald to think something was owed to him. That's not a good thing for a child."

"No, I guess not." She paused, not sure she should say what she was thinking, knowing how Ms. Geraldine revered her father. Finally she went on, choosing her words. "It sounds like your father's decision led to problems he probably didn't expect."

"That's right." Ms. Geraldine suddenly looked tired. "And now I have to make the decisions about what I'll do with it all. If Gerald did break into the house, I can't reward him for that."

Rachel had no idea what to say, but she felt so sorry for her employer. Her wealth seemed nothing but a burden to her.

"And there's Holly to be taken care of. Her future has to be secure, no matter what Julianne does." Ms. Geraldine fell silent, brooding about it. Then she stood up abruptly. "I shouldn't be bothering you about this, Rachel. It's my decision, and I must decide for myself."

She made her way out of the kitchen, looking older than she had when she came in.

Rachel's head was a jumble of thoughts. Wealth hadn't brought happiness. Still, as her mother used to point out when she longed for something she didn't have, we weren't put on this earth to be happy. Happiness came along when we were doing what we should.

All she could do was try to live up to it.

LATER IN THE DAY, when supper was over, the storm was close enough to make Rachel start preparations in case the power went off. At home, of course, no preparation was needed, as they got on very well without a connection to the power line, but things were different here. And she knew from some of the Englisch neighbors how easy it was for a branch or even a whole tree to come down on the power lines in a bad storm.

She was filling a bucket with water when Holly came in. She looked from the pitchers already filled to the bucket. "What's all this for?"

"In case the power goes off in the storm. Water in the pitchers to drink and to brush your teeth and wash with, and water in the bucket in case we need it to flush the toilets."

Holly looked horrified at the thought, and Rachel tried not to laugh. "But the water comes out of the spigots anyway, right?"

"Not out here in the country. This house isn't on town water. It has its own well."

"And there's a spring that comes off the ridge with fresh water in case we need it," Ms. Geraldine added, coming in just then. "Without electricity to power the pump, nothing will come out."

Holly shook her head, apparently not sure whether she was appalled or curious. "It sounds like *Little House on the Prairie*," she said.

Ms. Geraldine did chuckle at that. "Wait until we get out the oil lamps. Then it really will be old-fashioned." She glanced at Rachel. "The extra flashlights and the oil lamps are in the cabinet back in the corner of the pantry. We may as well be prepared. The local news said it hit hard over in Millertown and is headed our way."

Rachel glanced at Holly, deciding she'd be better off with something to occupy her mind. "Come and help me with them."

Holly didn't bother to delay, and when Rachel handed down a pair of oil lamps from the shelf, she took them cautiously. "You sure they won't start a fire?"

"Not unless someone knocks one over and breaks the glass that protects the flame."

"You actually use these at home?" She was clearly finding it hard to believe.

"Something like them, but we have newer lamps that can provide more light. And battery torches, too." They headed back into the kitchen with their burden.

"I'd rather the power stayed on." Her eyes widened as a rumble of thunder sounded.

Ms. Geraldine took one of the lamps and began to trim the wick. "It's an adventure, child. Don't you like adventures? I still remember how we sat and played games around the table by the light of oil lamps when the power went off. Freda would jump every time the lightning flashed."

"I'm not afraid of lightning," Holly said quickly. A spatter of rain hit the windows on the west side, punctuated by a flash of lightning and the rumble of thunder. "I didn't jump," she pointed out.

Another clap of thunder sounded, and the storm hit in earnest. Holly peered out the window. "Somebody's coming," she announced. "It's Jacob."

Rachel looked out while Holly ran to open the door. Jacob carried an armload of something, and his free hand clasped his hat to keep the lightweight straw from flying off his head.

Jacob reached the porch, stamped and shook the water off, and came inside. Holly quickly shut the door against the storm.

"Going to be a big one," he said. "I brought the flashlights and the battery light that were in the garage."

"Good." Ms. Geraldine took them from him and set them on the kitchen counter. "Holly, there's a stack of board games on the shelf in the study closet. Why don't you pick something out in case we want it?"

Holly went willingly enough, but she didn't look as if she expected to have much fun.

A half hour later, she would have surprised herself if she'd thought of it. The power had gone off moments after she'd come back with a Monopoly set, and the radio informed them that the same tree that pulled down power lines had fallen across the road, blocking the way to town.

But sitting at the kitchen table playing a game by the yellow glow of the oil lamps, Holly was giggling with joy when Jacob's man landed on her hotel and she demanded payment.

"You're taking pretty close to my last dollar," he complained. "How did you get to be such a shark at Monopoly? I thought you said you'd never played it."

"Beginner's luck," Ms. Geraldine suggested, and Holly gave a smug smile.

They might be a family, Rachel thought. Maybe, at the moment, they were.

Without warning, loud knocking sounded from the front door. Ms. Geraldine looked annoyed at the interruption. "Who would be coming out in this weather?"

Rachel was already on her feet and heading for the door. It might well be a neighbor coming to check on them. As she pulled open the door, a spatter of water hit it, startling her. A dark figure loomed outside, one fist raised. Panic ripped through her.

Then a flash of lightning showed her Richard Withers. His hair was flattened by the rain, and water dripped from

his shoulders. The panic was overtaken by a sense of…
what? Memory? Fear?

Just as quickly the feeling was gone, and she could laugh
at herself. She was imagining trouble lurking on the doorstep, acting like a child afraid of a storm.

"Come in, come in," Ms. Geraldine said from behind
her. "Goodness, Richard, what are you doing out in this?
You're soaked. Rachel, get some towels."

Richard started to protest, but Rachel was already running back to the powder room to grab a handful of towels
from the shelf. When she returned, they were in the circle
of lamplight in the kitchen. She handed over the towels.
Richard smiled his thanks and began to rub his head briskly
with one. He emerged looking much more like himself.

"That's better. Thanks."

"Sit down," his aunt ordered. "Tell me what you're doing
out on a night like this."

He took a seat at the table and reached across to clasp
Ms. Geraldine's hand. "The power's out in this whole area.
I wanted to be sure you're all right."

"I've gone through more power outages than you can
count," she said tartly. "Of course I'm all right."

But Rachel felt sure she was pleased at the attention, and
probably Richard knew it, too.

"You've had lots of visitors lately," Rachel pointed out.
"Gerald yesterday and Richard today."

"Gerald?" Richard frowned. "What did he want? And
if you said *nothing*, I'd be thunderstruck."

Ms. Geraldine's narrow lips twisted in a wry smile. "You
know Gerald. He always has some scheme to make money.
Too bad none of them include doing a job of work."

Rachel glanced at Jacob, wondering whether they, as
outsiders, ought to withdraw from this family discussion.

But Jacob was watching Richard intently. Maybe he wanted to hear where this led.

"What is it this time?" Richard asked.

"Someone he says is a friend of his wants to lease the land the quarry is on. There's an idea that the quarry should be opened again. Gerald says there's money in it."

"The quarry?" Richard's voice rose. "That's ridiculous, and I hope you told him so. They'd make a big mess and end up with nothing to show for it. And the noise of the equipment would drive you wild. You're not going along with this silly idea, are you?"

Ms. Geraldine was regarding him with what seemed to be surprise. Was it at the idea, or was it because of his vehement argument? Rachel suspected the even-tempered Richard rarely got upset.

"We'll see," Ms. Geraldine said lightly. "I told him I'd think about it, so I will."

Richard seemed to bite back further argument. "I'm sure you'll do what's best. I just hate to see you bothered by Gerald's nonsense." He stood. "You all look very cozy, and I can see you have everything under control. I'd best get back to Lorna."

Ms. Geraldine thanked him for coming even though, as she pointed out, it hadn't been necessary. Rachel moved to walk to the door with him.

Richard didn't speak until he had his hand on the knob. Then he smiled at Rachel in the way he had when she was a small girl. "I shouldn't have worried. You obviously have everything under control." He started to open the door and then paused, putting his hand lightly on her shoulder. "If there's ever a problem, you be sure to call me. I'm always here to help."

Rachel stood smiling for a moment after locking the door

behind him. He'd been kind as a young man, and clearly he still was. Ms. Geraldine might not agree, but she was fortunate to have him.

THE NEXT DAY, Jacob noticed that while everyone seemed tired after the late night, Ms. Geraldine, Rachel, Holly and even he were cheerful. They all had a new easiness with each other, as if going through the adventure of the storm had brought them closer. Ms. Geraldine actually made a joke and submitted to teasing by her young great-niece. Amazing.

Even the weather reflected this new atmosphere, with the damp grass unusually bright and fresh and the air clear and cool. Nothing like a storm to clear things out, it seemed.

He was leaning against the back porch railing, one foot on the step, as he talked to Ms. Geraldine about where to work next. Rachel, coming out to water the potted flowers on the porch, stayed to join the conversation.

A panel truck pulled in the driveway and parked. While they watched, the driver's side door opened. A man wiggled his way out—a hefty, middle-aged man wearing work clothes emblazoned with the words *Gray's Stone and Gravel*.

Frowning a little, he watched, wondering what this might have to do with the mention Ms. Geraldine had made about Gerald's big idea to open the quarry. And wondering, too, at Richard's reaction to it. Had he been upset because he had his own plans for the Withers property?

"Hey, there." The man approached, looking from Jacob to Ms. Geraldine and seeming to settle on her as the right person to talk to. "I'm Delmer Gray, ma'am. Maybe you've heard of me… Gray's Stone and Gravel?"

"No, Mr. Gray, I'm afraid I haven't."

Jacob controlled a smile both at Ms. Geraldine's expression and the man's reaction. Obviously he hadn't expected that. No doubt he was the *friend* Gerald had talked about, and Ms. Geraldine knew that as well as he did. What, he wondered, was she up to?

"Well, now, you are Ms. Withers, aren't you?" At her nod, he went on with more assurance. "I'm here to talk to you about the quarry that's way up there on the ridge. On your land, I understand."

Again she nodded, her face noncommittal.

"Fact is, Ms. Withers, that quarry closed because at the time, there wasn't much more need for stone, and the cost of getting it out was too great. So it was allowed to fall into disuse. All overgrown and maybe downright dangerous. I'm guessing you haven't been up there in a while, so you wouldn't know."

If he'd stopped long enough to study Ms. Geraldine's expression, he'd have slowed down, most likely, but he didn't.

"Now, you don't want a hazard like that on your property, just sitting there and not making any money for you. I'm here to take a lease on that piece of ground. I can work it properly, the way it should be, so it'll pay its own way. What do you say?"

Ms. Geraldine eyed him. "I'm aware of the quarry on my property, Mr. Gray. And my nephew Gerald had mentioned it to me. I'm assuming it was Gerald you talked with?"

"Well, yes, ma'am." He was clearly becoming aware of the fact that he'd made a misstep. "He indicated to me that you'd be receptive to my offer."

"I'm afraid that was wishful thinking on Gerald's part," she said drily. "I have no intention of leasing any part of my land."

Gray's face darkened when he heard the first part of

that. It looked like Gerald had stretched the truth in both directions.

The sound of a car in the driveway distracted both of them. Then Ms. Geraldine smiled, not very pleasantly. "Here is my nephew. Let's see what he has to say about the situation."

Jacob caught movement behind the screen door into the kitchen. Rachel appeared and hesitated, obviously not sure whether to interrupt or not. He shook his head just a little, hoping she'd get the message. It would be a shame not to hear Gerald's excuses at having been caught in his deception.

Gerald stopped the car, looked toward the porch and seemed to freeze. For a moment he clung to the steering wheel, but then he must have realized that driving away wouldn't help. He got out slowly and came toward them, arranging his face in an unconvincing smile.

"Gray. What a surprise to see you. What are you doing here?"

He smiled and nodded at his aunt, ignoring Jacob.

"Look, what's going on here?" Gray's square face took on a reddish hue. "You told me your aunt was all for my leasing the quarry. You said you just had to finalize all the details. Now it looks like you've been lying to everyone."

"Not…not lying," he said, stammering. "I wouldn't… Aunt Geraldine, you know I'd never lie to you, don't you?"

"On the contrary, Gerald. It sounds as if you've done that more than once. Were you planning to pay my nephew for his assistance, Mr. Gray?"

"I was, ma'am." He glared at Gerald. "Now I wouldn't give him a red cent." He looked like he'd have a few more words for Gerald if it weren't for Ms. Geraldine's presence. He turned back to her. "I'll be on my way now. I'm sorry to have bothered you, ma'am. Delmer Gray doesn't do business like that. If you ever decide to do something with that quarry, I'd be honored to take care of it. I'll be on my way."

He took himself off, and Jacob was impressed by the man's dignity. Unlike Gerald, who looked as if he wanted to weep.

"Well, Gerald? What else have you been doing? Putting wax on the stairs? Setting a trap in the attic?"

Gerald stared at her blankly. So blankly that Jacob was inclined to believe his denials, much as he'd rather ignore them. While he was still denying having anything to do with it, Jacob studied Ms. Geraldine's expression, realizing that she believed him, too.

"Enough," she said sharply, as Gerald went on and on. "Maybe you didn't do that. But you broke into the house, didn't you?"

"Not…not break, exactly." He was flushed and unhappy. "I mean, I wasn't going to steal anything. Honestly, I wasn't. I just…"

Understanding dawned on Ms. Geraldine's face. "Of course. You and your mother have been trying to take a look at the changes in my will, haven't you?" Her expression tightened, and she looked suddenly older. "You can certainly assume that my will is being changed now."

"Please, Aunt—"

"Enough." She gestured, and Jacob saw that her hand was shaking. He took a step toward her, but Rachel got there first. She pushed her way out the screen door and took Ms. Geraldine's arm, murmuring something about a rest.

The two of them moved slowly inside, with Rachel pausing for an instant to send an angry look back over her shoulder in the direction of Jacob.

Why was she angry at him? He hadn't done anything.

He turned to escort Gerald off the property, but Gerald was already trotting to his car as fast as he could go.

Glaring, he watched Gerald drive away, but his thoughts were on Rachel. If that wasn't like Rachel—blaming him for something that wasn't his fault at all. Why couldn't she be sensible?

CHAPTER EIGHTEEN

RACHEL GUIDED HER elderly employer inside, alarmed at the way she seemed to crumple after the confrontation with her nephew. But by the time they reached the hallway, Ms. Geraldine was her usual erect self. She walked toward the parlor, her hand resting lightly on Rachel's arm.

"I don't know why I'm falling apart because of Gerald, of all people." Her voice had regained its tartness as she settled in her favorite chair.

She seemed herself again, but Rachel could still see the strain in the way the lines deepened around her eyes. "It's upsetting to learn something like that about your own kin," she said. "Even if…"

"Even if I never thought very highly of this particular branch of the Withers family tree," Ms. Geraldine finished. She leaned back, looking tired. "I'm not surprised. Not about Gerald. He's been trying to manipulate people since he was in nursery school. It's surprising that he's never gotten very good at it."

"I'm sorry." That was all she could find to say.

"I know you are, dear." Ms. Geraldine patted her hand. "When I think what my father would have said…well, it doesn't bear thinking of." She glanced across the room, and her gaze came to rest on the portrait of her father over the mantel. "He was good at a lot of things, but most of all, he was an honorable man. People knew that he said what he meant and meant what he said. And that if he said he'd do something, he did it, no matter what."

"I'm sure you've lived up to him," Rachel murmured.

"That's the point, you see." She fixed her gaze on Rachel's face, but Rachel had the sense that she wasn't really looking at her. "There's always been some pride in being a Withers. In carrying on the tradition. And now, Gerald has betrayed the family and everyone will know it."

Rachel stared at her. "But…surely it doesn't have to be known to anyone outside the family, does it?"

"You're not thinking, Rachel. A crime was committed and the police called in. They're looking for the person who broke in. What if they arrest someone? I can't let anyone else take the blame for what Gerald did."

"I see," she said slowly. "No, you couldn't. That would be terrible." She shivered at the thought.

"And there's the rest of the family to consider. Richard's business depends on people trusting him and relying on him. Will anyone want to invest in his projects or buy a house from him if they're afraid he's not trustworthy?"

Her genuine anxiety was taking her too far, Rachel thought. "I'm sure folks wouldn't judge Richard by what his cousin did," she murmured. "They know him."

"You think I'm exaggerating, don't you? Well, maybe I am, but I know how people talk." She sighed. "Well, at least Holly's over at Leah's today. I'd hate for her to hear anything about this. But I don't know what I can do."

"Maybe there's something." She spoke slowly, feeling her way. "If you told the chief about this privately…well, he's a kind man. And after all, nothing was taken. Maybe he can arrange to just drop it."

"Maybe." She didn't sound convinced. "It's worth a try, I suppose."

"I'm sure it is. We certain sure won't say anything."

"I know. If only…" Ms. Geraldine seemed to turn inward, letting her thoughts move far away. "William was always worth twice what the rest of them were. If only he hadn't run off. I could count on him."

Rachel smiled a little, hoping the worst was over. "He was your favorite, ain't so?"

"One shouldn't have favorites," she mused. "I know that, but still… William was special." She shook her head and seemed to emerge from her memories. "Forgive an old woman's wanderings. You get back to what you were doing. I'll just relax here for a time."

Realizing she wanted to be alone, Rachel nodded and slipped out. Poor Ms. Geraldine. It must be hard to know your own kinfolk had plotted against you.

Rachel headed upstairs, intent on a thorough cleaning of the room where Jacob had finished working. She glanced up and saw him waiting at the top of the stairs. For her?

Apparently so. "Ms. Geraldine wants me to work next on the room you're in, so I'm supposed to move anything you want into the opposite one. You want to show me what to move?"

"I'm sure I can manage…" she began, but he was shaking his head.

"Ms. Geraldine's orders. You don't want to get me in trouble, do you?" His eyes narrowed. "Or maybe you do. What's the big idea of being mad at me for what Gerald did?"

The remembered annoyance sparked in her. "What do you think? I came outside and found Ms. Geraldine all upset and you standing there like it was…was a performance. You should have done something."

As soon as the words were out, she knew she was being

unfair. Ms. Geraldine had been determined. But surely he could have done something to help.

"What?" he demanded. "You're being unreasonable, just like always."

"What do you mean, 'always'?" This had flared up in an instant, but maybe that was just as well. "If you're still harping on what happened between us years ago, you're hopeless. And it's certain sure just as well we didn't get married. It would have been a mistake."

Jacob's face set, and his hand grasped the doorjamb so hard that his knuckles were white. "You…"

He stood there, frozen in place. And then a change swept over his face, and his lips relaxed into what was almost a smile. "You think that, do you? Well, maybe you're right. Come on, now. Let's do what Ms. Geraldine asked before she hears us and comes up here."

The words, so reminiscent of a brother and sister bickering, dissolved her anger as if it had never been, and she smiled. "Yah, all right. But I still say I can move things myself."

"I'll have to pull the furniture away from the wall, so you may as well be there. Make sure I don't damage anything."

"I'll do that," she said, opening the door. With her balance restored, she thought how foolish she'd been. They had both been. He could always make her more annoyed than anyone else, ever since they were children playing together.

"Everything that's hanging in the closet?" he asked, opening the closet door.

"Yah, I guess so. I don't want you getting sawdust all over it."

He grinned in response to her teasing and began gathering up her clothes while she concentrated on the things in the bureau. She'd never had a closet before she moved in here. Pegs on the wall were sufficient for her dresses, so what else did a person need?

Just as well Jacob had started there. She wouldn't want him looking in the drawers where her nightclothes were. Stacking the drawer contents, she carried them across to the other room. It was about the same size and had its own bed and bureau, except that it faced in the opposite direction.

She stood at the window for a moment, glancing across the drive to the lawn beyond. She could catch a glimpse of the grape arbor from here.

Rousing herself, she hurried back across the hall, passing Jacob, who carried her dresses in and put them on the bed. Then he followed her back.

"I'll strip the bed and find something to cover it," she said, picking up the few things that were on the top of the bedside table. "Will you need anything else?"

He shook his head. "I have some drop cloths to cover the other furniture. Now to get things away from the wall so I can get a gut look at the baseboard." He grasped the edge of the dower chest and then paused. "Don't you want this moved across the hall?"

"No, I don't need that." She went quickly to help, sensitive about the dower chest in relation to Jacob. But he probably didn't even recognize it for what it was…maybe had never known about the things she'd been storing for their wedding.

But even as she thought that, his grasp slipped and pushed the lid up a few inches, showing the wedding quilt that lay on top. He reached out, touching one of the patches.

"My mother made that one. From an old shirt of mine." He slammed down the lid and turned away. "You're right. You don't need that."

JACOB CHARGED OUT the back door, intent on working hard enough to chase away his annoyance. Truth was, he couldn't be sure whether he was more annoyed with Rachel or with himself. Or maybe he was sure, and he just hated to admit it.

His steps slowed as he considered it. Why was it still such a sore spot for him after all this time? If he'd stopped to think when he saw the quilt...

But he hadn't. He shook his head and tried to focus on something else. Anything else.

The two horses stood side by side in the paddock under the tree, head to tail. Each one swished his tail almost in unison as they kept the flies away from each other's head. His lips twitched in a reluctant smile. They were like an old married couple taking care of each other.

No wonder they'd sought the shade. It was going to be a hot day for June, and the humidity was building. The storm hadn't cleared the air for long.

Movement at the garage caught his eye. Mamm was sitting in her buggy pulled up at the side of the building. She saw him looking and waved, then swung herself down as easily as a girl.

"Mammi! I wasn't expecting you." He gave her a quick hug. "Is everyone okay?"

"Yah, no problems. I just thought you'd need some clean clothes by now." She pulled a large shopping bag from the buggy and thrust it into his arms. Taking a closer look at him, she frowned. "Was ist letz? What's wrong with you?"

He'd never found it possible to evade her sharp eyes. "Nothing." He nodded to the stairs, trying to distract her. "Come up and see my place."

She headed up the stairs and he followed, carrying the bag, which looked like it might contain a shoofly pie in addition to the clothes. At the top, he pushed the door open. "Here it is."

"Very nice." Mamm walked around, touching each piece of furniture as if to approve it and then looking in the small bathroom. "Very nice for one."

"There's only one of me," he said lightly. He lifted out the shoofly pie and set it on the dresser. If he wasn't careful, she'd start talking about how he should be married. "You didn't need to bring food. Rachel keeps everyone well fed."

"I'm sure she does, but a little extra never hurts. Take it into the kitchen for the family." She pinned him with a mother's frown. "Now tell me what you're so annoyed about or I'll think it's me."

He shrugged, giving up. "You know it's not you. I just… I happened to notice that quilt. Rachel has it here. You know, the quilt you helped make when we were courting."

Mamm's frown deepened. "I can guess the rest of it. You got annoyed with Rachel. Why? For still having a quilt that was given to her?"

He found he was turning away from that frown, feeling as if he were ten years old and caught in some mischief. "I just…reacted without thinking."

"Aren't you getting a bit old for that?"

Defensive, he blurted out the thing that really stung. "She said that if we'd married, it would have been a mistake."

"She's right."

While he was still gaping, she went on. "Come, now, Jacob. You know that your father and I thought you were too young at the time. You were caught up in the wonderful glow of first love, but besides your age, Rachel was still grieving her mother and you…you were too young to have learned to compromise."

He took a breath and tried to speak calmly. "Her father wouldn't let her go, and she went along with him. That's what happened."

"Yah, I know. He panicked at the thought of raising those boys alone. But did you try to work something out? You could have married and moved in there, or into the daadi haus, or built a place of your own nearby. You didn't even think of it, did you?"

He opened his mouth to argue. And shut it again. She and Daad had known him better than he knew himself. If they'd suggested it at the time... But he couldn't put it on them. He didn't even think of it—that was the point she was making.

He looked at her ruefully. "Was I really that young and that stupid?"

"Not stupid." She patted his cheek, smiling a little. "Just young and foolish, thinking what you felt was all there was to loving someone and building a family. Real love is much deeper—part affection, part friendship, part attraction, part caring. Not as exciting, but much more satisfying. You'll see."

"I don't know," he said slowly. "I hope so, but I don't know if I'm brave enough to risk it again."

She laughed at him gently. "When you are, you'll know it. Don't worry."

Jacob hoped she was right, but he wasn't that sure of himself. Not at all.

RACHEL CLIMBED THE stairs to the second floor more slowly that afternoon. The heat continued to build, and the window air conditioners were struggling to cope with it. The downstairs was bearable, but something had to be done about the upstairs if they were to sleep that night. So she was going to the attic to bring down the window fans Ms. Geraldine said were up there.

She went up the attic stairs at an even slower pace reliving those moments when she'd plunged down them. At the top, she paused to check again the one that had been tampered with. No one would try the same thing again, surely, but she checked anyway.

The heat in the attic hit her like a blow. Fortunately the window fans had been neatly stacked to the side not far from the steps. Someone had foreseen the need to bring them down in a hurry.

The metal fans clattered together when Rachel moved them, and almost immediately Holly called out.

"Who's up there?" Her voice wasn't entirely calm—maybe she was reliving something, too.

"It's just me. I'm bringing some fans down to put in the windows to try and cool off the rooms."

"Good idea." Holly came running upstairs. "I'll help you."

Now that she seemed comfortable with the idea of staying here, Holly was as helpful as anyone could expect of an eleven-year-old girl, Rachel thought. She handed a couple of the fans to the girl.

"There are plenty of these, I think. We should be able to get it cool enough for sleeping tonight."

"Good. I was thinking of sleeping out on the porch."

"You'd be eaten by mosquitoes," Rachel said, following her down the stairs.

Holly grinned. "Yeah, I'd be one big lump by morning. Where should I put these?"

"Let's start with your aunt's bedroom."

They started to work, but Holly objected when she saw Rachel close windows and pull the shades down. "Hey, wait." She blinked in the suddenly darkened room. "I thought you were going to put the fans in the windows."

"That would bring in all the hot air. If we do it this way, we keep the rooms as cool as possible, and then when the sun starts to set, we'll open the windows and start the fans. The rooms will be cool by bedtime."

Holly looked doubtful, but she nodded. "In the meantime we roast. Can't we do something now?" Her face lit up. "I know. Let's go up to the woods. We can swim in the pond."

Rachel shook her head with a quick motion. She didn't want to go to the woods. Not today. The house felt oppressive enough, and the woods would be much worse. She didn't know why she felt that way, but the feeling was too strong to ignore.

"I don't want to go that far in case your aunt needs me. I'll tell you what. If you go down that flagstone path through the lilacs, it ends in a little creek that's just right for cooling off. Why don't you go down there?"

Holly made a spirited effort to get Rachel to change her mind, but she finally gave in cheerfully and set off with a bottle of lemonade, a towel and a book. Rachel just hoped whatever ended up in the creek, it wasn't the book.

With Holly gone, she set about finishing the upstairs windows, hurrying so she could check on Ms. Geraldine. Her employer looked a bit strained today, maybe because she hadn't heard from Julianne yet. Ms. Geraldine was as eager to have things settled for Holly to stay here as Holly was.

Her hands on the window that looked out on the porch roof, Rachel paused, staring. What was that funny-looking piece of metal extending under the window? She raised the window and gingerly touched the object, then picked it up and looked more closely.

It took a moment to figure out what it was for, but then it struck her. With the metal extending on the outside like a handle, it would be fairly easy for someone on the porch roof to open the window.

Her first instinct was to call Jacob in and ask him to do something about it. But she cringed at that, not wanting to see him or speak to him until they'd both had time to cool off. Her anger welled up again just thinking of it.

Jacob had been completely unreasonable. As annoyed as she was with him, she was even more annoyed with herself. She'd let him provoke her into anger, into venting that anger at him. She felt a flush of shame at the thought. No, definitely not. She didn't need or want his help to deal with this.

She knelt, looking at the metal piece more closely. There was no doubt in her mind. Someone had put it there. It couldn't have been by accident. Someone who wanted to come into the house from outside had fixed on this way of entering.

Gerald? He might easily have set this up for his break-in project, but then decided the downstairs window was better. He couldn't have known what Ms. Geraldine's idea of a safe hiding place was, any more than she did.

Or someone else—someone who was still waiting for a chance to break in.

Rachel shivered, feeling the oppression seep into her from the house. The walls...even the roof...seemed to close in on her.

Stop it. She stood up quickly, the piece of metal in her hand. Then she shut the window and locked it firmly. Just to be certain, she wedged the thin edge of the metal piece between the window and the frame. There. Whoever he or she was, it wouldn't be an easy trick to get in there now.

Ms. Geraldine would expect Rachel to tell her about anything like this. She went down the stairs quickly, intent on doing what she knew she should.

But outside the study door, she paused. Should she? It would be upsetting, and would it serve any good purpose? If Gerald had done it…well, she'd already dealt with Gerald. And if someone else, at least that entrance was now barred. Ms. Geraldine already intended to put in an alarm system, and that would take care of the rest. Was there any sense in worrying her?

She was turning away from the door when it suddenly opened and Ms. Geraldine stared at her, startled. "Rachel? What is it?"

"Nothing. I mean… I was wondering if you wanted something cool to drink today instead of your afternoon tea. If seems so hot."

"Yes, that sounds delightful…" She stopped when the phone rang and went to answer it.

Since Ms. Geraldine sat down at the desk, Rachel realized she intended to talk for a time, so she went to the kitchen to prepare the tray. But before she could take it in, Ms. Geraldine followed her. Her smile chased the signs of strain from her face.

"That was Julianne at last. She's in Los Angeles now, but she gave me an address and phone number. And she's agreed that Holly should stay here with us, at least until school starts."

"Ach, that is good news," Rachel said, feeling as much pleasure as if they talked about one of her siblings. "That dear child should be able to count on something in her life."

Ms. Geraldine lifted her lemonade glass to Rachel in a mock toast. "Thank you, Rachel. I couldn't do it alone, but with your assistance, I'm sure we'll be fine." Carrying the glass, she turned toward the study. "Now I'll call Enid Hastings. She's on the board of the local recreation center, and she's always talking about their programs." Her eyes twinkled. "This time I'll listen to her. It's time Holly had an opportunity to make more friends."

The door swung shut behind her. Rachel was still smiling, but she felt her burden increase with Ms. Geraldine's confidence. Ms. Geraldine relied on her. Holly relied on her. She just hoped she could live up to their expectations.

And that meant no more brooding over Jacob. It was useless. He belonged in her past, and this was her present.

SHE WAS WALKING slowly through the house in the darkness. Total darkness, with not a glimmer of light anywhere. She had that feeling again—the feeling that the house was closing in on her.

Worse. That she wasn't alone in the darkness. Someone or something lurked there, following her, step by step with her. Coming closer. She opened her mouth to scream, but nothing came out. Her throat was paralyzed. She couldn't make a sound. She could only flatten herself against the wall as the movement came closer and closer, until she could reach out and touch—

And suddenly she wasn't in the house any longer. She was in the woods, on the trail that led up to the quarry. No. She didn't want to go to the quarry. There was something there…something waiting for her…something terrible. She didn't want to see it. She couldn't see it.

She spun to go back down the trail, but she hadn't taken a step before she knew there was something there, too. Something between her and safety. Something that moved through the shadowed woods stealthily, coming closer and closer.

No. She couldn't wait for it to catch her. She had to run. The only way was to head for the quarry. But she couldn't. She couldn't force her legs to move. If she went to the quarry, she would see...whatever it was. It waited there, waited to be seen.

She opened her mouth again, and this time the scream came, loud and shrill.

Rachel sat bolt upright in bed, gasping, the scream echoing in her ears. Had she really screamed, or had she dreamed it? She sat silently, trying to still the thundering of her heart. She strained her ears, and finally she settled. Either she hadn't screamed out loud or no one had heard it.

She let out a long breath, reaching for a state of calm. Slowly her thoughts stopped spinning. It had been a dream. A nightmare, maybe, but nothing more. No one was here. No one followed her. But her nightgown was soaking wet with perspiration, and she shivered when the air from the fan hit her.

Get up, change clothes, change the bed. Then, maybe, she'd be able to go back to sleep. But not to dream. Not that.

CHAPTER NINETEEN

RACHEL GOT UP when the sun began to streak through her window. Up, but not fully awake and certainly not rested. After the nightmare and its aftermath, it was a long time until she was willing to trust herself to sleep.

Even once she got moving, she couldn't entirely shed the remnants of the dream. It kept haunting her, making her feel as if there was something she should remember. About the dream, or about something else? She didn't know. It was elusive, slipping away like a minnow in the stream just when she touched it. Trying to erase the feeling didn't work. She couldn't get rid of it.

Holly, on the contrary, was bouncing around as if all her problems had been solved. Of course they hadn't, but Rachel wouldn't intrude on her pleasure for anything. Holly should enjoy the feeling as long as she could. It was a measure of how uncertain her life had been that she was so happy just to know she was settled for the rest of the summer.

"Rachel, did you hear?" Holly skipped into the kitchen, letting the door swing behind her.

Rachel had just finished the lunch dishes, and she'd started mixing up some homemade noodles to have with the chicken she planned to fix for supper when Holly burst in on her.

"Heard what?" she asked, holding the rolling pin in a flour-covered hand.

"Aunt Geraldine fixed it up so I can take tennis lessons this summer at the rec center. I always wanted to learn to play tennis." She swished an imaginary tennis racket. "The lessons start next week. Isn't that great?"

"It is, that's certain sure." She couldn't help smiling at the pleasure in the child's face.

"And Aunt Geraldine's friend has a granddaughter who's taking them, too, so we can ride back and forth together."

Holly was bubbling over, relaxed and happy. She looked like a different child from the sulky eleven-year-old who hadn't even wanted to put her backpack down when she'd arrived.

"And…" Holly dragged out the word. "Ricky called me." She gave an extra bounce.

Rachel tried not to laugh. "That's nice. What did Ricky have to say?" She slapped the dough onto the bread board and began to roll it out.

"I told him about the tennis, and he said that was a great idea." Holly leaned on the table, dangerously close to the floury board. "He played on his high school team—did you know that? And he said he'd come over next week, and we could practice together. He said the only way to get good is to practice."

"I'm sure that's true of a lot of things," Rachel commented. But obviously when Ricky said it, it was worth remembering.

"Yeah, I guess." Holly's elation seemed to slip. "Only thing is, I asked him about the berries, and he said I should go ahead and pick them myself. He doesn't have time to do it this week, because his friend from school is here."

Rachel tried to find the right thing to say, but she

couldn't be sure what that was. Holly had a crush on her older cousin. That wasn't surprising. It would be more surprising if she didn't. He was, as Ms. Geraldine said, a charmer.

He was too old for her. He was being kind to his little cousin. Those things wouldn't help if she were to point them out.

"But he's going to meet you next week, remember. Maybe pick you up in his car to go to the park for practice."

"Yeah." She brightened. "I know I'll be here next week."

She said it as if that were an unusual thing—to take being in one place for granted. Rachel's heart lurched. Such a common thing to be able to count on.

"For the rest of the summer," Rachel reminded her. "A lot of things could happen by the time school starts again."

Holly seemed to pursue that thought. She nodded. "Maybe even my mom would come and live here. I know Aunt Geraldine wants her to. Wouldn't that be great?"

"It would." She struggled to speak over the lump in her throat. "We'd all love to have you live here for good."

For a moment, Holly's expression seemed too old for her. "At least then, if she went away, I'd have someone."

Holly's fear came through so clearly when she said that… the fear of being left. That was behind everything, and it hurt Rachel's heart to think about it.

Still distracted, Holly put one finger in the flour and began drawing circles on the board. Rachel didn't speak, accepting her need to think about what she'd just said.

Just as Rachel's mind kept harking back to what she'd said. She'd told Jacob that it would have been a mistake if they'd married. She'd said it out of anger, but it was still true. Marrying then would have been a disaster. Now…now that they were both more mature…well, it didn't matter about now, because Jacob no longer wanted to marry her.

Holly, rousing herself from her thoughts, clapped her hands together, sending a drift of flour into the air. She went to the pantry and returned with a small plastic pail.

"Okay if I go up and pick any strawberries that are left? I can check on the raspberries, too."

Rachel caught herself on the verge of saying yes. Was it really a good idea to let Holly wander into the woods by herself? Gerald would be too afraid, she'd think, to cause any more trouble, but still…

"How about waiting until I finish getting this dough rolled out? Then I can go with you."

Holly looked rebellious, and Rachel hurried on.

"It won't take long. I just have to roll it out flat and then cover it with a tea towel. Then I can go with you."

Tapping the plastic pail against her palm, Holly studied her face. "I'll be outside waiting. Don't be long," she said. When Rachel nodded, she marched out the back door, swinging the pail.

The noodle dough, with the perversity of just about all objects when you were in a hurry decided to be difficult. She had to adjust and readjust the amount of flour and water. Finally it rolled out, stretching to the required thinness without any further struggle. Rachel covered it with a couple of tea towels, washed her hands and went to tell Ms. Geraldine where they were going.

When she returned and went out onto the back porch, she found it empty. Holly was gone.

EXASPERATED, RACHEL WENT back inside. She thought she'd have seen Holly if she'd come in, but she could have gone to the side door or even the front. Unlikely, but she'd better call. She went to the bottom of the back stairs.

"Holly? I'm ready to go."

Nothing. She closed the stair door and, after a moment's hesitation, went through to the front staircase to call again. The only response was silence, until Ms. Geraldine opened the study door.

"Is something wrong?" She stood, framed in the door, looking concerned.

"No, nothing." Rachel made her tone reassuring as she walked back. "I thought Holly was going to wait on the back porch for me, but I must have missed her. Don't worry. I'll find her, and we won't be gone long. I don't think there will be many wild strawberries left after the storm."

Hurrying, she went toward the back door and then out onto the porch, mentally reviewing the other possibilities. The grape arbor, the stable...

Jacob was likely to be in the stable, working, so she tried the arbor first. It was pleasantly shady, but Holly wasn't there to take advantage of it.

When she came back around the house, she saw Jacob standing in the stable door, watching her. As she approached, he raised his eyebrows in a question.

"Lost someone?"

She shook her head, still feeling uncomfortable after their quarrel the last time they were alone together. "I don't know. I thought Holly was waiting for me on the back porch, but she's not there. Have you seen her?"

"Yah, about ten minutes ago, maybe." He nodded toward the woods. "She was headed up there, carrying a bucket. I guess after berries."

"Denke." She started to turn away, but he was studying her face so intently that she didn't feel able to. She should apologize…tell him how sorry she was she lost her temper. Keep it light, because after all, he'd started it.

But she didn't have time right now. She didn't like to have Holly up in the woods alone after everything that had happened.

Rachel finally turned away just as Jacob said her name. "Rachel…"

She looked back at him, but he didn't seem able to go on. "I'd best go find her." She hesitated. "I'll talk to you later, yah?"

Without waiting for a response, she scurried off.

Unfortunately, she couldn't leave Jacob behind in her thoughts. Even as she strode up the path, she pictured his face and wondered what he'd intended to say.

She'd reached the branch off to the spot where wild strawberries grew before she could push him out of her mind. Some of the meadow grasses had been flattened by the storm, convincing her that it would have dashed any hope of the wild strawberries, as well. Still, she had to check. For all she knew, Holly might have found a treasure trove.

She rounded the flank of the hill to find that her forebodings had been correct. Where the berries had been, there was only crushed vegetation and a few smashed berries. Holly was nowhere in sight.

She called, briefly, but could hear no one. Holly must have gone on up the hillside. Returning to the path as quickly as she could, Rachel hurried on toward the woods, realizing that she seemed to be heading toward darkness. The western sky was masked by dark clouds again. Surely they weren't going to have another storm. Well, all the more important to find Holly.

At the point where the path branched off to the left, just

before the woods started, Rachel paused. If Holly intended to check on the raspberries, she'd have gone off that way, but the tall grasses didn't look like they'd been disturbed by anyone passing. She turned to look up the path toward the ridge top and the quarry.

One way or the other? Pausing, undecided, she looked up the path to where it disappeared into the deeper woods. She started to call, but her voice seemed to get caught in her throat.

Ridiculous, she told herself. *Just because of a dream you've turned into a coward.*

"Holly? Holly, where are you?"

She stood still and listened. Nothing for a moment, and then she heard something rustling up ahead. Up toward the top of the hill and the quarry.

Well, she wasn't going to let herself be ferhoodled. If Holly had headed toward the quarry, she'd best go after her. She'd said that they'd come together. *Now stop wasting time.*

Determined, she strode under the shadow of the trees, her head up and listening. If Holly was there, why hadn't she answered? Annoyed at Rachel for delaying their walk? Or maybe just out of earshot. Or pulling her into a game of hide-and-seek.

The farther she went, the denser the trees and the darker it grew. Here and there she walked through a spot where the sun broke through, and once she spotted a bramble of raspberry canes. Nothing ripe yet, it seemed, but quite a few berries. They wouldn't grow where the sun didn't penetrate, but the wild ones were hardy enough to pop up wherever they had a chance.

Rachel thought about raspberries on the surface of her mind, while underneath her apprehension grew. She couldn't seem to fight off the sense of foreboding. As the woods grew thicker, it was like walking into her nightmare. Memory teased at the corner of her mind.

What was it? What had she forgotten? It slipped into view for an instant and vanished before she could focus on it. Something she had seen—something recent? Or something from the past?

She forced herself to move forward. The woods lightened ahead now, and she knew she approached the quarry. She stepped out into the clearing where the quarry dropped off in a sharp cut to the rocks below. Water glinted.

"Holly?" She called out again, looking from one side to the other.

No answer. But then someone stepped into the open farther up along the rim of the quarry. For a moment she was frightened, and then she saw who it was. It was Richard. Her breath whooshed out in a sound of relief.

"Are you looking for Holly?" he asked, moving out to the edge and peering across its depths at her.

She nodded. "But what are you doing up here?" Surely it was a workday for him, judging by his clothes. The light wool slacks and the dress shirt and tie weren't suitable for a walk in the woods.

"I haven't seen her." He hesitated, frowning, and then pointed at the cliff face below her feet. "What's that?"

"What?" Her heart missed a beat. She leaned forward, trying to see the side of the quarry but she couldn't. "I can't see anything. What is it?" Fear edged her voice. If Holly had come to harm, she'd never forgive herself.

"You're at the wrong angle. I'm not sure—there's something, a bit of color, something else. You'd better come and look. My eyes aren't so good."

He leaned forward, craning to see, and fear mounted to

panic in her. Heedless of the sharp drop-off, she hurried along the edge, trying to see, stumbling and nearly falling. The gap reached toward her, and she grabbed a tree limb to steady herself.

"Careful," he said, extending his hand toward her.

Sucking in a deep breath, Rachel advanced from one handhold to another until finally she reached him. "Down there." Richard stooped, pointing to a spot below where she'd been standing. "Just look about fifteen feet down the cliff."

Rachel stooped the way he had, her hands on her knees for balance, searching the rocky, seamed face of the quarry. "I can't see anything."

"You'll have to get a little closer to the edge." His voice came from right behind her. As if a cold wind had hit her, Rachel shivered.

"I can't…" She looked up and saw Richard above her and behind him only sky.

Fear ripped through her, worse than anything she'd ever felt. She was revisiting her dream, but this time the danger was real. It wasn't lurking behind her in the dark, it was here, in front of her, hands reaching.

"No!" She lunged to the side, hoping to evade him, but there was no space, nowhere to go with the drop-off behind her, and his hands grabbed her arms, tightening.

"You saw it. I was always afraid you had." He sounded sad.

She shook her head, trying to pull her arms free. "I didn't. I didn't see anything. Just you, with the sky behind you."

"Yes." His hands began to push her toward the edge.

"What…what…" The memory came back, the memory she'd buried all these years. She'd seen…

Rachel dug in her feet, pulling against his hands. "William. You and William were tussling. And then… William wasn't there anymore." Sickness rose in her throat. She knew where William had gone. Over the edge, into the depths of the quarry.

"He didn't make a sound." Richard's voice was calm, as if he'd been through it so many times it had lost the power to shock. "I couldn't believe he was gone. It was an accident. You saw that. It was just an accident."

Was it? Or had there been some thought in his mind that if William, his aunt's favorite, were gone, he'd step into William's place?

"An accident," he insisted, as if intent on proving it. "But what could I do? Everyone would have blamed me. So I had no choice. I wrote a short note and hid his clothes. I didn't want to, but I had to."

She managed to nod. "It was an accident." Her mind raced. She was alone. No one was coming to help her. She had to help herself. "It wasn't your fault. I'll tell everyone that."

"No!" He shoved, and her foot twisted under her, throwing her off balance. She was inches from the edge.

"It was an accident. People will understand. I'm sure they will." What else could she say or do to divert him? She sent up a silent prayer for help.

"I don't want to do this." He looked at her as if pleading with her to understand. "I don't. When I found out what Lorna did, I told her it must never happen again."

"Lorna? You mean Lorna was the one who put that slippery wax on the stairs? And loosened the attic step so I would fall?"

"She was trying to help me. A wife wants to help her husband. You must see that. If Aunt Geraldine went into a care home, I'd be able to go ahead with developing this land.

Lorna knew how much it meant to me, but she'll never do it again." He shook his head. "It's too late for me."

"It's never too late. You can stop now."

But he was already shaking his head while she spoke. "I'll never be safe as long as someone knows. And you're the only one who knows."

His hands tightened. She pulled back, resisting, but her feet slid on the loose gravel. She would go over the edge. She'd never be able to tell people how much she loved them—her family, her friends, Jacob. *Please.*

"She's not the only one!"

The shout echoed from the quarry, ringing in her ears. The pressure on her froze, holding her there on the very edge of the chasm. Jacob's voice. She didn't dare turn her head to look, but she knew he was there. Strength and hope surged through her.

"And I know, too." The second voice was younger, lighter, but just as determined. Holly.

"You can't do it, Richard." Jacob's tone was almost conversational, as if he spoke to a friend. "You don't want to, and it won't do any good. Stop now."

The pressure didn't ease, but Rachel, infused with hope, got her feet under her and threw her weight toward solid ground. Richard released her, and she staggered forward, stones and gravel stinging her hands as she landed. Gasping, she rolled to her side and looked back at Richard.

He still stood on the edge, with the sky behind him, the way she'd seen him when she knew the truth. He seemed to shake his head. She thought his lips moved, but she couldn't be sure. And then he took a long step forward into space.

No scream. Nothing for what seemed a long time, and then a rattle of rocks. Silence gripped them—even the birds were still.

Now, at last, Rachel could close her eyes. She let her head rest on her arm and tried to erase that last image from her mind.

Then she heard the clatter of footsteps, and Jacob was there beside her, his arms around her. An instant later Holly's strong young arms circled her, too.

"Be all right, Rachel." Her voice shook. "Please be all right."

Someone needed her. She couldn't let herself drift away into numbness. She had to be there when someone needed her.

"I'm all right." Her voice sounded almost normal to her. She struggled to sit up, and Jacob helped her, his strong arm supporting her.

"That's my girl," he murmured, his voice almost as shaken as Holly's. "You're fine."

She looked from one dear face to another. "Yah. I am." She tried not to look toward the edge, but she couldn't help herself. "Is he…"

Jacob nodded. "He hit the rocks." He didn't need to say more. No one could hit the rocks from that height and survive.

"Serves him right," Holly muttered. "He deserved it."

"No." Rachel patted her cheek. "But he chose it."

"Komm, Holly, help me with her." Obviously he could lift Rachel alone, but he seemed to know that it was best for Holly to do something.

Once she was on her feet, Rachel took a tentative step and then another. "I can make it."

"Gut." Jacob seemed to force lightness into his tone. "Holly and I don't want to carry you all the way."

Holly managed to smile, clearly trying to copy Jacob. Trying to take care of her. Rachel's heart swelled with love.

She paused for a moment, giving a brief glance over her shoulder to the space where no one stood now.

Jacob seemed to read her thoughts. "He probably couldn't see any other way out."

She nodded. She understood, she supposed, but she felt sure his family would rather have gone through anything other than losing him. It was such a terrible waste of two lives—both William's and his.

CHAPTER TWENTY

JACOB'S STEPS QUICKENED as he approached the house later with Chief Jamison. Rachel was all right—of course she was. But he wanted to see for himself. He'd have been with her already if not for the need to help the police and emergency squad. He'd had to guide them to the best way to bring in what they'd called the "recovery equipment." It wasn't easy to get machinery up to the quarry.

Rachel and Holly still sat at the kitchen table with Ms. Geraldine. Ms. Geraldine had a cup in front of her, but she didn't seem to be drinking from it. She looked worn and ravaged, but something of her indomitable spirit showed when she raised her head and looked at them.

"Well?" she asked.

"The equipment is there, and the men are working. They'll notify us once they've brought the remains to the surface." Chief Jamison paused. "I'm sorry."

She nodded, seeming to hold whatever she felt inside herself. "You must have questions."

"Yeah." The chief glanced around the table and then pulled out a chair, nodding Jacob into another. A uniformed officer stood by the door, a pad and pen in his hands. Ready to take down whatever they said, he assumed.

"Rachel, let's start with you. I know basically what happened, but I don't know what sparked it off. What made a person like Richard do such a thing?"

Rachel blushed at being put on the spot, but she nodded. "It… I guess it started with something that happened when I was a child and my mother brought me with her to work when the Withers children were here. I didn't really see very much." She frowned, as if trying to sort it out in her mind. "But Richard and William… You know about William?"

Chief Jamison nodded. Jacob had already told him everything he knew about the situation, and it was only twenty years ago. Jamison had been a young patrolman then.

"William and Richard were scuffling…just playing, you know. They were laughing. And then… William wasn't there anymore."

She put her hands over her eyes for a moment, and Ms. Geraldine reached out to pat her arm. Rachel nodded and raised her head, regaining her composure.

"I didn't realize what I'd seen, I guess. But I knew it was something bad, and I ran back down the trail. I don't remember what happened after, but I…I think I kind of put it away in my mind and buried it, not understanding." She paused, giving Ms. Geraldine an apologetic look.

She nodded. "Go on, Rachel."

"There's not much more. I guess I started to remember something when I came to work here, but I still didn't know. I think Richard assumed I had seen and remembered."

Ms. Geraldine spoke. "'The wicked flee when no man pursueth,'" she murmured.

"That all seems pretty clear with what I've heard from Jacob and Holly." Jamison frowned. "We can figure out what he intended, but how did he know you'd be up in the woods this afternoon?"

"I think that was me." Holly spoke in a small voice. "I

was talking to Ricky, and I could hear his dad talking in the background. And I told Ricky that I'd get Rachel to go looking for berries this afternoon."

"Why didn't she find you, then?" Jamison asked.

"I got there first, and when I saw there weren't any, I started down what I thought was a shortcut. Jacob found me."

Now it was his turn. "I got worried when they didn't come back, so I went looking. When I found Holly, we looked for Rachel, and then we heard voices up at the quarry."

There were noises outside, voices talking. The chief nodded to the officer, who went out and then leaned back in the door to gesture to him. Jamison followed him out, and they sat in silence until he came back a few minutes later.

Jamison cleared his throat and focused on Ms. Geraldine. "They've retrieved the… Richard's body. It will be taken to the hospital morgue for now." He stood for another moment and then planted his hands on the back of the chair. "They also found some…other remains, probably William's. They'll be brought up shortly."

Ms. Geraldine took the blows with composure. She nodded. "I will make the arrangements when it's allowed." She focused on Jamison. "About your report."

Jamison paused for a long moment. Then he nodded for the young officer to leave. Once he was gone, a wordless message seemed to pass between them.

"In tragic situations like this, all we can do is try to spare the families as much as possible. I'm sure we're looking at nothing more than a terrible accident."

Ms. Geraldine must feel relief, but she didn't show it. She simply nodded. But Rachel moved to stand by her chair.

"Best you all get some rest now," Jamison said. "There's

nothing you can do. If I need anything, I'll check with Jacob." He went out.

"Come," Rachel said gently. "You heard the chief. There's nothing you can do now." She looked at Holly, who immediately jumped up and went to help her with Ms. Geraldine.

"Yes," she said, leaning on them. Then she shook her head. "Secrets, too many secrets. If I'd known...if Richard had just told me what happened, we would have been spared so much." She looked from one to the other of them. "Families shouldn't have secrets from one another. Remember that."

"We will," Rachel said, comforting as always. "Come and rest now. Holly and I will go up with you."

He watched them make their slow way toward the stairs. Rachel wouldn't have time for him for now...not when someone needed her. Taking care of people who needed her, that was his Rachel.

THE REST OF the day didn't go much better, but so many people turned up to help. Ricky came and was closeted with his great-aunt for a time, but when he emerged, although he had been crying, he looked relieved and stronger. He hugged Holly and then went off to be with his mother. Ms. Geraldine seemed better for talking with him.

Several friends of Ms. Geraldine's turned up to offer support, and Sammy and his wife came bringing dishes that could be warmed up as needed. Sarah took over the kitchen, serving coffee to the various emergency workers who were in and out. All in all, it was just what happened in any Amish home after a death, reminding Rachel that good people were good people whoever they were.

Finally everything grew quiet. Ms. Geraldine refused the sleeping medication the doctor had left for her. She went to bed but probably not to sleep. Heart aching for her, Rachel checked on Holly, reassuring her again that she belonged here, with the people who loved her.

Tired, but feeling she wasn't ready to sleep, Rachel stepped out onto the back porch. Jacob was sitting on the swing. He got up and came to put his arm around her shoulder.

"Everyone settled?" Jacob drew her gently against him, and she felt his breath moving against her temple.

"As much as they can be," she said. "It's been a hard day. I haven't even had a chance to thank you. You saved my life."

He hugged her a little closer. "When I saw you…well, let's say I never prayed so hard in my life. I knew that if I lost you, I'd lose everything. I love you, Rachel. I always have, and I always will." His lips moved against her cheek, filling her with warmth.

But there was something she must say before this went any further.

"You remember what Ms. Geraldine said about not keeping secrets from people who love you?"

He nodded, his cheek moving against hers.

"There's a secret I don't want to keep anymore." She pulled in a deep breath, trying to find the words to tell him what she'd learned. "I always thought that we couldn't marry because of my family, and I was angry at you for not understanding. But the truth is, I was relieved. I think I knew in my heart that we weren't ready. I never doubted our love, but we truly weren't ready to marry."

"I know." He made a sound that was almost a chuckle. "I always knew, but I couldn't admit it until my mamm practically knocked my head against it. I was so immature and selfish it's a wonder you had anything to do with me."

Sure now, she nestled against him, shaking her head. "I loved you. In spite of it."

"I think we're ready now," he said. "What do you think?"

She was quiet for a moment, thinking of all there was to get through in the coming days. As if Jacob was reading her mind, he added, "Ms. Geraldine asked me to stay here as long as I want. To set up my business in the old stable and work from there. I think it would be fine with her if my wife was there. Besides, we have to be here to keep an eye on Holly. They need both of us."

He turned so that he faced her, still holding her in the circle of his arms. "We have to take care of people who need us, ain't so?"

She nodded, studying the dear lines of his face in the dim light. "Yah, we do." She put her hand on his cheek. "And take care of each other, too. We can, as long as we love enough."

Jacob smiled, and then his lips covered hers and she realized they didn't need any words to say everything that they felt.

* * * * *

IF YOU ENJOYED THIS BOOK
WE THINK YOU WILL ALSO LOVE

LOVE INSPIRED
INSPIRATIONAL ROMANCE

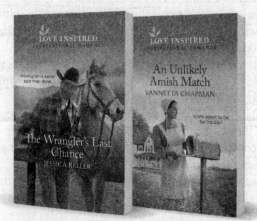

Uplifting stories of faith, forgiveness and hope.

Fall in love with stories where faith helps
guide you through life's challenges, and discover
the promise of a new beginning.

6 NEW BOOKS AVAILABLE EVERY MONTH!

SPECIAL EXCERPT FROM

❦

LOVE INSPIRED
INSPIRATIONAL ROMANCE

Running a small Amish coffee shop is all Lydia Stoltzfus needs to be satisfied with her life—until her next-door neighbor and childhood crush, Simon Fisher, returns home with his five-year-old daughter. Now, even as she falls for the shy little girl, Lydia must resist her growing feelings for Simon…

Read on for a sneak preview of
A Secret Amish Crush by Marta Perry.
Available March 2021 from Love Inspired.

"You want me to say you were right about Aunt Bess and the matchmaking, don't you? Okay, you were right," Simon said.

"I thought you'd come to see it my way," Lydia said lightly. "It didn't take your aunt long to get started, did it?"

His only answer was a growled one. "You wouldn't understand."

"Look, I do see what the problem is," she said. "You don't want people to start thinking that you're tied up with me when you have someone else in mind."

"I don't have anyone in mind." Simon sounded as if he'd reached the end of his limited patience. "I'm not going to marry again—not you, not anyone. I found love once, and I don't suppose anyone has a second chance at a love like that."

His bleak expression wrenched her heart, and she couldn't find any response.

He frowned, staring at the table as if he were thinking o something. "What do you suppose would happen if I hinted t Aunt Bess that I was thinking that way, but that I really neede to get to know you without scaring you off?"

"I don't know. She might be even worse. Still, I guess yo could try it."

"Not just me," he said. "You'd have to at least act as if yo were willing to be friends."

Somehow she had the feeling that she'd end up regrettin this. But on the other hand, he could hardly discourage her fron trying to help Becky in that case.

"Just one thing. If we're supposed to be becoming friends then you won't be angry if I take an interest in Becky now, wil you?"

He nodded. "All right. But…" He seemed to grow mor serious. "If this makes you uncomfortable for any reason, w stop."

She tried to chase away the little voice in her mind that sai she'd get hurt if she got too close to him. "No problem," sh said firmly, and slammed the door on her doubts.

Don't miss
A Secret Amish Crush
by Marta Perry, available wherever
Love Inspired books and ebooks are sold.

LoveInspired.com

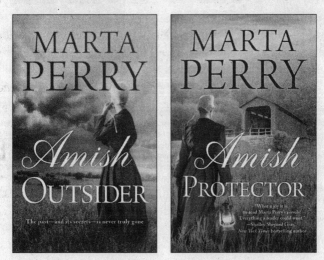

Get 4 FREE REWARDS!

We'll send you 2 FREE Books plus 2 FREE Mystery Gifts.

FREE Value Over $20

Both the **Romance** and **Suspense** collections feature compelling novels written by many of today's bestselling authors.